HUNTING
for the LAMB
of GOD

JAMEY O'DONNELL

authorHOUSE®

AuthorHouse™
1663 Liberty Drive
Bloomington, IN 47403
www.authorhouse.com
Phone: 833-262-8899

Published by AuthorHouse 05/08/2023

ISBN: 978-1-6655-3304-1 (sc)
ISBN: 978-1-6655-3303-4 (e)

EDITED BY
KATHLEEN KLINE
DRAGONFLY PUBLISHING AND EDITING

DEDICATED TO MY SON
RORY JAMES O'DONNELL

CONTENTS

I had not read too deeply into Jamey O'Donnell's *Hunting for the Lamb of God* when a novel thought crossed my mind. As a fan of the post-apocalyptic genre in both print and film, I knew enough to be concerned about supplies of food and water and batteries and gasoline and guns and ammo, but O'Donnell made me think about something more basic: is my bicycle in working order? Following an EMP attack, a bike is about the only thing on wheels that will be working. A shopping cart would help too! It is this kind of attention to everyday detail that separates *Hunting* from so many other works in this genre.

But a bicycle and a shopping cart are not the only things I would need to have at the ready. A good paper copy of the Bible would be even more helpful. My e-Bible would be as useless as my subscription to Netflix. If the bicycle provides mobility, the Bible provides hope. It is their hope and faith that distinguishes our protagonists, basically a two-family cluster, from America's dwindling number of survivors. It is hopefulness, too, that makes any post-apocalyptic novel readable. By contrast, after slugging through a book like Cormac McCarthy's *The Road,* the reader looks for the nearest cliff to jump off.

Of my sixteen published books, two have been novels, and these were the hardest to write. The first, published in the year 2000 and called *2006: The Chautauqua Rising,* imagined a functional but dystopian America in the very near future. The second book, *The Hunt* published in 2019, featured a Christian father and his two sons ensnared in an unexpected battle against a terrorist cell in the wilds of Colorado. Both books had positive endings. Both were well received.

While writing *The Hunt* with my co-author Mike McMullen, a skilled outdoorsman, I came to understand the essentials of successful male-oriented fiction. Those essentials start with likable, relatable protagonists. O'Donnell scores high on this one. In fact, he scores high on all the essentials: a credible plot, believable dialogue, flawless technical details, logical behavior, abundant suspense, and, finally, yes, a touch of romance. It never hurts. Not to turn Jamey's head, but I would argue he does a more credible job imagining a post-apocalyptic future than Stephen King does in the morally inconsistent novel, *The Stand*.

As a fan of TV's *The Walking Dead*, I watched in dismay as the writers forgot the essentials after the first few seasons. What had started out as a highly credible examination of how people behave when all social order breaks down, became increasingly ungrounded and even woke. Without a logical thread and a moral code, the genre quickly degenerates. O'Donnell honors the essentials in *Hunting* as he will, I am sure, in the planned sequel.

The reader of any novel has to want the characters to succeed, and he wants them to succeed without betraying the principles they have absorbed as Christians and Americans. In fact, as the reader will come to understand, the characters in *Hunting* will survive only if they stick to those principles.

Jack Cashill

"There are those who rebel against the light;
They do not know its ways, nor abide in its paths.
The murderer rises with the light;
He kills the poor and needy and in the night he is like a thief.
The eye of the adulterer waits for the twilight, saying

"No eye will see me", and he disguises *his* face.
In the dark they break into houses

which they marked for themselves in the daytime.
They do not know the light, for the morning

is the same to them as the shadow of death;
If *someone* recognizes *them, they* are in

the terrors of the shadows of death."

Job 24: 13-17 NKJV

ONE

The Bright Light and the Big Swoosh

B rian had just blasted through the gauntlet of soldiers on his way to the church tower and was now positioned to take out the sniper at the top where the church bell hung above him. Rocky was playing alongside Brian and was making his move to flank the sniper in hopes of distracting him, giving Brian enough time to load his RPG to take the sniper out.

Two rounds pinging off the church bell was all it took to draw fire from the sniper, and according to plan, the sniper fired back, enabling Brian to fire the RPG.

BOOM! Direct hit!

It was no sooner than the tower and its inhabitant exploded into pieces when the bunker shook violently for a split second, and everything, including the Call of Duty game they were playing on the Xbox, went dark.

"Aw man...what the heck" muttered Brian.

The lights, monitor, Xbox, fan...everything had suddenly lost power and the two boys, along with Brian's older brother Mark, were sitting in complete pitch-black darkness in the doomsday bunker their dad had built in the backyard five years ago.

It was approximately 1:16 p.m. EST on May 24, 2022, when the lower forty eight of the United States, most of Northern Mexico, the southern half of Canada, along with Cuba, Belize, and the Caribbean Islands saw the big bright light.

There were technically three bright lights that spanned from the East to West coasts, with the east light appearing first, followed by the west light, then lastly the center light between the two.

It was at that moment that the world took a quantum leap backward and nothing would ever be the same. Three nuclear warheads had just exploded 200 miles in space into the thermosphere over the United States within minutes of each other.

The first thing people saw was the blinding light that overtook the sun and everything else in view. A loud swooshing sound followed, accompanied by a massive shock wave-powerful enough to knock people to the ground that were outside.

These effects were the result of three nuclear explosions strategically positioned over the United States, designed to create a super electromagnetic pulse (EMP) and cripple the U.S.

Cars on the roads and highways immediately stopped dead in their tracks, all things that ran on electricity came to a screeching halt, computer screens went black, phone conversations ended, television and radio broadcasts stopped, and 3200 jet airliners began to fall from the sky over America, Canada, and Mexico.

Over 2000 satellites were immediately disabled, and because the International Space Station was orbiting within only 227 miles of the Earth, it also lost power.

In the blink of an eye, the Northwestern Hemisphere of Earth had been thrown back into the Stone Age, all at the hands of Iran, being directed by North Korea.

These two countries had been secretly working together for years to implement this exact plan at this exact moment in time. Leading right up to the minute and hour of this day.

It went off seamlessly without a hitch.

North Korea constructed the warheads and Taepodong-2 ballistic missiles, whereas Iran made the rocket launchers. Two were designed to be launched from shipping containers loaded onto freighters, moored off the east and west coasts of America.

The third missile and launcher were to be assembled and launched from inside Mexico after being smuggled in. This had needed to be the first pivotal warhead put into position, placed a full year before launch day.

All the construction for the container launchers had been completed by the end of 2020 and was ready to go. The constructed warheads/missiles were smuggled into Iran by submarine from North Korea, then moved to Tarragona, a small burg outside of Barcelona, Spain. This is where the containers were modified for the mission, to be loaded onto two separate freighters, along with six soldiers of Iran's Revolutionary Guard …one inside the container with the missile and launcher, the other five as passengers. One soldier would be needed to unlock the doors of the container for the launcher to extend outward to fire its missile, with the other five soldiers to provide cover should any of the ship's crewmen try to prevent the launch.

The shipping containers were modified to allow the launchers to electronically extend out past the doors once they were opened, enabling the missiles to position themselves upwards for launch.

For this to be pulled off successfully, the container loading operators at the Barcelona port had to place the containers on the very top of their cargo. This meant a couple of the dock workers and the shipping manifest had to be part of the plan, which they were.

One freighter was set to travel toward the Port Authority in New York, and the other would travel south to traverse the Panama Canal before it was piloted north toward the Port of San Diego. Both freighters would drop anchor fifty miles short of the ports as their goal was to launch from the sea.

Before any of this happened, the first missile, warhead, and launcher had to be successfully smuggled into Mexico and assembled for launch, a task that would prove to be much more involved than anticipated.

The launcher was the first to be smuggled into Mexico in pieces. It came by way of boat, then was loaded on a truck and driven west to San Fernando, then north to a hangar in Matamoros, where it would be constructed and prepared for launch. To ensure a successful undetected delivery, the pieces for the warhead and missile were brought in by submarine, loaded onto a boat, then onto a truck to be taken to the same location as the launcher-to the launcher's final destination.

Two scientists from North Korea accompanied the warhead and missile. They were assigned to complete the assembly of the missile and the attachment of the warhead to the missile.

The assembly operation started in January of 2021 and was completed in six trips, ending in June of the same year.

As the Mexico operation was beginning, Joseph Biden became President of the United States. Shortly after he took the helm, he signed Executive Orders ceasing the construction of the border wall that had been in development during the previous administration. This, combined with new policies that were perceived by many as a "Come In, We Are Open for Business" sign, created a vacuum of people that came from around the world in record numbers, all in hopes of crossing into the United States in search of a better life for them and their families.

In March and April of 2021 alone, the U.S. Border Patrol

apprehended over 180,000 illegal immigrants each month, completely exhausting all of the Border Patrol's manpower and resources. Officers were pulled off of the border, leaving gaping holes for cartel coyotes (human smugglers) to bring women into the U.S. to be sex trafficked and their mules to transport drugs.

This created chaos unlike anything ever seen in the history of the U.S./Mexico border and posed a perfect opportunity to conduct an operation such as the one being conducted by Iran and North Korea. If there was ever a time when the U.S. would be distracted from other events in the world, it was now, so these two countries struck while the iron was hot and they began their operation that would conclude the following year.

Iran had been suffering under crippling sanctions imposed by the United States for years as punishment for its aggressive nuclear program. While these penalties were devastating to their economy and their people, Iran continued their plan to construct a nuclear weapon that could be launched and delivered by an intercontinental ballistic missile reaching anywhere in the world, namely the United States.

They never ceased being the number one state sponsor of terrorism around the world. Iran continued funding Hamas along the Gaza Strip, Hezbollah in Lebanon, the Islamic Jihad, Al Qaeda, and later ISIS.

In July of 2015, the Obama administration facilitated the release of 150 billion American dollars it had been holding in frozen assets since 1979 when Iran took fifty American hostages. On top of that, it had been reported that Obama secretly flew 1.7 billion American dollars in cold hard cash on pallets to Tehran in the dead of night. The release was done as a good-faith gesture as part of the Iran Nuclear Deal, which required Iran to halt its enrichment of uranium and give unfettered access to the United Nations to all of Iran's nuclear sites.

The deal was doomed from the start.

America and the world were destined to get the short end of the stick. Iran never stopped enriching uranium fully, and full access to the nuclear sites was never given to the U.N.

Many condemned the deal. It was common supposition that a good portion of that money would be used for the continued funding of terrorism around the world, namely the groups previously mentioned whose sole mission was the destruction and elimination of the state of Israel, our fiercest ally in the Middle East, and of course, the United States.

On January 20, 2017, Donald Trump became President of the United States. One of the first things our new president did was pull America out of this flawed deal with Iran, while reinstating the sanctions that were there previously, then adding more crippling sanctions to those already existing.

The final nail in the coffin for Iran was the execution of their highest military officer in command, Qasem Soleimani, who was taken out by a targeted drone strike on January 3, 2020, in Baghdad, Iraq.

Soleimani was personally responsible for the deaths of over 600 U.S. servicemen during the Iraq war, so he was a high-priority target.

Enter North Korea.

Since the days of North Korea's former leader Kim Jong-Il, this country has embarked on an aggressive nuclear program as well. This prompted an agreement signed in 1994 by then President Clinton entitled the "Agreed Framework", which gave North Korea four billion dollars in energy aid in exchange for the halt of their quest for nuclear proliferation on the Korean peninsula. Unfortunately, this agreement broke down in 2003 and they resumed their quest for nuclear proliferation. Many believe they never stopped.

Since that time, there have been massive sanctions placed on North Korea that steadily increased up until now.

Fast forward to the death of Kim Jong-Il in December 2011.

He was succeeded as Supreme Leader by his son, Kim Jong-Un, and like his father, he has ruled his country with an iron fist. Jong-Un appeared to learn well how to show little to no regard for his people. Like his father, he believes he and his country's continued existence rely upon the possession of their nuclear weapons program.

One of President Trump's priorities was to get North Korea back to the table to negotiate an agreement that would finally end their desire for nuclear weapons. For a short time, it looked as though President Trump was making significant headway with the young leader...and just might achieve what past administrations had been unable to do.

President Trump and Kim Jong-Un met a total of three times, in June 2018 in Singapore, in Hanoi, Vietnam, and then finally at the DMZ (Demilitarized Zone) between North and South Korea on June 30, 2019, where President Trump became the first president in history to step foot in North Korea by stepping over the DMZ line into that country. He was met by Kim Jong-Un there, where they shook hands and posed for pictures, then immediately crossed over to the South Korean side and had a meeting at The Freedom House.

Afterward, Trump escorted Kim Jong-Un back over to the North Korean

This was an ongoing process that had its setbacks for sure, but it was more than any president had been able or willing to accomplish.

Had Trump won re-election, who knows how far the process could have gone, but once Trump was defeated in November 2020, this changed the dynamic between North Korea and the United States. Consequently, this led to the decision by both Iran and North Korea to move forward with their plan to once and for all destroy the United States and rid themselves of these economically crippling sanctions that had flatlined both countries for so long.

The relationship between these two countries did not begin here and had been ongoing for years, beginning in the 1980s.

Over the last four decades, North Korea has been sending missiles to Iran via air transport with stops in China and Pakistan, (lending to the belief that those countries were aware of what North Korea was doing, which should come as no surprise since China was and is heavily dependent on Iranian oil. Not to mention China has the final word over anything North Korea does).

The two countries decided to strike almost immediately after the 2020 United States presidential election, based on its results and the overbearing sanctions, but also because America was at its weakest.

At the beginning of 2020, the world was hit with a deadly pandemic, a coronavirus engineered in a lab in Wuhan, China, but not known to come from there at the time of its release.

In the beginning, it was thought to have originated in a wet market in Wuhan, then spread across the world by its citizens traveling abroad. Soon it made its way to the U.S., and by 2021 there were over 33 million cases reported with almost 600 thousand deaths.

Worldwide there were 178 million cases reported with over 3.5 million deaths.

Covid 19, as it was named, devastated a thriving American economy, with travel shut down for months to China, Europe, The British Isles, and eventually South America.

The airline industry had almost come to a screeching halt because no one was flying.

Restaurants, hair salons, fitness gyms, and any government deemed non-essential businesses were prohibited from doing business as usual, The workforce was thrown out of work and onto unemployment benefits that were supplemented by hefty money provided by the Federal government. Several emergency stimulus packages were passed by Congress that amounted to over 10 trillion dollars, increasing the national debt from 20 trillion to over 30 trillion dollars.

Combine that with the Biden administration slashing jobs by canceling the Keystone XL pipeline, thereby constricting America's ability to be the number one energy producer in the world, and halting construction on the border wall, hyperinflation beginning to take hold in virtually all goods bought and services performed in America, the immigration crisis at the border, and the attacks on Israel (sustaining over 4000 rocket attacks from Hamas in the Gaza Strip), America was at a tipping point-and seemed to have no answers under the current administration.

If there was a bright point in this time, it would be the vaccines that were created for Covid 19 under the Trump administration in late 2020. By mid-2021, nearly half of the population in America had been inoculated, and the rest of the world was not far behind.

Things were beginning to open again with mask mandates being eased.

Had this not happened when it did, there is no telling how bad things would be in the world at the time of the attack.

In mid-2020, it started to become apparent that the Covid 19 virus did not originate in one of the wet markets in Wuhan but instead escaped from the Wuhan Institute of Virology, ten miles from the suspected outdoor market, thus shifting the focus and blame onto China.

Up until this point, China, and the World Health Organization (WHO) had dismissed claims of this being the case. Further research and investigation showed that scientists in the lab were hospitalized with Covid-like symptoms back in November of 2019, just before the virus started to spread. It was also discovered that this laboratory was in the process of specifically working with coronaviruses. In essence, they weaponized the virus…putting China in the spotlight. Furthermore, it exposed them to hundreds of thousands of lawsuits from the American people alone, so how upset would China be if something happened to the United States, thereby taking the focus off China, and putting it elsewhere?

To believe that China knew nothing about the impending attack is a stretch, even to the most China-friendly skeptics. Regardless of how much they knew, they did nothing to stop the attack, even with the worldwide ramifications that taking the United States off the global stage would present to the world's economy, and potentially result in a worldwide economic collapse, let alone elevate China to be the sole superpower in the world. This is something China was planning on achieving by the year 2050 anyway, so having knowledge of this and not trying to prevent it would only strengthen its position in the world and speed up its timeline.

The most amazing thing about this operation is how they were able to fly this under the radar of the free world. Had there not been the pandemic, combined with a new administration overwhelmed with the results of their new policies leading the United States, chances are more likely than not it would have been discovered, exposed, and thwarted.

This is how the end of America as we know it took place on May 24, 2022.

Everything about the launches was pre-planned, right down to the second.

Both freighters were anchored outside New York City and San Diego and were in position, as was the missile launcher in Matamoros, Mexico.

The first missile launched was off the freighter outside of New York City. The doors of the container were opened, and the warhead was moved into position, ready to head straight for the heavens. After its deployment, it was immediately picked up by the United States missile defense system and Patriot missiles were deployed to intercept it, but because the intercontinental ballistic missile (ICBM) was set to head straight out to space and had no land target, it was unable to be intercepted. Plus, the defense missiles were chasing a projectile that had a good head start to its atmospheric destination.

Within seconds, the ICBM off the coast of San Diego was deployed into space with the same results as the first.

Seconds later, the missile was launched from Mexico.

When all three missiles reached the thermosphere at 200 miles above the earth, all three exploded within seconds of each other, creating a super electromagnetic pulse sent to the earth, frying every single power line, transformer, cell phone, battery, radio signal, automobile, airplane, computer, and appliance.

Everything immediately stopped.

Medical equipment, such as ventilators stopped ventilating.

Pacemakers stopped, causing those who had them to fall dead in their tracks.

Elevators stopped between floors, trapping occupants inside them.

Freezers with meats and medical supplies in them began to thaw..

Phone conversations were abruptly interrupted by silence.

Surgeons in the middle of an operation were suddenly left in pitch blackness holding their scalpels in hand, not knowing what to do next.

Subway cars filled with people became dark. The only electronic devices to survive the blasts were those shielded by being underground or in an encased concrete enclosure.

Stoplights ceased working.

Cars went dead on the highways, over 3200 jet airliners fell out of the sky, lights and air conditioning came to a halt, tv, and radio stopped transmitting, and water stopped running.

Fail-safe and fail-secure locks went into effect, locking prisoners in jails and prisons, and locking bank vaults. Conversely, doors were unlocked in public buildings, markets, theatres, and any other structure that relied on fail-safe locks for their security.

The more urban the area, the harder it was hit.

Big cities and their suburbs across America immediately became a collection of death zones, and the rural areas of America suffered the same circumstances, only not as condensed.

Farmer's tractors stopped in the fields, dairy farmers suddenly lost their milking machines. The only living things happy for this respite were the livestock about to be slaughtered.

Trains were affected too-their engines quit and they coasted to a stop on the tracks.

Ships (cargo, vacation cruise ships, and personal crafts) in the blast zone stopped at sea, leaving their precious cargo to float aimlessly.

Semi-trucks on the highway came to a rolling stop and their refrigerated goods stopped getting the air conditioning they needed.

Gas stations stopped pumping gas.

There were no police or ambulances to come to the aid of its people, and no way for them to reach you even if they could.

The Cavalry was not coming.

The president and the United States Congress would not be arriving to our aid.

From that moment on, there would be no government programs to rely on.

The only vehicles and buildings hardened to withstand an attack of this magnitude were in the military, a few located in Washington D.C., and others sparsely positioned across the 3000-mile expanse of this country. The citizens of the United States were not going to be able to depend on them. To do so would be an act in futility and signing your own death warrant. Besides, even if they could reach you to help, what would they help you with?

It would take weeks, possibly months before the rest of the world could respond and come to our aid. As bad as it was for America and most of Canada, it was so much worse for Northern Mexico and the other lessor developed countries in its wake. The EMP created a horrific disaster of biblical proportions. After all, we are talking about 550 million people in dire distress that were affected.

Unless you were a doomsday survivalist and planned for a situation exactly like this, the cold hard facts were that you would probably be dead in the not-too-distant future.

The horrible reality is that close to ninety percent of Americans would be dead within the year. This is exactly what Iran and North Korea were counting on.

Diabetics would not have the man-made insulin they have become accustomed to survive on, many others would die of thirst, cancer patients would not get their treatment, infections normally treated with antibiotics would result in many deaths, food would become extremely scarce in a matter of weeks, and diseases would go untreated.

Then there is the criminal element to consider.

Though America was one of the most humane societies in the world, it has had its fair share of evil incarnate in the form of mankind. Throughout the years, society had disintegrated into human beings that had lost all sense of goodness or never had it to begin with.

Men walked the streets with no more regard for human life, or any life for that matter than they would have for walking through the door of someone's home and stealing their possessions.

These are men and women living their lives without God. Some of them may not knowingly embrace Satan, but they most certainly will embrace his evil.

Many of them have help being this way due to their dependence on drugs…with methamphetamine being the number one drug employed by this element.

Ironically, the most equipped to survive a nightmare such as this are the homeless, many of whom are the very meth addicts described here.

They are used to living with next to nothing, dealing with whatever weather they find themselves in, living hand to mouth, taking what they need to survive, and victimizing anyone standing in their way of getting whatever it is that they want or need.

If there was a saving grace for the rest of society, it was the fail-secure locks that kept the prisoners in all the jails and prisons behind bars, saving all their potential victims from being savaged by these beasts upon their unwanted release into the world.

Since we are talking about the Four Horsemen of the Apocalypse, we must spend some time on pestilence.

With all the immediate deaths that would happen, there would be diseases running rampant upon what was left of society, infecting millions with no recourse or way to be treated.

What would happen with the dead? Would they be buried, moved, burned…or eaten?

All these scenarios would come into play.

Though it's an overused adage, it had never been truer than during this time…only the strong would survive.

Because the world had become so reliant on things and people to take care of them, the population had collectively lost their ability to survive the way our ancestors were able to, braving the elements with no electricity or creature comforts they had become accustomed to, not unlike the soft underbelly of today's society.

Other than the occasional plane falling from the sky, the screams of people in disbelief of what was happening, or the occasional dog barking, the northwestern hemisphere became quiet.

Eerily quiet.

Church mouse quiet.

๑๛ﾍﾚ

"Don't move," said Mark. Then there was light as he turned on the flashlight on his cell phone, illuminating the underground bunker that he, his little brother Brian, and Brian's friend Rocky from across the street were in.

"Man, you got to be shitting me. A circuit breaker must have broken or the power's out in the neighborhood. Brian…go up top and check the breaker box."

As Brian whisked up the stairwell and opened the big lead-coated door to the outside, daylight splashed into the bunker, illuminating the inside and all of its contents.

"Wow, it was creepy down here when there wasn't any light" exclaimed Rocky as Brian went up the stairs to open the steel door leading to the backyard outside.

"Hey, you guys…come out here!" yelled Brian down the stairs. "The telephone pole is on fire!"

Both boys ran up the stairs and out the door to look up and see the transformer Brian was talking about ablaze up the top of the utility pole at the back corner of their backyard.

"Jesus…does it look different out here to you guys?" whispered Mark.

All three were craning their heads, with Brian and Rocky nodding in agreement.

The air had an electric blue tint to it, and the sky was brighter than usual.

"I guess this explains why the power went out," said Mark.

Just then, Mark and Brian's mom came out the back door of the house and yelled to the boys "I just tried to call the fire department, but the phone's dead. My cell phone won't work either."

Mark walked over to her and said, "Let me see it, Mom".

She handed the phone over to him and it was black...dead as a doornail.

He reached into his pocket and pulled out his phone and it was working fine, then he tried calling his mom's phone, but got nothing. No sound, no busy signal, no "call can't be completed as dialed" statement...not anything at all.

He then tried calling his dad in D.C.

Again, nothing.

Just as he was about to comment, they all heard a strange sound from the sky and looked upward to see a big passenger jet about 15,000 feet in altitude to the northwest falling from the sky like a bird that had just been shot dead in flight.

"OH MY GOD!" screamed his mother in horror as she pointed up to the sky.

Within a few seconds, it dropped out of view behind the very tall willow tree at the side of the house and was followed by an enormous explosion that you could hear in the distance, maybe about five miles away.

"DID YOU SEE THAT?" screamed Rocky.

Then you could see a plume of black smoke rising above the trees and filling the sky.

"What is happening?" said Mom, her words barely audible as she whispered in terror.

It was then that Rocky bolted through the side gate toward home across the street, yelling behind him that he is going to check on his sister and brother.

At this point, the boy's mother Viv would have gotten her husband on the phone, who was most likely at work for the Department of Agriculture in Washington, D.C., to update him on what had just happened, but without a working phone, that was impossible now.

"Let's go into the house and turn on the TV. There should be something about that plane we just saw crash!" Brian suggested, so Viv walked into the house with Brian right behind her, leaving Mark in the backyard pondering.

Mark tried to make sense of the burning transformer on the pole, the blue tint to the air that surrounded him, the phones not working, and now the plane falling out of the sky...almost simultaneously.

"Power's out in the house. TV isn't working, nothing is working... not even the water. I can't get it to turn on. Refrigerator is off too," shouted Brian out the window to Mark.

Power is out too? This might be something serious. He was wishing he could call his dad right now. He'd know what to do.

His dad was a prepper of sorts...someone that prepares for the end of the earth kind of stuff; hence, the doomsday bunker in the backyard. Five years ago, his dad Bill began to pay attention to that kind of stuff, shortly after he took that job in Washington working for the government. Suddenly one day Bill decided that they needed to be prepared in case something catastrophic were to happen, so after discussing it with Viv, he invested in a whole bunch of freeze-dried food; meals that had a shelf life of twenty-five years, and it was enough to feed the family for more than a year.

Mark was seventeen, so that made him only twelve at the time. He remembers the day the truck pulled up to the house and delivered all those boxes with different food dish labels on them because he, his dad, and the delivery driver spent close to an hour unloading the boxes out of the truck and stacked them along the back wall of the garage.

A couple of days later a truck pulled up, this time with a driver and a helper with him, and they were there to deliver 500 cases of bottled water, stacked and shrink wrapped on pallets, and the only place to put them was in the garage. It was that day his mom and dad began parking their cars in the driveway and out on the street because there was no room for them in the garage, at least until the bunker was created.

A month later a crew showed up early in the morning, took down the section of the fence alongside the house, and drove a backhoe into the backyard, then proceeded to dig a giant hole fourteen feet deep, fifteen feet wide, and thirty feet long.

A room was created when the cement truck showed up a couple of days later and poured cement into forms that had been constructed using plywood and two-by-four's. When finished and cured, the room was approximately fourteen feet wide, and twenty feet long, with an eight- foot high ceiling, and a very long, wide, and exceptionally steep stairwell.

The backhoe came back a few days later and filled the remainder of the hole on top of the room with the dirt that had been pulled out originally, and a smaller little tractor showed up to remove the rest of the dirt from the backyard, which was then loaded into a trailer, then hauled away from the house.

Next, Bill had a special door made for the entrance that had a lead coating, then he had an electrician run conduit into the bunker to provide electricity.

Throughout the remainder of that year, Bill and Mark finished the bunker themselves by painting, carpeting, and making it a home away from home for the boys.

When they had completed the finishing touches, the two of them assembled some metal shelving against the back wall, unloaded the cans of freeze-dried food out of the boxes that contained them, then toted them down the stairs, filling half of the shelving with the cans of food. Next, they carried fifty cases of bottled water off one of the pallets in the garage and loaded the other half of the shelving with those, then stacked the other 450 cases of water up to the ceiling against the back wall of the garage where the food had been, which is also when the cars could once again be parked inside.

The bunker was not made to live in but was merely a place to survive should the unthinkable happen, a disaster, such as a tornado, or something else they could not imagine.

They brought down an old couch and coffee table, a TV with an Xbox, a boom box for music, some board games, and an electric heater for the wintertime.

After re-sodding over the dirt patch on top of the bunker, you would never know the bunker was there, except for the lead door that was painted green to match the grass.

Over the next five years, the bunker became a place for Mark, Brian, and their friends to hang out and play video games or watch TV, and it was also a great place to beat the heat in the summer because it was naturally much cooler temperature-wise due to its subterranean nature.

The bunker was like an insurance policy that you never expect to use, but the peace of mind that came with having it made the expense of it all worthwhile to Bill.

One thing that Bill had stressed to the boys was keeping the bunker on the down low.

Should an emergency ever happen, and they needed to retreat to it, the last thing they needed was to have the neighborhood at its door trying to get inside. It was only big enough for the four members of the family, so it was better not to tell any of their friends of its existence.

Well, boys will be boys, and it did not take long for some of their friends to be invited into it by Bill's sons, but for the most part, it remained pretty much a secret to the neighborhood, which is what Bill wanted all along.

So, it remained that way through the next few years.

It never really occurred to anyone that this bunker would turn out to be a lifesaver for the family, but it was indeed.

There were other things in the bunker as well, such as a Faraday cage.

A Faraday cage is a box or case made with wire mesh, metal sheets, or both, and its purpose is to shield anything kept inside it from electromagnetic waves, such as batteries, phones, computers, flashlights, radios… anything electrical.

The Faraday cage in the bunker possessed items that would come to be useful over the coming days, weeks, and months, and these items were worth more than their weight in gold.

"Mom…I'm going to drive over to see where that plane crashed and see if I can be of any help. Maybe Brian wants to come with me?" Mark queried as he winked at Brian.

"Yeah…I'll go with you," said Brian as he was already halfway out the front door.

"Ok boys. Be careful. I'm sure it's going to be dangerous if you get too close to it if you find it, so DON'T GET TOO CLOSE!" Viv snapped back.

When Mark got out of his car parked on the street in front of the house, Brian was already sitting in the passenger seat. Brian liked riding with his older brother, and it never mattered where they were going, as long as the car was moving.

Mark got in behind the wheel, then turned to his brother and said, "Brian, what do you think we are going to see when we get there? A lot of dead bodies. That's what. Are you ready for that?"

"I have no idea, to be honest with you, but I'm sure whatever it is, I'll be able to handle it. If anyone is still alive, they're going to need help, and if I can help someone, I want to be able to be there to do that, so let's go, big brother."

Just as Mark was going to put the key in the ignition of his 2005 Honda Accord, he noticed a car in the middle of the street. The car had its hood open with a man leaning inside the engine compartment.

"Maybe our neighbor needs a jump. I'll ask him when I pull up next to him", Mark said under his breath.

Then he turned the key...nothing. No lights came on, the engine did not turn over, not even once. Nothing happened at all.

"What the heck? I just had this baby serviced last week and the last time I drove it was last night and it was running perfectly."

He tried it again. Again, nothing.

He looked up the street at the car in front of him stalled, looked at his hood, then noticed two more cars further up his street...both seeming to be dealing with the same issues as the guy leaning over his engine compartment, and then it hit him like a ton of bricks.

WE'VE BEEN HIT!

This is exactly the thing his dad had been talking about all these years.

We've either been hit by a solar flare or something manmade, but this looks and feels like an EMP, at least how his dad had always described it, which meant that not only was he not driving anywhere, but neither would anyone else be.

To think of it, he hadn't heard an automobile since they came out of the bunker twenty minutes ago, or anything else.

He stopped Brian as he was getting ready to say something with a "shoosh" hand wave as he opened his car door to listen outside…and he heard nothing…nothing at all.

No cars, no planes, no sirens in the distance, nothing.

It wasn't even this quiet at night, let alone at noontime during a workday.

He just stared out the window and began to see what was happening on his street.

There were some people in their front yards just looking around, some other neighbors standing in the street talking to each other, with some of them making hand gestures toward the sky, but what became sobering was that Mark could not remember the last time he saw this many people outside their homes at this time during the week, figuring to himself that with most of his neighbors at work, these people he was seeing outside must have constituted just about every single person that was home.

That was kind of shocking to him, since the only time he would see this many of his neighbors outside would be on a weekend, with most of them mowing their lawns or washing their cars.

These people were just standing in disbelief, not knowing what to do or think about what was happening.

"Come on man, let's go in the house. We need to talk to Mom," Mark barked to Brian as he was already out of the car.

The two ran inside to find Viv in the kitchen over the stove heating some water.

Mark put his hand on his mom's shoulder and asked, "Mom. Do you know what's happening?"

Before she could answer, Mark continued, "Mom, I think this is more than the power going out. I couldn't get my car to even turn over…no lights, nothing!"

Then he noticed the flame burning under the pot of water under the stove.

"Dad always said that if we were hit by an EMP, the gas would continue to come through the line for some time after, right? Mark asked.

"Is that what you think has happened?" she asked.

"The transformer is on fire, the air has a blue tint to it, the power lines are smoking, nothing electrical is working in the house, the car won't start, there are other cars stuck in the middle of the street, the phones aren't working, and a jet fell out of the sky…isn't this what Dad has been preparing us for all these years?"

"Lord Jesus. I need to get a hold of your father," Viv said as she backed into a kitchen chair to sit down.

TWO

Prayers for the Dead

Rocky's older brother Jack had been in the shower when the power went out, so he was not up to speed with the situation like Rocky and their sister Kate was. He did not notice anything from the upstairs bathroom, except that the light went out.

"Rocky! Are you downstairs? Bring me a towel please!" yelled Jack.

Jack had just completed his junior year at Benedictine College, a Catholic institution in Atchison, Kansas and he was now home for the summer, getting ready to meet some friends for lunch at the local Applebee's down University Blvd., a couple of miles from the neighborhood, then go do something later while enjoying the late spring day. Springtime in the Rockies was something he looked forward to after a harsh Kansas winter.

With a knock on the door, Jack opened it slightly as Kate stood in the hall with a towel in hand, then gave it to him as he stood behind the door naked and dripping wet.

"You better come downstairs when you are dressed. Something bad happened," he heard her say as he closed the door.

Across the street, Mark and Brian were in the kitchen doing their best to calm their mother down, while outside the sky started to fill up with black smoke from the plane crash miles away.

"I'm going to ride my bike over to where I think the plane crashed and see what I can do to help if anything," stated Mark. "I'm going to go by myself, Brian. You need to stay here with Mom."

Brian shrugged his shoulders. It was obvious from the body language that he wasn't excited about that plan, and with that, Mark walked down the hall to his bedroom and grabbed a day pack, then filled it with a first aid kit and an ace bandage he had in his closet, along with some bottles of water from the refrigerator.

Mark was an Eagle Scout and had a basic knowledge of first aid, but there was no way he could imagine what he was about to deal with. He then opened the kitchen door and walked into the garage.

With the power being out, Mark had to reach up above his mom's car and manually unlock the garage door to pull it up to open it. When he got it open, he could see Rocky and his older sister and brother out in the street looking up at the now-blackened sky, with Jack desperately trying to get his cell phone to work.

He pulled down his old beach cruiser from the rafters and carried it out onto the driveway, then coasted out to the street where they were standing.

"Hey Jack...pretty crazy, huh?" Mark stated.

"Where are you going?" answered Jack.

By this time Rocky and Kate had filled Jack into everything happening as they knew it, not nearly as informed as Mark and his family were, but Mark would take care of that.

"I'm going to ride my bike over to Broadway and head north till I run into that plane that crashed. They are probably going to need some help."

"I'll go with you. Give me a minute so I can get my brother's bike. I left mine in Atchison for the summer." Jack announced.

Rocky nodded his permission to Jack as the oldest of the three went to the side of the house to get Rocky's bike. Seconds later he was straddling the bike in the street next to Mark.

They then both started peddling down Cook Way to make their way out of the Cherry Knolls subdivision, while Mark filled Jack in with all the information, he believed he knew that Rocky and Kate did not have.

Mark had known Jack for years from living across the street from him, but Jack was four years older, so they never really hung out together. Besides, even if they were the same age, they were different from each other. Mark was more of the jock type that played football and rugby for Arapahoe High School, whereas Jack was more the studious type and not much interested in contact sports.

Still, they liked each other and were always respectful.

As the two made their way onto Arapahoe Road, Mark and Jack both became 100 percent convinced that what had happened was in fact, an EMP.

There was not a single car moving on the road. The only cars they could see were cars stopped dead in their lanes as far as they could see, with their drivers either standing next to their cars or sitting on the side of the road, some talking to each other, some very mad and yelling at their cars, and some even screaming at each other as if this was the other person's fault.

None of the signal lights were working either, and other than the occasional dog barking or the human voice, there were no sounds audible.

It was so quiet, the loudest sound they could hear was their bicycle chains as they peddled down the middle of the road.

"I've heard of EMPs, but I never thought we would see one. I'm really worried about my mom and dad", Jack said. "I have no idea how they are going to get home."

Jack's mom and dad both worked at Denver Health, formerly known as Denver General Hospital…a good ten miles north in downtown Denver.

His dad was a pharmacist in the outpatient wing of the hospital and his mom worked in billing, close to the main entrance.

Jack had only been home a couple of weeks from college. His dad had taken a couple of days off and drove to Atchison in his truck to pick up Jack and his belongings, bringing him home for the summer before his senior year began. Jack was majoring in Business Management and had managed to make the Dean's List every semester, putting him in Magna Cum Laude territory. When it came to matters such as EMPs, Jack knew as much about that as Mark knew about college, which wasn't a whole lot.

They were on their way to their destination when Arapahoe Road dead-ended into Broadway, where they would be taking a right-hand turn, and when they got there, they stopped peddling.

Looking to the north, they saw the carnage up ahead. It was beyond their comprehension as both of their mouths were agape in disbelief. They were also close enough now to the crash site that they could smell the smoke of burning homes, jet fuel, and burning flesh, making an almost stomach-churning stew of odors that was anything but inviting.

It was Southwest flight #1952 coming out of Los Angeles, heading into Denver International Airport for landing. It wasn't supposed to land until 11:35 a.m., but it caught a jet stream and was about ten minutes early. Including the pilot, co-pilot, and flight crew, there were two hundred twenty-three people on the plane that had met their fiery deaths.

Looking about a mile and a half up ahead, all they could see were fires and thick black smoke, and this is what they were about to bike into.

Mark pulled a couple of bottles of water out of his day pack and handed one to Jack. Both were thirsty after peddling through the early afternoon heat of the day. They got off their bikes and sat down in the grass not far from a couple of women standing next to their car stopped dead in the street at the intersection, apparently from waiting to turn at the light.

"You got any more of that water?", asked one of the women.

Mark drank half of his bottle, then handed it to the woman.

"I'll share what I have with you", he responded, as she gratefully accepted his gift.

Jack drank half of his bottle and walked over to the other woman who responded in kind.

Both boys pulled their shirts up over their noses and mouths and began biking north up Broadway. The smell got worse with every few feet they got closer.

Ten minutes later they were gasping as they searched for pockets of cleaner air to breathe into their lungs, and after finding a decent place to stop their bikes, they took inventory of what they were on the threshold of.

The only sights in their vision were city blocks of leveled homes on fire, pieces in varying sizes of jetliner, seats (some empty and some with people still strapped in, all dead), cars on fire, and bodies and body parts everywhere, so many to the point that you could hardly take a step without having to step over them.

There were also people not involved in the crash that were stepping through the wreckage, looking to help anyone that showed signs of life. There was a policeman comforting someone he had just extinguished, as flames had been burning this person alive, and all he could do now was hold this person's hand as he died...another person was holding an arm that had been severed from a woman still alive in shock. Those still alive were so few and far between the massive number of deceased, occupying virtually every square foot of ground around them, leaving both Jack and Mark feeling helpless.

The crash took out approximately four square city blocks, just missing the King Soopers supermarket at the corner of Littleton Blvd. and Broadway, but the market did not go unblemished. Parts of the roof were on fire from scattering debris from the crash. Soon the market would be ablaze, but no one would be there to put out the fire.

There were no sirens to be heard, and no ambulances or fire engines were on the way. Normally the air would be filled with the sounds of sirens, horns honking, and first responders making their way to the victims.

The two volunteers started to make their way around the outer perimeter of the crash site looking for someone...anyone...anyone to help at all. Jack almost tripped over the upper torso of a man with nothing more than his head, neck, and left arm attached. Through the smoke and haze, Mark heard the muffled cries of someone to his left. Mark pushed aside a drink service cart that had the Southwest logo emblazoned on the side of it and found a man in delirium crying out for help, bleeding profusely from a gaping wound above his left temple.

He sprang into action by emptying his pack on the ground, then picked up his first aid kit, opened it, grabbed a handful of gauze bandages, then started to apply pressure to the man's wound, but he failed to notice that the man's entrails had spilled out of his viscera and the poor soul probably only had moments left to live.

Jack came up behind him and grabbed his shoulder, saying, "Mark... stop. Look at his guts."

Mark looked down at the man's body and eased the pressure he'd been putting on his head, realizing he was fighting a losing battle because the man was surely going to die. He then grabbed the man's hand and held it tightly in his bloody hand, and then silently began to weep.

Wrapped momentarily in his sorrow, he didn't even notice that the man had passed away. Jack then bent down and put his arms under Mark's, lifting him off of his knees, and holding him up until he could get his balance.

"There's nothing we can do here for these people Mark" whispered Jack. "They are all dead or going to die. Even if we could keep them alive, there is no help coming for them. All we can do is pray for them."

So, they walked over to the front yard of a house next to the crash scene and got down on their knees in the grass, as Jack led them both in prayer.

"Please Lord, accept these souls into your beautiful kingdom of Heaven and spare them any more pain and suffering that they would endure. Please watch over their families wherever they are Lord and let them feel your love, kindness, and mercy. In Jesus' name, Amen."

With that, they both made the sign of the cross, then rose to their feet, and could not help but notice the middle-aged woman sitting in a chair on the front porch of the yard they were in, looking out over the carnage of the crash scene with not even a smidgen of care or compassion at the tragedy unfolding before her…instead, it was as if nothing unusual had happened on that day and she was doing what she always did, sitting alone on that porch like every other day before.

It was unnerving to both of them, yet neither one of them said a word to her, nor she to them.

Between the passengers on the airliner, the people living or doing business in that vicinity, and the people trapped in the cars driving by, there had to be close to a thousand people dead or dying.

It was overwhelming and unlike anything this town had ever seen before, and the only ones on the scene were a few scattered concerned citizens trying to help, or they were just there to witness the moment. No news camera crews were reporting, no first responders, and nobody was there to save the day…but there were people there also that did not have the best intentions.

Off to the north, Mark saw them first. Two people. One man and one woman, going from body to body, rummaging through their pockets and purses, looking for wallets or anything of value.

The man was taking rings off the fingers and necklaces off the women, and it was too much for him to bear.

"HEY!!! WHAT ARE YOU DOING???" Mark screamed over at the man.

The man doing the pilfering looked to be homeless, as did the woman.

The man quickly stiffened up, looked up at Mark, said something under his breath, and continued what he was doing.

Jack was going to urge Mark to get on his bike but then noticed to the north that there was another giant source of black smoke about ten miles away, just outside of the downtown Denver area, and it made him think about his mom and dad that were probably stuck at the hospital. He wondered if they were ok and what they were doing.

The thought crossed his mind he should keep traveling north to where they were, but his better judgment took hold. He needed to get back to see to his little brother and sister.

"Leave it, Mark. There's nothing you can do to stop them, short of staying here until they leave, and even then, they will come back when we are gone. Let's go back home and help our families. They need us more than these people do."

Jack then reached into Mark's backpack, still on his back, and pulled out a bottle of water.

"Take off your shirt Mark. You're covered in blood."

Mark looked down at his chest, and he was indeed soaked with the blood of the man he was trying to assist. Both the front of his t-shirt, his hands, and his arms looked as though it was he that was bleeding.

Jack took the day pack off Mark after taking off his shirt for Mark to dry off with, then Mark took off his shirt and dropped it to the ground.

"Hold out your hands Bud" commanded Jack as he opened the bottle of water and started lightly pouring the water over Mark's hands as Mark scrubbed the blood off his hands, arms,

face, and chest, followed by Jack handing Mark his shirt to wipe off and to catch the remaining residue of blood.

And with that bit of sage advice given a minute ago, the two bare-chested men got on their bikes and headed south on Broadway toward Arapahoe Road, back toward home.

Little did the grave robbers know that any money they pilfered off the dead would be worthless. The money would have no value to them or anyone else.

The world would revert to gold, silver, trinkets, services…anything useful to the seller and buyer…the rarer it was, the more value it would have.

Paper money might as well be toilet paper, which would have more value than the money itself. The banking system stopped about an hour prior and would not be coming back anytime soon.

It was close to four in the afternoon when the boys rolled up into Mark's front yard, tired from pedaling in the afternoon sun. Brian and Rocky were in the garage rummaging through some boxes, looking for something that seemed important. Brian caught a glimpse of the two as they laid their bikes in the yard.

"What did you guys find? Were there a lot of dead people? Who else was there?" asked Brian as he walked out of the garage toward the two.

"You don't even want to know" muttered Jack.

Then Mark spoke, "What are you looking for in the garage?"

"Dad's Ham radio."

Brilliant! That was the thought that ran through Mark's brain.

"Well...it's not in the garage, thank God. It's in the Faraday cage down in the bunker, and it's a good thing it's not in the garage, otherwise, it would be fried like everything else. Good thinking Brian!" answered Mark.

The Faraday cage was something Mark hadn't thought of until Brian brought up the idea of the Ham radio. It was an addition to the bunker their dad made a couple of years ago just in case something like this had occurred. It contained the radio, a couple of brand new car batteries, six or seven flashlights, a ton of D-size batteries, a cell phone, and a 200 ft. spool of wiring.

The cage was designed to protect any electronics from frying in case of an EMP attack such as this.

Just then, Viv walked out of the front door, followed by Rocky's older sister Kate.

"You boys must be starving. I'm cooking up all the meat from the freezer in the basement before it all goes bad. I'm barbequing in the back yard and Katie's frying up bacon and sausage on the stove. I've also got a roast in the oven" announced Viv.

"Jack... you, your brother, and your sister will eat with us tonight."

She got no argument from Jack.

Pretty smart. Hopefully, the neighbors were barbequing as well before any meat they have goes bad.

Viv didn't much know what was in the bunker, let alone the Faraday cage and its contents, so she had already thought ahead and located every single candle, both big and small, and set them each on plates to be distributed strategically throughout the house for when the sun went down along with the daylight.

"If you don't need any help, we are going to hook up Dad's Ham radio and see if we can make contact with anyone and try to find out what's going on. Who knows…maybe we can even get a hold of Dad?" Mark informed his mother.

"Oh my God, that would be so wonderful if I could talk to him. I'm so worried about him. Don't worry about me and Kate. We've got the cooking taken care of…speaking of which, we need to get back to it, so nothing burns. You boys do what you have to do." she responded.

And with that, she turned around and followed Kate back into the house.

All four boys then walked through the gate to the backyard, walking past Viv at the barbeque as she was turning a grill loaded with steaks, then making their way down the steps of the bunker.

No one had eaten anything that day, so the aroma of the meat cooking on an open flame was enough to make their mouths water with anticipation, which their mouths were indeed watering.

Though Rocky had spent countless hours with Brian in the bunker, Jack had heard about it, but never saw its location, let alone stepped foot inside.

Mark turned on a couple battery operated lights attached to the ceiling that gave off a decent amount of light, enabling Jack to see everything inside.

"Wow…this is really cool in here. I'm impressed," exclaimed Jack. "Your dad really is smart to have done this. I'll bet you guys are the only ones in the neighborhood to have something like this."

Mark got down on his knees at the foot of the shelving and reached in under the bottom shelf, pulling out a large metal box covered in tin foil, then unlatched the lid from the box, revealing its contents.

"What the hell? What all is in there Mark?" asked Jack as he scanned over everything inside.

"Stuff we are going to need," Mark answered as he pulled out the Ham radio.

He then pulled out a brand-new Interstate car battery, then another one just like it, along with a giant spool of copper wire, some wire cutters, and some clamps.

"What's all the wire for?" asked Brian.

"We're probably going to have to rewire the antenna on the roof. I'm sure the existing wire got fried like everything else," said Mark.

Mark then pulled out a book on Ham radios. Since he never actually operated one before, he would need to take a crash course in operating one. Thank God his dad thought to put this in the cage with everything else.

"It's going to be dark in a couple of hours, so we probably won't get this up and running tonight, but what we can do now is make sure the radio works. I'll hook up the radio to the battery, and Jack, maybe you can run some wire up to the roof and attach it to the antenna. We won't be able to contact anyone out there until we position the antenna just right, and that might take an hour or more, so we will have the light to do that in the morning. Besides, I have to read this book tonight to find out how this thing works! Sound good?" Mark asked.

"You're running this show, Bud. I don't know a thing about Ham radios, but I'm damn glad that you do. Just tell me what you want us to do." retorted Jack.

Mark then reached back into the cage and pulled out a large Mag light, then another seven flashlights, followed by what had to be at least fifty D-size batteries still in their wrapping. He handed Jack the next biggest flashlight, then handed Brian and Rocky each a flashlight of their own.

"Turn on your flashlights to see if they are working. Brian, take these other four flashlights and bring them into the house for Mom and Kate, and Rocky…you take all of these batteries and put them on the utility table inside by the back door," said Mark, and with that request, all the boys turned on their flashlights as Mark pulled up the last item from the box…a hand crank AM/FM/National Weather Emergency Alert radio, something they would surely need if they could not get what they needed from the Ham radio.

"We're going to need these flashlights when it gets dark."

All flashlights were working perfectly.

As they rolled out of the bunker heading to the house, Viv turned to the boys and said, "We should be done cooking up all the meat in an hour, so whatever you boys are doing now, be done with it by then, because we are going to eat afterward."

Mark had been fiddling with the radio after he connected the radio cord to the battery posts, providing power to the Ham, but getting no signal.

Jack had set a ladder up to the roof over the garage where the Ham radio antenna was located and had been unspooling the wire so he could connect to the antenna, then drop it down to Mark so he could walk it to the back door, where Mark had set up the Ham radio on the utility table inside the back door next to where Rocky had set down the batteries for the flashlights.

While Jack was on the garage roof, he had a rather good line of sight over part of the neighborhood, including the next street over, and he could see the smoke wafting up skyward from various other barbeques in the backyards of the people that were home, people that had the same idea Viv had about cooking any meats they had before they thawed and rotted in their freezers.

Normally at this time he might expect to hear TVs in the distance, music playing, cars and motorcycles up and down the streets, jets flying over at high altitude, and even traffic in the distance from either University Blvd. or Arapahoe Road, both carrying vehicles either to or from The Streets of Southglenn, the local shopping mall less than a mile away, but he heard none of that. It was quiet, just like the quiet he would hear if he were in the mountains camping, but he did hear the children laughing in the near distance.

On the next street over, he could see several elementary school-age kids riding bikes in the street, screaming and laughing, without a care in the world as if it were summer vacation, which it was.

Go figure.

Without the serenade of sounds the kids were providing, it would have been so quiet that you would have been able to hear someone cough in a house three doors down, as long as they had a window open.

Cherry Knolls was a big subdivision with over 700 homes, but from his view from up on top of the garage roof, he could only see maybe twenty other homes due to being blocked off by the second story of the home he was on, combined with the vast number of trees in the neighborhood.

One home he was curious in particular about was Mr. Parsons, his next-door neighbor.

Mr. Parsons was in his 70s, a widower who had lost his wife to cancer a few years back.

He was usually out in his yard watering his flower bed at the foot of his front porch, but Jack had not seen him out there since yesterday evening at this same time.

"Come on in and eat boys…it's on the table," yelled Viv out the kitchen window.

That's all they needed to hear as the four of them were hungry enough to eat the ass out of a rhinoceros. Jack finished clamping the wire onto the antenna, then shimmied down the ladder as the other three were entering the back door.

"Wash up in the kitchen sink. You'll have to use the bottled water I sat next to it. Dish towels are hanging on the door of the frig." she said.

On the counter next to the stove were stacks and stacks of cooked meat wrapped in foil, the rewards reaped from their marathon cooking session.

On the table in the dining room were six place settings, each with a plate consisting of a steak, baked potato, and bowl of salad next to each plate. In the middle of the table was salt, pepper, some salad dressings, a butter dish, sour cream, and an assortment of pops and bottled water.

When they had all washed up, they sat at the table and joined hands as Viv said a prayer over the food they were about to eat.

As they buttered, salted, and peppered their potatoes, Viv brought up the plane crash.

"How bad was it? You boys haven't said anything about it, nor how you both lost your shirts."

Jack looked at Mark, waiting and hoping he would be the first one to speak, but he didn't say a word.

Finally, Jack spoke up.

"It was horrific. I can't even express in words how horrible it was. It was like something out of Saving Private Ryan, but much worse. It was a Southwest Airlines jet, and it took out four to six, maybe seven blocks. Everything was flattened and on fire, and just about everyone we saw was either dead or dying. Mark tried to give first aid to a man, but the man died before Mark could even put a bandage on him. It was sad beyond words. We both used our shirts to clean the blood off of Mark."

Viv then made the sign of the cross, followed by Brian and Kate.

After a long pause, Viv again spoke.

"Jack, how do you think your parents are doing?"

Jack flashed back to the huge plume of black smoke he saw coming from Downtown Denver, thinking about that very same thing Viv had just asked about.

"I'm thinking they are probably ok, even though they are not home," he said. "I'm sure Mom is with Dad since they work at the same place. They are either still at the hospital or they are walking home, but I really don't think they will be walking with Mom's bad knees unless Dad is pushing her in a wheelchair, which is entirely possible, but if I had to guess, I think they are probably still there to help out because of all the sick people there. I can't even imagine the chaos they are dealing with. I wonder how many people died who need medical equipment to live. All the dead people there…I don't even want to think about it."

It was then that typically quiet Kate blurted out, "Jack…you've got to go get them!"

Kate then broke down and started weeping.

Viv was sitting next to her and slid her chair over next to Kate, putting her arms around her and holding her tight.

"If they don't come back tonight, I'm going to take the bike and ride to the hospital. Dad and Mom are probably tending to the sick, so I'll probably have to search the hospital to find them. I just hope that Dad remembered to lock up the pharmacy. I'm also going to bring a big backpack to load up on stuff we will need, like ibuprofen, Tylenol, cold medicine, and especially antibiotics. I'll bet Dad already has some put aside for us." Jack said.

"I'll go with you. I'll bring my backpack I use for scout trips." Mark chimed in.

Jack nodded his head in appreciation, and after Kate was properly consoled, they all began to eat their dinner like ravenous wolves.

Just as Mark was getting up from the table, his mother said to him "I want you to take over that plate, a couple of bottles of water, and the candle on the plate sitting next to the dinner plate over to Mr. Parsons."

"When I was up on the roof, I didn't see Mr. Parsons out there like I normally do. Since he is always out there watering his flowers, he probably wasn't out there tonight because there's no running water," said Jack.

Mark put the two bottles of water, one in each pants pocket, grabbed the plate in one hand and the candle in the other, then walked out the front door and headed across the street as everyone else was finishing their dinner.

The sun had now set to the west and everything on their street was getting dark. The streetlights would normally be coming on by now, but they were black as the rest of the houses on his block.

When he got to the front door, he knocked and waited, but no one came.

He knocked again and still, no one came to the door.

He set the candle down on the chair next to the front door and opened the screen door, then opened the front door and yelled, "Mr. Parsons?"

Nothing.

"Mr. Parsons? It's Mark from across the street. My Mom sent some dinner over for you."

Mark then walked into the house and stood alone in the living room, then walked around into the kitchen…and there he was…lying on the kitchen floor. Mr. Parsons was dead on the floor in front of the stove. He set everything on the counter and immediately began to give the old man mouth-to-mouth but stopped immediately when he felt Mr. Parsons's ice-cold lips on his mouth. It was obvious that Mr. Parsons had been dead for hours, as he was cold as an ice cube, and by how hard it was to get his neck to bend upward, rigor mortis was already setting in.

Mark didn't know that Mr. Parsons had a pacemaker put in his chest five years ago, right before his wife had died and it became fried that morning when the EMP hit. He never saw what hit him and was probably dead before he even hit the floor.

Mark stood there in shock for a second, made the sign of the cross, then got his wits about him and began looking for something to cover him up.

He found a blanket folded up on the living room couch, grabbed it, unfolded it, then gently laid it over the body of his neighbor, covering his head and body, leaving the top of his shoes exposed. Not knowing what else to do, he left the food and candle there on the counter, picked up Mr. Parsons's cat Whiskers, and carried it out the front door, closing it softly behind him, then walked slowly across the street back to his home, thinking about how he was going to break this tragic news to his mother and the rest, especially the fragile Kate, who had just broke down and cried because she is so worried about her parents.

This would undoubtedly send her over the edge.

Maybe the cat would help.

THREE

D.C. and N.Y.C.

To say that D.C. was in utter chaos would be a gross understatement, but it was not unlike every other major metropolitan city across the U.S. When the bright light struck, everything in that city shut down except for the White House and some Federal buildings housing specific Federal agencies, as they had been hardened against an EMP attack.

Both houses of Congress stopped what they were doing immediately on their floors. One Senator and three Representatives dropped dead where they were sitting or standing due to pacemaker failure.

A jet airliner that had just taken off from Ronald Reagan airport had circled and was over the Capital when it lost all power and began falling from the sky, narrowly missing the Capitol building, but falling squarely on the Supreme Court across the street, completely leveling the building and its inhabitants.

Washington D.C. is a restricted fly zone, except for scheduled commercial flights flying to and from Ronald Reagan airport, about four miles outside of D.C.

In a split second, all nine Supreme Court justices, their staff, reporters, law enforcement, attorneys, building maintenance, and visitors, along with the 236 occupants of the airliner… were smashed to bits and instantly killed.

Under normal circumstances, the air would be filled with sirens and the streets would have hundreds of emergency vehicles on their way to the scene, but May 24 was unlike any other day because all normal transportation had ceased to function.

It would be over two hours before the National Guard would make their way through the congested streets of D.C. to respond to this national catastrophe, but only being able to hopelessly sift through the wreckage of twisted metal, rubble, human remains, and jet fuel.

At the White House, the president and his staff, along with the prime minister of England visiting that day, were ushered quickly to the elevator, leading them down to the secured bunker deep underneath the White House, which was standard protocol in case of a perceived threat to the president.

This began minutes before the EMP hit, as the White House was notified in advance of the missile launches.

The attack happened just moments before the president and the prime minister were about to make a joint statement from the Rose Garden concerning the progress both countries had made one year later regarding the battle against Covid 19.

In the bunker, the President could stay informed of the latest information and still make decisions based on keeping America safe and up and running to the best of its ability.

Also with the President were the heads of both FEMA and The Department of Homeland Security.

At the time of the attack, all that was known was that three ballistic missiles were fired into space and unsuccessfully pursued by our patriot missiles, thereby exploding above the Earth's atmosphere.

They were also somewhat confident that the missiles looked to be North Korean, and ships were on the way to both coasts, to the general area where they believed the missile launches had taken place, to intercept the freighters that had launched two of them.

What they did not know is that both freighters had been set ablaze and were on fire after the Iranian Revolutionary Guard had murdered the crews of both freighters, then exited the ships onto hardened boats that had been trailing the freighters nearby.

It was still too early to tell exactly who was behind the attack and why, and the evidence left behind would do little to shed any light once the naval vessels eventually found the ships burning at sea.

The trains underneath the Capitol that normally transported Senators and Representatives to their respective office buildings, such as the Russell, Hart, and Dirksen buildings for the Senate and Rayburn, Longworth, and Cannon buildings for the Representatives, were not working, so that meant they all had to walk city blocks from the Capital to their offices, leaving them exposed to the people on the street. Like the rest of America, none of their cell phones were working, so they were also in the dark as to the condition of their families or the states they were sent to D.C. to represent. All felt a sense of helplessness as they talked among each other in the groups that were heading to their offices, not knowing what they would do once they got there, but it would be a starting point for their next move. Most of them were not sure what had just happened and were in shock at what they were seeing transpiring before them, whereas a few of the others knew exactly what had just happened, and because of that knowledge, were frightened of the images they saw in their minds concerning the following days and months ahead.

As the last out of the Capital trailed behind, along with the few that walked across the street to witness the horror happening before them where the Supreme Court used to stand, they could see the armored trucks of the National Guard approaching from Constitution Avenue, at least ten trucks filled with soldiers ready to do the work as first responders, absent the ambulances and fire engines that would normally be deployed for such a grim task, trying to avoid the burning trees and grass set on fire from the lit jet fuel that exploded out of the plane.

Over on Independence Avenue was the Department of Agriculture (USDA), where Bill Jenkins's office was. He was employed there as a Supervisory Statistician. As he looked out the window onto Independence Avenue, he could see that the street was clogged with vehicles not moving, and the endless parade of citizens, both Federal workers and non, marching aimlessly up and down the boulevard to destinations unknown, he ruminated in thought, wondering, and hoping his son Mark remembered what to do if a situation like this ever arose.

Bill knew exactly what had just happened, and he was kicking himself for waiting to take that position in Aurora, Colorado only miles from his home, instead of the 2000 miles that currently separated him from his family.

He was also thanking God that it was late Spring and not the dead of Winter. If something like this had happened in January or December, the only heat source in the house would be the gas stove in the kitchen and the living room fireplace. Living in Colorado certainly had its perks, but the winters could be mighty cold in the Mile High City. He thought about the love of his life, his wife Vivian, and his boys Mark and Brian, both great kids thanks to their mother mostly, but also because of the great mentoring he had done with them.

Bill had spent time teaching both boys what he knew but had spent more time with Mark because he was the oldest. Mark was whip-smart when it came to all the prepper stuff Bill passed on to him. Being an Eagle Scout like his dad, Mark knew how to survive, and he naturally possessed critical thinking, which is a lost art among today's generation.

If the family were to survive without Bill there, it would be because of Mark and his intuitive ability to map out the situation and act accordingly.

Racking his brain, he tried to imagine some way he could get in touch with his family, but like everyone else in D.C. he knew, he was in the same situation as the rest.

He tried calling home, but there was no signal through the line, both on the landline and his cell phone. He tried a couple of other cell phones borrowed from other employees, ending with the same results.

Though he had not gone to the parking garage to try starting his car, even if he had and got it started, there was no way he would find gas on the way home to Colorado to make it.

The only reason Bill had taken a job so far from home was that the pay and benefits were excellent, plus he had been working shit jobs that held no interest to him, making barely enough to pay the bills and put food on the table.

Raising two boys, both with expensive extracurricular activities outside the home, he just couldn't see how he would make ends meet, and he hated the fact that Vivian had to work instead of being home for the boys when they got home from school, so flashback to just over five years ago, when one of his oldest friends that worked for the Department of Energy in D.C. contacted him about a job, he would be perfect for, paying a six-figure salary and great bennies, so he applied, and because of his friend's influence, he got the job.

Though it would cause him to be away from his family for a substantial part of the year, the tradeoff would be Viv staying at home and the boys after school programs would be paid for along with the rest of the bills. To make it even sweeter, Bill was also paid a housing stipend to live in D.C.

Seemed like a no-brainer at the time, and it still was, but a position had come up in the Aurora office he was getting ready to apply for. He just wished he had done so a couple of months earlier. If he had, it is most likely he would be there now instead of inside that stuffy office;

stuffy because the a/c had shut down and was not circulating cold air on that extremely hot and humid early afternoon.

Just after everything had shut down, he heard a voice down the hallway screaming that a plane was falling out of the sky. He barely got to his third-floor window, then to the right, he saw a glimpse of a passenger jet fall in the vicinity of the Capitol building, followed by a huge ear-splitting explosion and fireball, filling the sky with fire and thick black smoke. He couldn't tell exactly where it landed…if it hit the Capital building, the grounds in front of it, or maybe even the Supreme Court building across the street.

All he knew for sure was there would be death and destruction.

It had been two hours since the plane had dropped from the sky, when one of the staff from Homeland Security had come by the office, letting Bill and his staff know that it was confirmed that America was hit by a manmade EMP device, taking out the East Coast, and maybe the rest of the country. It was then he told his staff they could go home if they could, leaving him alone in his office.

He thought back to the Faraday cage he constructed and its contents. Mark should have everything he would need to establish contact with the outside world, as long as the Faraday cage did its job and protected what was inside of it. Besides, it was in the bunker, and the bunker alone without the cage should have protected everything.

Bill knew they had everything they needed to survive for the better part of a year.

There was a year's supply of food, water, and paper products, but knowing Vivian, she would be feeding the neighbors around them, dwindling their supply down to a month or two.

What they did not have is what haunted him…they had no supply of antibiotics. That was just something he did not have access to at the time he was putting together their survival stash.

There was one more thing…they did not have any weapons to protect them should those with ill intent should attempt to overtake the household. It was true that they did not live in the city, but lived instead in the suburbs where life was slower and just a little safer, but depending on how long their situation would last, it wouldn't take long for the criminal element in Denver to make their way south through Englewood, Littleton, then eventually into Centennial where they lived. From there they would head south to Highlands Ranch.

Denver would run out of goods on the shelves of the stores quickly, driving potential marauders down south into the wealthier neighborhoods populated by more preppers such as himself…fueled by the sheer will to live, letting nothing or no one stop them. The gun stores would most certainly be looted of their inventory.

Bill's absence of weapons was by design. One of his and Viv's greatest fears at the beginning of parenthood was having a gun in the house to be found by one of the boys, ending in a tragic accident. It was one of the few things they solidly agreed on when it came to raising their children. They both agreed that Bill and a machete would have to suffice should anyone break in if they were home.

Relying on Bill to smite the dragon with his sword was not as far-fetched as one would think. Before meeting Vivian while attending CU Boulder, Bill had worked at many nightclubs in Denver as a bouncer, having more than his share of fistfights at the door and inside these clubs while breaking up alcohol-induced fights between patrons having too much to drink, or the occasional tough guy looking to beef up his cred by beating up a bouncer, but Bill was known for his fighting skills among the nightlife.

Unfortunately for them, it never went as planned and almost always ended up with them having their heads stoved into the passenger door of a car parked in front of the club…and most likely getting a set of cuffs slapped on them with a ride to the Downtown Denver hoosegow.

Bill was not there to fight for his family now and it was killing him.

His son Mark was sure tough enough, being a lineman for the school football team, but probably not tough enough to fight with the barrel of a Smith & Wesson pointed in his face.

Bill was projecting into the future now. Today was Day One and that kind of a situation was hopefully far enough down the road that he would find a way to get home way before the chance of something like that ever happening.

There wasn't much he could do or was expected to do, so he gathered up his briefcase and headed down to the outdoor parking lot to see if he could start his car, if for nothing more than shits and giggles.

As expected, the car wouldn't open by hitting the unlock button on his key fob, so he removed the actual key from the fob, opened the door, inserted the fob into the ignition switch, and turned the ignition, which produced nothing at all. It was as if the car had no battery or ignition switch.

Slamming the door shut, he began to walk the ten blocks to his modest one-bedroom apartment off 7th and G streets, south of the National Mall, and it was the tensest walk of his life.

The humanity Bill was hit with was mind-shattering, and he could only imagine how bad things were in other cities around the country that did not have the EMP hardening that D.C. did.

Walking west on Independence was like walking through a gauntlet. He came upon a man not much older than him lying dead to the world on the sidewalk within his first block, with no one attending to him, or seeming to even care.

The sidewalks were full of tourists visiting the city as they always are every summer, going in and out of the various Smithsonian museums and office buildings of Congress, going somewhere in particular, but today was different. No one was going anywhere. They were all trying to figure out what to do next.

They all saw the plane go down by the Capital but did not know the full ramifications of what it meant. Some speculated it had been shot down out of the sky or was purposefully crashed, conjuring up memories and visions of 9/11.

Had they been inside, they would have known that the power crashed. All they knew from outside was that there was a blinding light for a few seconds, then the cars had stopped, the signal lights were not working, followed by discovering their cell phones weren't working either.

On the next block, he came upon a man screaming at the top of his lungs at another man for a wrong he perceived was perpetrated on him. It looked like the two were going to come to blows, but Bill walked on by as if they were not even there. The last thing he wanted was to become involved in something as stupid as a fistfight when he had other fish to fry, such as getting home.

It wasn't the same as it used to be when people fought with their fists. Nowadays someone would just as soon pull out a pistol and start shooting someone for something as insane as cutting you off in traffic.

He couldn't wait to get off of Independence Avenue and was relieved to make a right-hand turn onto 7th.

Before he turned, he noticed across the mall several large military vehicles filled with soldiers heading west on Constitution Avenue toward the Capital, undoubtedly toward the crash site.

He could feel it in the air…a sense of insanity magnified by the heat and humidity.

That was one of the things he most missed about Colorado, the dryness of it. You could stand under a shade tree in Colorado on the hottest of days and cool off about ten to fifteen degrees, unlike in D.C. where the sticky oppressive air seemed to hang on you like a cheap suit.

Today there would be no cooling off. Once he got to his apartment, he could open a window and that would be the best he could do. There would be no a/c or even a fan to plug in.

❧

"Just hang on! We're going to get you guys out of there" yelled the building superintendent down the elevator shaft from up above. Stuck in an elevator car between the fourth and fifth floors were five people: a young man and his wife, both in their twenties, their six year-old daughter and ten year-old son, and a very portly middle-aged man in a business suit with his briefcase. They had been in there most of the day and were miserable, tired, thirsty, and hungry.

They had been yelling for hours, hoping someone would come to their rescue. When the elevator stopped, everything immediately went dark except for their cell phones and the businessman's Rolex watch. They had tried calling for help on their phones, unsuccessfully, but at least they knew what time it was because of the watch. Their phones were all working, but none of them could get a signal.

Being in the concrete of the elevator shaft, they were spared the effects of the EMP that had blasted New York City, other than the failed power causing the elevator to stop.

It was now 5:25 in the afternoon and they had been stuck for over four hours.

The little girl had pissed her pants, with the rest of them having to go to the bathroom, but they managed to hold it so far.

"OK...come on though. We've got people that have to go to the bathroom in here!" said the father.

Things could have been worse. They could have been stuck up toward the top of the shaft on the forty-seventh floor.

All were guests of the Doubletree Hotel located on the corner of forty-seventh and seventh in Times Square. The family had just arrived the night before to spend a few days visiting N.Y.C. from Seattle, Washington, whereas the businessman had been there since Sunday night…in town to negotiate a merger between two companies on the verge of failing, hoping to revive both companies to ensure their survival.

It wasn't until someone on the fourth floor trying to summon the elevator heard their pleas for help, prompting them to run down the stairwell to the front desk in the lobby and alert the hotel staff. From that point, it was a matter of trying to find the building superintendent. They searched for him for an hour and a half because he had been taking an afternoon siesta in one of the un-booked rooms, something he did more often than anyone knew.

He only did this when he had eaten a large lunch, which he did that day.

They found him coming out of a room on the fourteenth floor, he was alerted to the emergency and jumped into action.

He had managed to manually open the elevator door on the fifth floor, where he was yelling down to them to hold on, help was on the way.

In the meantime, one of the desk clerks had run outside and grabbed one of New York's Finest off the street, beckoning him to come to the aid of these people, and of course, he did.

When the officer got to the sixth floor, the Super was glad to see him and brought him up to speed with the situation. They both determined that a ladder was needed, so the Super headed up the stairwell to the seventh-floor utility closet to retrieve one. He kept a ladder in the utility closet for situations such as these.

"This is Officer Moretti with the New York Police Department. We're going to get you out of there! The building Super is going to get a ladder and we will take you out through the roof of the car you're in. How many people are in there?" said the cop as he had just arrived.

"There's five of us in here. Three adults and two kids!" shouted the businessman.

"Ok….is anyone hurt? Are any of you disabled? Are you able to climb a ladder?" answered the Cop.

The businessman turned on his cell phone flashlight and looked at the father, then shined the light on his face tilting his head while looking at the dad expecting him to answer the cop.

"I've got a six-year-old down here…and a ten-year-old. I can help the little one up the ladder and I'm sure the ten-year-old can make it on his own" answered the father. "How far up the ladder will we have to climb?"

"About five feet. That's it. Easy peasy. As soon as he gets here with the ladder, I'm going to set it down on top of the car, then I will come down there and open the panel above you. I will help you all out of there" said the police officer.

Thankfully, this was happening while it was still light outside. Though it was darker in the hallways than usual, there was light coming in through the windows at each end of the hall, but in a couple of hours that light would be gone, and they would be immersed in total darkness.

Scenarios like this were playing out all across town, as there were over 63,000 elevators in the five boroughs of New York City, and just about every single one was stuck with people trapped in them. There were about 500 rescues taking place in various phases throughout the city, mostly by citizens and building Supers, some assisted by first responders, but the vast majority were left alone in the dark crying out to be saved…and no one was coming to help them.

Inside the elevator, they heard the abrupt sound of the ladder hitting the top of the car, then the officer climbing down the ladder into almost pitch blackness. His flashlight had gone dead, so the only source of light he could muster was his Zippo lighter.

He struck a flame and could see the panel, but he would need a special tool to unlock the bolts that held the panel in place.

"Hey man," he spoke to the Super leaning out through the open door above him. "I'm going to need a fireman's tool to get this thing open. You don't have one, do you?"

"Yes," said the Super. "I've got one in my desk drawer in the utility room. Give me a minute to go get it."

Five minutes later he was back with the tool and handed it down to Officer Moretti.

"No, no, no, no. You're going to have to come down here with me and open it. It's too dark for me to see. I will hold the lighter for you." the cop said.

The Super shimmied down the ladder and stood next to the cop, then got down on his knees and proceeded to use the tool on the panel. After a couple of minutes, the Super managed to lift the panel off and set it aside, only to find five very frightened and unnerved faces looking up at him, illuminated by the flashlights of their three cell phones.

They then broke into a cheer.

The policeman kneeled and stuck his head inside the car.

"You guys ready to get out of here? he asked.

In unison, they all shouted a resounding YES!!!

"Give me the boy first", the dad lifted his son up above his head and handed him to the cop, then the cop pulled the boy up through the hole in the roof, setting him next to the Super.

The Super then instructed the boy to climb up the ladder to the desk clerk who had come up to be of assistance, ushering the boy to safety.

"Ok, now the girl" ordered Moretti.

Moretti could not help but notice that the businessman in the car was a portly 280 pounds at a minimum and he would have an issue getting him out of there.

The little girl came through the hole and the cop could tell that she had gone to the bathroom in her pants, smelling the acrid scent of urine. She too was set aside by the Super.

"Now let's get your wife out of there. Can you pick her up by the waist and lift her to me?" Moretti asked.

The dad did as he was asked and hoisted his wife with all the strength he could muster up to Moretti, as Moretti then brought her up through the hole, setting her by the ladder where she then climbed up, leaving her daughter next to the Super to be brought up by her husband.

"All right...now you Dad. Can you jump up and pull yourself up? If you can do that, I can help get you up and out of there" Moretti asked.

"I think so," the dad said, and with that, he jumped up and grabbed the lip of the hole, where Moretti then grabbed his arms and pulled him up to where the man could push himself the rest of the way out of the hole in the roof. The Dad had to be around 160 to 170 pounds and took everything Officer Moretti had to pull him up through.

Once the dad was out of the car, he picked up his little girl in one arm and ever so slowly, then crept up the ladder and handed his daughter to the waiting arms of the desk clerk standing by, then brought himself up into the hallway.

The only one left now was the businessman. Four down and one to go.

"Look mister," said Officer Moretti. "I'm not going to bullshit you. I don't think you're going to be able to jump up to the ladder, and even if you could, I don't think I'd be able to pull you up. What I'm going to have to do is bring the ladder down here and slide it down into the car, then you can walk up here and climb your ass up out of there. Once you are up here with me, I'll pull the ladder back up, then we can both climb up out of this elevator shaft. Capiche?"

The businessman nodded his head in agreement.

The cop then had the Super get off the car and back in the hallway. He grabbed the ladder and slid it down into position inside the elevator car. First, the man handed up his briefcase, then began walking up the ladder. When he reached the top, he realized there was no way he would be able to fit through the hole to get out of the car. He was just too big of a man.

He first reached his arm up through the hole, but then could barely fit his head in alongside his arm. There was no way he was going to be able to push his body out of that car.

It was not even a close fit.

"Shit," said the cop.

It was simple mathematics. Getting this guy through the roof would be like trying to squeeze 280 pounds of sausage into a 100-pound casing. It wasn't going to happen.

"What the fuck???" barked the businessman as he was stepping down the ladder.

"Hey Super" yelled Moretti up the shaft. "Is there any way we can make this hole bigger?"

A few seconds had gone by as the super purposely paused before answering "No…unless we cut it open. Fat chance of that since there's no power to run a saw."

Some bottled water had been brought up to the fifth floor and the super handed the cop a couple of bottles, one for him and the other for the man in the elevator. The family had been ushered down to the lobby, so the only ones up there now were the Super, the cop, and the businessman.

The cop threw down a bottle of water to the man, but instead of immediately opening it and drinking it, the man must have forgotten how thirsty he was due to his reality staring him dead in the face. All he could do was hang his head and start to weep. He knew how his life story was about to end.

"Hey Pal...don't give up yet, because I'm not," said Moretti with all the compassion he could muster, but he also knew how this was going to end.

All across New York City, people were dying or on the verge of death, and this was a microcosm of that first day's tragedy unfolding.

It would be dark soon, and what would normally be a Times Square brilliantly lit with all the neon signage, would instead be a city wrapped in total darkness, creating a changing of the guard, turning the city over to the dark angels, where they would exercise their dominion.

※ᴧᴧᴧ

Off Lenox and 125th Street, there was a scene transpiring that duplicated the riots seen across America in the summer of 2020.

It was bedlam. It was just before dusk and all the storefront windows had been smashed in by rioters in their element, taking what they wanted and disregarding the rest, leaving store owners helpless to do anything to stop them. Those that tried to stop them were beaten senselessly and left bleeding, lying in the broken glass of their life's work and savings.

New York City was once one of the safest cities in the world when it was run by Mayor Giuliani, but under Mayor DeBlasio, the city had gone to hell in a handbasket.

The mantra of the far left of society had demanded the defunding of the police, and the mayor listened, stripping the NYPD of one billion dollars of funding in 2020 and another billion in 2021, leaving the police department a shell of what it once was.

No one wanted to be a police officer anymore, so they quit or retired if they had the time in. The police academy enrollment was down in epic numbers.

NYPD at full strength, before everything started to unravel, was over 35,000 strong.

Now they only had little more than 20,000 officers for all five boroughs…almost half of what they once were.

Cops no longer walked a beat because it was too dangerous for them. All of them were now in patrol cars, some even four to a car, especially in Harlem. Many of them had to move out of Manhattan if that's where they lived. Cops were being targeted and harassed, along with their families.

Central Park was not even safe to be in during the daytime, let alone at night, and the cops didn't go in there at night either.

For any reason. Period.

The gangs, both local and national, had taken over the city and made it whatever they wanted it to be. Stories were circulating that ritual murders were being committed at night near the reservoir, and the only reason they were stories is that no one wanted to go in to confirm it for themselves.

The cops occasionally flew in drones, but as soon as they were spotted, they were always shot down.

There was one time in the summer of 2021 that a tactical team of eight had gone in on foot at night dressed all in black, wearing night-vision goggles to do reconnaissance and assess what it would take to take back the park, but the mission failed miserably.

All eight were captured and hung naked from the chain-link backstops of the ball fields.

All had their scrotums removed and their tongues cut out, left to bleed out on the dirt behind home plate.

These were bloodthirsty savages running the park now, and it was nothing short of a miracle that more cops had not ended up the same way as these eight men in blue.

Many of the storekeepers had left the city, but there were still the stubborn few that refused to relinquish ground to these factions of evil. Most of them were born not far from where their businesses were and had lived in NYC all their lives.

Die-hard Yankee and Knicks fans...all of them.

They stayed, even though the police, the same ones their taxes were paying for, were not going to, or be able, to protect them should they need it.

And so it was that the scene on 125th Ave was playing out without a cop anywhere in sight.

One storefront operator got the brunt of it and was coughing up blood in the gutter in front of his store. He had been kicked in the stomach so many times that his stomach had ruptured, sending bile and blood up to his esophagus and into the sewer system. He also had been bashed in the head with a metal stand used to hold velvet rope, forming crowd management lines for the public, and what showed was a gaping hole in the back of his head that was pouring out blood, matting the thick black hair on his Syrian skull.

All he ever wanted was to become an American citizen and be a success for his wife and his children. Ten years ago, he came to America from Damascus with his family and his life savings after getting his green card to stay.

He went to school every night during the week after working for his father-in-law, learning English and how to be a United States citizen.

It went on that way for six years and he became adept at speaking

English. He also got help from his children, who learned to speak the language better than he did from being in the public school system.

His name was Ahmed, and he was proud to be an American, and that's what he finally became after passing his test in 2019, becoming a United States citizen.

Now it was all going to be for nothing, because fifteen minutes later he would die in that street, in front of the little market he opened right after passing his test.

What makes this even sadder is that there was no need for this man to die, as he put up no struggle to save his store or its contents. The taking of his life was a thrill kill by these savage cowards. After trying the door that Ahmed had locked after the power failed, one of the thieves immediately threw a metal chair Ahmed had kept outside to sit in while taking a smoke break during slow periods, sending it through the plate glass window of the store. In came three men with the intent to rob him of the money he kept in the cash register.

Ahmed showed no signs of resistance and even backed away from the register to stand up against the wall, letting them take what they wanted unfettered.

He had less than a hundred dollars in the till, and that was not enough for one of the craven robbers, so in retaliation for his short-haul, Ahmad was thrown to the ground and beaten with closed fists, then kicked repeatedly in the stomach as his assailant laughed with glee. He then finished his victim with a blow to the back of the head with the heavy metal object.

This was only the first day of the blackout, and it was not even dark yet.

This was the new N.Y.C....and it was about to get a million times worse.

FOUR

Little Plastic Jesus on the Rear-View Mirror

I t was 6:00 in the morning and Jack was sitting at the kitchen table, sipping on a bottle of water...worried sick about his parents. They didn't come home last night, and he imagined all kinds of horrible scenarios too terrible to think about, yet there he was thinking about them just the same. He tried to empty his mind, telling himself it was just his over-active imagination running away as usual.

His dad was getting up there in age, with his mom not far behind. His dad Paul was sixty-four and was coming up on his sixty-fifth birthday in August. He never knew his dad to be a fighter, and rarely had seen him angry. He couldn't picture his dad in a fight, so likewise he couldn't imagine him having to defend himself from a mugger on the streets of Denver while pushing his mother in a wheelchair down Broadway trying to make it home...in the dark.

Both of his parents were pacifists and didn't believe in corporal punishment, meaning neither of them ever spanked or paddled Jack, his little brother, and especially not his sister. Instead, they were given plenty of time-outs, and restrictions, and had lots of things taken away from them, but never were they slapped or struck in any way.

Truth be told, Jack might have preferred a smack instead of having to stay up in his room on a Saturday afternoon, missing out on playing with the boys outside at Cherry Knolls Park.

His parents were not big drinkers either, except for the occasional glass of wine with dinner, or a few more glasses with friends and family during the holidays, so there were no momentary slips of character resulting in anything of a violent nature.

In short, they were great parents and their kids reflected that in their behavior.

Everybody has their way of raising children, some with an iron fist, and they still produce the same result with great respectful kids, while others go over the line and show they never should have had kids to begin with.

Knowing that Mr. Parsons was next door lying dead on his kitchen floor was more than Jack could bear, but it did keep his mind off his parents for the moment. If Mark was right about the EMP, no ambulances or coroner would be coming to collect his body, so that left him, Mark or both of them to do something with him. What would that be? Would they bury his body in his backyard?

One thing was for sure…Jack and Mark would not be going up Broadway again to look for his parents. They would go up University Blvd. this time to Speer Blvd., making a left onto Speer, then heading northwest to the hospital, the same way his parents traveled when going to work. If they could not find his parents there, they would be forced to take Broadway back down toward home in hopes of finding them. He certainly did not want to think of the other possibility, not finding them at the hospital.

Jack got up from his chair and went upstairs to look in on his little sister and brother. Stopping at his sister's bedroom, he looked in on her, lying so peaceful as she slept…different than a few hours ago, as she was weeping at the thought of her parents not home and possibly in trouble somewhere. Jack went to sleep listening to her crying, wishing he could go into her room and tell her something to soothe her, but he was in just as much fear as she was and he could not let her, or Rocky, see his fears escaping through his eyes. Now she was sleeping soundly and the last thing he wanted to do was disturb her slumber, so he tiptoed down the hall to check in on Rocky.

There he was, lying on his bed, eyes wide awake, looking at the ceiling, then he turned his eyes toward Jack as he caught view of him.

"They didn't come home last night, did they?" Rocky asked.

"Nope," Jack answered back at him. "I'm going to leave here in a bit to go find them. I'm going to sneak over into Mark's backyard. He told us last night he would be up at sunrise messing with the Ham radio at the table inside their back door. He's going to come with me."

"I wanna go with you guys," said Rocky. "It's super boring just staying here".

"I need you and Brian to stay here to protect Kate and Brian's mom. I promise…I'll take you with me next time I go somewhere" answered Jack. "Promise."

After throwing on a shirt and a pair of shorts and tennis shoes, Jack went out the front door, crossed the street, and opened the side gate of Mark's backyard surprised to find him outside digging a hole in the yard.

"What are you doing Mark?" he asked. "Are you digging a hole to bury Mr. Parsons?"

"No…I'm digging a latrine" Mark replied.

This was the resourcefulness his dad had thought about in D.C.

The toilets wouldn't be able to flush but one time without running water to fill the tanks back up, so his quick thinking got him out to the garden shed to grab a shovel and start digging.

The hole was three feet deep, one foot wide, and a couple of feet long. Next to the hole on the ground was one of the toilet seats he had just removed from the bathroom in the basement. The plan was to hammer together a bench and attach the toilet seat to it, then set it over the hole.

"That's good thinking, but what is everyone going to do? Come out here in broad daylight, drop trow, and take a dump?" he jokingly asked.

"We've got a big family tent in the garage that I'm going to set up over it. You can stand up in it and everything. I'm going to pitch it over the hole and then cut a hole in the floor of the tent. You'll be able to go inside the tent, zip it up behind you, and then do your business with total privacy" explained Mark.

"Dude…that's some total Eagle Scout shit right there" Jack laughed back. "I don't suppose you've had a chance to mess with the radio yet?"

"I wanted to get this done before we headed out today, so no, not yet, but I did read through that Ham instruction book last night. I think I might have the gist of it. I still need to hook up the wire you installed on the antenna to the radio, but that should only take a minute. We can do that and get on the radio today or tonight when we get back. Did your parents come home last night?" asked Mark.

"Nope," said Jack.

"Oh no…where do you think they are? Still at the hospital?"

"I hope so. I'm hoping they didn't try to leave the hospital yesterday because that would probably mean they are in trouble" Jack answered.

"Well, let me finish building this bench for the toilet seat real quick, and then you can help me set the tent up over it, then we'll leave." Mark then walked over to the garden shed and grabbed a hand saw, then he walked over to the woodpile behind the garage to grab a few choice pieces of old lumber.

"I think my Mom is in the house cooking up some breakfast," Mark said, as Jack suddenly noticed the smell of BBQ everywhere. People in the neighborhood were firing up their grills everywhere, as they could see smoke in any direction they looked, and by the smell of it, it was more than breakfast meats cooking. Most stoves in the neighborhood were electric, which meant they were cooking their meals on either a BBQ grill, a Coleman stove, or over an open fire.

Mr. Parsons's cat Whiskers was sitting on the window sill, looking out the window at the two men, probably wondering why he was there and not home.

After Jack and his crew had gone home to sleep in their beds last night, Mark went back over to Mr. Parsons's house to fetch Whisker's food bowl, bags of cat food and cat litter, and his litter box, all in the kitchen where Mr. Parsons laid. It was dark in the house, so stepping over his dead body to open the cabinet door under the sink where he searched for the cat food was creepy beyond belief, and Mark was glad to have found what he came for as quickly as he did and relieved to be out of there once he shut the door behind him.

He knew he'd have to go there at least one more time. He would need Jack's help to get Mr. Parsons off the kitchen floor, and into the ground, assuming no other help was coming their way.

After assembling the bench as Jack watched, Mark set it over the hole he had dug, it was perfect.

"I'm going to need your help putting up this tent," Mark said to Jack.

Mark walked back over into the garage and came out with a family-size twelve person tent, then emptied the contents of the bag next to the newly constructed latrine. After laying the tent over the hole, they staked it down and erected it with the poles that came with it. Mark unzipped the tent and went inside. He reached into his pocket and pulled out his Buck knife, then proceeded to cut a hole in the tent floor over the hole he had dug, then placed the funky, but functional toilet seat bench he constructed over the hole, and voila! Just like downtown.

"Jack and Mark! Come inside and eat" yelled Viv out to the two of them.

"Thanks, Mrs. Jenkins. You've been great feeding us. Appreciate it" thanked Jack.

"I would expect nothing less from your parents if the tables were turned. Besides, they'll be home today, right? You guys will find them and bring them home where they belong." She offered.

Not only would she be feeding the kids across the street, but probably their parents as well if this thing lasted more than a couple of days. Viv would be breaking out the freeze-dried food kept down in the bunker, which was designed to last four people for a year, but with a total of eight mouths to feed, that supply would be cut in half, turning it into six months' worth.

Bacon and eggs were just what the doctor ordered, and the boys wolfed everything down in short order.

There was no milk, as it had already turned sour, but the lunch meats, cheeses, and vegetables were good for a couple more days. The condiments, except for the mayo, should last until they ran out of them.

"I'm hoping we are all wrong about this being an EMP and the power comes back on today" Viv hoped but knew deep down inside that sentiment was nothing more than wishful thinking. Mark had the only working cell phone of the bunch since he had been down in the bunker yesterday, and everything electrical was fried, plus there was no running water.

"I dug a latrine out in the yard Mom. It's inside the tent!" Mark proudly announced.

Not a moment too soon either. Everyone had already used the toilets once, flushing the water in the toilet tanks down the drain, leaving them bone dry. Any waste left in the toilet bowls after that would sit there, creating a not-too pleasant aroma.

"We're already crapping in King Soopers grocery bags," said Jack, prompting a disgusted look from Viv.

"You guys can come to use the latrine, but only for number two. If it's number one you can pee in the backyard, except for Katie...she can pee in the latrine," said Viv while pointing at the kitchen counter. "I made you boys some sandwiches, cookies, and chips to take with you. They are in those paper sacks"

"I was thinking we'd take a different route today. My parents always drove up University Blvd. to go to work, so I'm thinking they would probably go the same way walking home. I can't see my dad wanting to deal with Broadway" said Jack to Mark. "What do you think about that plan?"

"Whatever you think is good with me" Mark answered." I just want to find them, probably almost as bad as you do.

Paul and Julie Price had watched Mark grow up across the street from them and had gone to most of his football games at Arapahoe High School, attended many of his birthday parties, and were even at his Eagle Court of Honor the year before.

Julie and Viv were always very tight, and they both were good Christians. Viv had always tried to get Julie to come to her church, Most Precious Blood, over on Colorado Blvd. in Denver, which meant she was trying to convert her to Catholicism.

Viv had always sung in the church choir and would have loved to have Julie join her, but Julie was torn between going to Viv's church or going to their church off Dry Creek Blvd. with Paul and the kids. Paul was adamant about not going to a Catholic church. Catholicism as he saw it was breaking one of the Ten Commandments, worshipping a false idol as God, meaning the Pope was the false idol. Julie, of course, would never repeat that to anyone, especially Vivian. Catholics see things from a different point of view, but it never became a stumbling block in their friendship.

So, Viv, not aware of this, figured she would just keep gently nudging her, and eventually, she would come around and join her one day and see how great it was, and then she would become a member.

Viv had always been a devout Catholic, along with her husband Bill and the kids. These last few years, she had hung on to the church more than she ever had, with Bill being away in Washington D.C. two-thirds of the year.

Calling his job a strain on their marriage wouldn't exactly be accurate, but she did miss him every time he was away, and it didn't get any better with time. When she was feeling especially lonely, she would flashback to when she met him in college at the local Starbucks off-campus working behind the counter as a barista and Bill would come in, always early in the morning right after they opened, and get a Grande Café Americano and sit close to the counter. She would always catch him checking her out, and she was waiting for the day, what seemed an eternity, for him to get up the nerve and ask her out, which he eventually did.

After their first date catching a movie, she knew that he was the man she was going to marry. There was no doubt in her mind and she was already making wedding plans in her head after their third date.

Bill Jenkins was a catch for sure back then. He was studying advanced mathematics and was attending CU Boulder on both athletic and academic scholarships, playing football for the school as an offensive lineman.

As far as Vivian was concerned, he was still the strapping,

sandy-haired, good-looking young man she had married, though it was fair to say that she saw him through slightly different lenses.

Bill was still in damn good shape, but he had taken on some of the sins of the world, and his face showed it. He now had some serious luggage under his eyes due to less sleep than his body and mind required, and he was beginning to show the unmistakable signs of a potbelly in the works.

His hairline had also receded just a bit, but he was far from being bald.

All in all, Bill had held up fairly well throughout the years. He too was missing his wife and kids terribly, and there were many days on the job that he heard a voice in his head, telling him the job wasn't worth it, that he should quit and go home. It was just awful, some days needing to hold his wife closely and share his day with her like he used to.

They did the next best thing instead, and that was to spend at least a half-hour on the phone after dinner, filling each other in on the day's events. -- but it just wasn't the same.

One thing Bill <u>had</u> slacked off on was going to church regularly while in D.C.

It felt different going to church without his wife and two boys trailing behind.

"Ok…you ready to see what's going on in the world?" asked Mark as he pulled the red Midland ER210 emergency radio off the shelf above the kitchen counter.

It was a hand-crank radio but worked on batteries as well, and the batteries inside the unit had just been changed about a year ago. Mark pushed the power button and it turned on to static, as it was set to AM.

"That doesn't sound good," said Viv.

"Hold on Mom. It's not even on a channel yet" Mark replied to her. "Let me try to find one"

Mark moved the dial through the numbers and there was absolutely nothing. He then switched it over to FM, and still, there was nothing.

Then he turned it to one of the NOAA weather channels and... JACKPOT!

They had just caught the last few words, followed by a few seconds of silence, and then a voice started to speak.

"Yesterday at 1:16 p.m. Eastern Time, the United States, Southern Canada, Northern Mexico, Cuba, Belize, and all of the Caribbean Islands suffered a massive electromagnetic pulse due to several nuclear explosions 200 miles into the thermosphere over said countries, causing catastrophic loss of infrastructure to these affected areas. You may currently be experiencing a loss of power in all aspects, including electricity, phone, radio, television, internet, running water, electric and gasoline-powered vehicles, including but not limited to cars, buses, boats, airplanes, motorcycles, and any machine operated on electricity, gas, or other fuel sources. Use extreme caution in your daily activities. If your area has been affected, there are no first responders that will come to your aid. If you have no bottled water, boil all water before drinking, regardless of where it is from. President Joseph Biden will make a statement on this channel at approximately 6:00 p.m. Eastern Standard Time. This announcement will repeat in five seconds.

"OMG!" Viv gasped.

The three of them sat at the table, looking at each other stone-faced.

"I guess that answers your question Mom," said Mark. "It looks like the power isn't coming on anytime soon.

"Thank you for breakfast, Mrs. Jenkins," Jack thanked Viv as he was beginning to stand.

"Sure Jack," she said while putting the paper plates in the garbage. "Do me a favor, Jack. Take the garbage out to one of the cans behind the garage so I can talk to Mark for a minute, will you Hun?"

"Sure thing" he replied and proceeded to get up from the table and grabbed the garbage out of its can and walked out the back door.

"We've got enough food and water to last a year, correct?" she asked Mark.

"Not really. Since we are taking on Jack and his family, that cuts our supply in half. We've got six months' worth…seven if we conserve. Every person that we bring into the fold cuts our supply down. We can't take in anymore Mom. Period." Mark explained, and with that said, he got up and left the kitchen to go outside.

Outside Mark was loading his backpack with bottles of water from the garage and the lunch his mom had made for him, while Jack headed across the street to his house to grab Brian's bike and backpack.

Jack noticed the street they lived on looked the same that day as the day before when everything went sour. All the cars were in the same position as they were then, and none of the sprinkler systems were on, so none of the lawns were being watered. There was no one outside, with no white noise from any of the streets close by, even from Arapahoe and University. No children laughing or screaming. Nothing but dead silence, and it was eerie.

Jack grabbed the big hiking backpack from the garage that he had only used once before…the trip he took with his church camp during the summer in 11th grade. He picked up the bike in the front yard, then hustled back over to Mark's backyard to load his stuff up as well.

After Jack loaded his pack, they both put their packs on, and though the packs were pretty much the same size, Jack's looked bigger, whereas Mark's was proportional.

They were both four years apart, and Mark was as tall as Jack, but his frame was quite a bit different. Mark took after his dad, and for a 17-year-old, he was built like a brick shithouse.

What made Mark different from Jack was his girth.

Being a lineman on the high school football team, Mark worked out in the weight room regularly, so he was muscle-bound, especially in the upper chest area.

As huge as Mark was, he was a pussycat at heart and always stuck up for the little guy.

Everyone that knew him loved him, and quite frankly, most expected big things from him in the future. He was extremely popular with the rest of his team and was always quick to crack a joke, but never at anyone's expense.

He was also an exceptional student. He always engaged in whatever class he was in and was eager to help his fellow students that might be struggling with a particular subject.

Mark was the kind of boy every parent would be proud of, which is part of the reason Paul and Julie cared for him as much as they did. Secretly they hoped Mark would influence their youngest son Rocky, who by all accounts, was the troublemaker of the family and known to be the class clown.

Rocky also seemed to have a penchant for fighting in school, which was frowned upon by his teachers, especially his dad.

Rocky's real name was Henry, but someone gave him the nickname Rocky after one of his fights, and it stuck from that point on.

"Maybe you should grab your little plastic Jesus off of your rear-view mirror?" Viv yelled at Mark. "Couldn't hurt"

Mark opened the door of his Honda and grabbed it off the rear-view mirror, showed it to Jack, then put it in his pocket.

"We might need all the help we can get today," said Jack as they rode off down the street.

FIVE

"This Wasn't Supposed to Happen"

As Jack and Mark were coasting down Elizabeth St. just before Arapahoe, Mark noticed Sean McAdams and his dad Kevin on their front porch, waving them down to stop and talk with them.

Sean was a couple of years older than Mark and had graduated from Arapahoe High School the year before. He decided not to go to college right out of high school, but instead became a river raft guide for a rafting company out of Buena Vista, a mountain town in central Colorado. Normally he would be there guiding trips down the Arkansas River, but he had driven across SouthPark over to Centennial to spend a few days with his parents before the brunt of the summer season began.

"How are all of you holding up," asked Mark.

"So far, so good" Sean replied. "But I don't know how much longer. We're down to our last case of water and pretty soon the meat we barbequed will go bad. Mom's in the house. She's not feeling well this morning."

"Where are you guys heading?" asked Kevin McAdams, Sean's dad.

Jack did not know them at all and had never spoken to them, so Mark chimed in on his behalf.

"Mr.McAdams…Sean…this is the neighbor that lives across the street from me, Jack Price.

After shaking hands, Mark continued "Jack's parents never came home yesterday from work. They work at Denver General downtown, so we are heading there to see if we can find them and bring them home."

"Aw man…sorry to hear that" offered Mr. McAdams, as if he knew something bad had happened to them.

"Working at a hospital, I can imagine they are completely overwhelmed. They are probably working non-stop just trying to keep people alive" he continued. "What do your parents do there?'

Before Mark could say anything, Jack spoke up for himself.

"My Dad is the Head Pharmacist, and my mom works in the administration part of it, you know, billing? Stuff like that."

"Pharmacist huh? We talked to the neighbor next door last night that works down there. He had walked home from downtown Denver. Had to leave his car there. He said as soon as the sun started going down, it started to become extremely violent, with homeless people marauding the stores and taking what they wanted. He said there were no police anywhere to stop them or protect anyone from them. It was like they had free reign over the city.

He said he made the mistake of walking down Lincoln Ave. on his way to get home and had to keep making detours. He said he hid in some bushes and behind some cars along the way to avoid them. He saw three guys run up to a guy sitting on his porch, and they just stabbed the shit out of him for no reason, then went into his house and left a few minutes later with a jug of water and some jewelry. That was it! They killed a guy for next to nothing.

He told me he should have made it home a couple of hours earlier than he got here, but because of those kinds of people out on the street, he had to keep hiding to avoid them. It's just getting crazy out there" said Mr. McAdams. "I hope your dad is ok in that pharmacy. I imagine those kinds of places are being looted by drug addicts."

That last statement Mr. McAdams offered up didn't make them feel any more secure about what they were attempting to do, but it only strengthened Jack's resolve to complete the mission, and Mark wasn't about to bail on him.

They then said their goodbyes and headed over to University Blvd. on Arapahoe.

Jack wished he had more air in his back tire, but there was enough to make the trip. When they got back home, he'd be sure to put more air in the tires with the hand pump in the garage.

It was pretty much smooth sailing up University Blvd. There were still plenty of vehicles on the road that they had to maneuver around, but what they didn't have to negotiate was that plane crash on Broadway, which they were thankful for, especially Mark.

It took them maybe forty-five minutes to get to the Cherry Creek Mall, where they would turn left on 1st Street, which turned into Speer Blvd.

They noticed a lot more people on the street than they did the day before and everyone had the same look about them. All were disheveled, with their clothes crumpled and their hair uncombed. They also saw a few more dead drivers behind the wheel of their vehicles as well.

The further and longer they rode, the more cars and people they spotted, and it felt to Mark like they were bike riding into a war zone with no one going anywhere, but instead stumbling and mumbling aimlessly.

They were in the heart of Denver now and had traversed a few inner-city neighborhoods on their way through more of them when First Street turned into Speer Blvd.

Other than all the cars on the street, Denver was beautiful at this time of year. It was a late spring morning with the trees in full bloom, and there were lots of them providing shade along the way.

It was starting to warm up pretty good and they were almost to their destination when they decided to stop at the corner of Speer and Lincoln to catch their breath and drink some water. They were only a few minutes away now. Both leaned their bikes up against the concrete barrier that separated them from Cherry Creek down below, a highly popular place for runners to run alongside the creek on a cement path, but it was also a place to find the homeless camped underneath the vast number of bridges along the creek's expanse throughout the city.

Both were enjoying their bologna and cheese sandwiches Viv had made for them, then down at the creek directly below them, Mark was the first to spot her; a woman, probably homeless herself in her twenties, performing a sexual act on an older man that was leaned up against the retaining wall directly below them.

Mark put his finger across his mouth, as to suggest silence to Jack, then motioned for him to look down below to see what he was seeing.

"Whoa," said Jack. The woman heard him and stopped what she was doing momentarily, but then resumed without reticence, right there in broad daylight…not caring who saw her.

They both then slid down the barrier to sit down on the sidewalk, shielding them from the view below. They looked at each other and smiled but didn't say a word…they just kept eating.

When they finished their sandwiches and bottles of water, a guy came up to them almost out of nowhere and asked them if they had any water. He didn't look like he was homeless, but instead, someone that got trapped down there, seeming to belong somewhere else, and he looked as though he hadn't slept at all that night.

"Sure. Sit down with us for a minute" Mark suggested to the man, handing him a bottle of water out of his pack.

The man sat down and accepted the water gratefully, then began gulping it down as if he hadn't had any fluids for quite some time.

"I'm from Omaha. I'm here checking on one of my clients. The power went out and the guy I'm dealing with dropped dead…right in front of me…simultaneously. It was the weirdest thing," said the man. "I tried calling on the phone for help, but none of the phones were working at his place of business…not even my cell phone. I had to get out of there and I've been walking around this area all night and found an unlocked car to hang out in. I had to get off the street because of what was going on out here" the man said.

"What was going on?" asked Jack.

"People were beating other people and killing each other. I must have seen five people bite the bullet last night. It was horrible…and there haven't been any police around here to be found" the man answered. "This is really a fucked-up town you guys got here"

"Do you know what happened yesterday?" Mark asked the man. "America got hit with an EMP and the whole country is shut down. It's like this everywhere mister. I can't imagine what the big cities are like, such as L.A., Chicago, and New York. It's probably the same as this, only on steroids"

The man was puzzled because he had never heard of an EMP before.

"What the hell is an EMP?" he asked.

"An electromagnetic pulse of energy…never mind. It was bad… really bad" Jack retorted.

The boys then stood up and wished the man well, then continued their bike ride to the hospital. The woman down below must have finished her business because she was now out of sight. The old man was sitting in the grass below, leaning against the retaining wall fast asleep.

They were only a couple of blocks away now and the hospital was in view.

Jack led the way and Mark followed, as he was unfamiliar with this part of town or the layout of the hospital.

A couple of minutes later, they rolled up at the main entrance and neither was prepared for what came into view. The first thing they witnessed was a gurney being rolled out of the front doors with a body on it, covered with a sheet, and pushed by two men in scrubs. They pushed the gurney toward the roundabout in front of them to an exceptionally long line of bodies of the dead, all lined up in the street leading to the roundabout. They watched in horror as the two men reached the end of the line, then lifted the body off the gurney, but instead of carefully setting the body down at the end of the line, they just dropped it in place with no regard for it, as if it were a sack of potatoes instead of a human being. In fairness, these guys looked to be dog tired and were probably doing this most of the night, obviously becoming de-sensitized to the task at hand.

It was a crap job, but someone had to do it. There had to be at least twenty-five to thirty bodies out there lying next to each other, with many more still inside.

Jack then asked the men "What are you going to do with these people"

One of them answered him "We're probably going to have to put them in a pile and burn them. If we don't, they are going to smell a whole lot worse than they do now and attract flies and diseases. See those dogs over there?"

The man pointed to a large pack of hungry stray dogs at the edge of the parking lot, some feral and some let loose by their owners.

"Those dogs are starving, and we won't be able to keep them off these bodies before long. It's either burn the bodies or these dogs are going to start eating them, and I don't think it's a good idea to let dogs acquire a taste for human flesh" finished the man.

The death that Jack and Mark had seen these last two days was staggering to them, yet they had not been de-sensitized to it like these two hospital workers had become, which had frightened them both.

To the left of the main entrance was the outpatient building that housed the hospital pharmacy. The boys both walked their bikes to that building and leaned them up against the big window on the side of the entrance of the building. They then walked inside with their packs on their backs, down the main hall to the front door of the pharmacy next to the elevator doors.

When they got to the pharmacy, the door was opened wide, and Jack started to panic as some of the upright shelving holding the medicines behind the counter were knocked over, and there was a big spray pattern of blood on the wall and a pool of coagulated blood on the carpet below it.

There wasn't a soul inside, but it was obvious what had happened here.

The pharmacy had been ransacked.

"DAD!!!! DAD!!! WHERE ARE YOU???" Jack screamed at the top of his lungs.

He searched everywhere and could not find him. He wasn't underneath the toppled shelving, or in the bathroom, nor was he in the break room. He was relieved for the moment not to find him dead, and since he was not in the pharmacy, there was a shot that he was somewhere else in the hospital, maybe helping with the dead or dying.

As Jack and Mark stepped out the door of the pharmacy and into the main corridor, they could hear a faint voice calling Jack's name.

"Jack...Jack...is that you?" the voice almost whispered from down the hall.

It was Julie, Jack's mom, and she was half hanging out of an office doorway a few doors down, lying on the floor looking half dead herself.

"OH MY GOD…MOM!!!" Jack screamed, running down to her and falling to his knees to embrace her.

His mom was now sobbing uncontrollably as Jack cradled her like a baby, stroking her disheveled hair as he tried to soothe her.

"Mom…are you hurt? Can you get up? Where's Dad?" he asked her with a quavering voice, and she began to cry even louder. "Where is he?"

"Your Dad is dead Jackie…they killed him" she spoke softly. "These men, three of them…they came into the pharmacy yesterday before it got dark. After the power went out, I left my desk and came over here to be with your father. I stayed with him all day and we were about to leave and start walking home when these men came in wearing hoodies and demanded that your father start filling a bag with drugs that he handed to your Dad, and then started naming off the ones he wanted. Your father refused, then the man punched him a few times in the face, but your Dad still wouldn't do it, so the man pulled a gun out of his shirt and shot him in the back of the head. The man tried to get me to fill the bag, but I told him I didn't work there and didn't know anything about drugs, so he slapped me hard on the side of my head. I fell next to your Dad on the floor, then the men just started looking for the drugs themselves. I managed to drag myself from behind the counter and out the door. I crawled down here to this office and locked myself inside. I've been in here all night, then I heard your voice screaming for Dad" Julie recounted, then resumed crying in the lap of her son.

Mark was speechless and did not say one word, but instead just looked at the two of them with tears rolling down his cheeks.

The only thing Jack could do was just sit there on the floor with his mom, holding her tight while crying with her.

"Mom…Dad wasn't in the pharmacy when we got here." Jack whispered in her ear. "Are you sure he's dead?"

"Didn't you see that big spray of blood on the wall?" she asked.

"That was from him being shot in the head. He was lying in a pool of his blood. If you are suggesting he could have walked out of there, I don't think it's possible. He must be dead. Oh Lord, I wish he weren't, but I saw it all happen right in front of me…all of it."

What none of them knew was that Paul Price's body was found earlier that morning by someone that came in looking to have a prescription filled. The hospital staff was alerted, and the body was carried out to the roundabout before the boys ever got there, by the same two men carrying dead bodies out of the hospital and laying them in the street.

Paul Price had already been brought out hours earlier and was one of the closest bodies to the boys, but since he had been covered with a blanket, they couldn't possibly have known he was there.

"C'mon Mom…let's get you home" urged Jack, helping her to her feet.

Mark had gone to the main entrance and found a wheelchair just inside and wheeled it over to the doorway where they were. What he didn't notice was that their bikes were gone from the front where they had been leaning against the window. Two men had stolen them and rode off almost as soon as they had left them there, which the boys discovered as they walked outside with Julie in tow. Bikes were at a premium now. They were the only mode of transportation other than your feet.

"Great. Now, what?' asked Mark.

"Looks like we hoof it" replied Jack. "I would have had to leave mine here anyway. There's no way I could have taken a bike and pushed a wheelchair at the same time."

Jack reached into his backpack, pulled out a bottle of water and opened it, then gave it to his mother. She could barely hold it up to her lips, but she managed to take a few sips, then began drinking it down.

She was severely dehydrated, and frankly, looked like hell. Her pretty peach tennis shoes were splattered with her husband's blood and her knees were red and scuffed from crawling on the floor. Her shorts were dirty, and her blouse was torn from the collar to the second button, but otherwise, she would recover physically.

The jury was out on the mental part.

He couldn't leave the hospital without looking for his dad first, so he asked Mark to search the hospital while he stayed with his mother. Besides, he would not have been able to bear the sight of his father dead with his brains blown out.

Mark spent the better part of an hour scouring the main part of the hospital on all floors, looking in the emergency rooms, the ICU, where none of the people there were still alive, every bathroom, patient room, cafeteria…everyplace he could think of. He even talked to anyone that might know the whereabouts of the pharmacist that had been shot. That's when he was able to confirm Jack's mom's recounting of what happened.

One of the women behind the desk on the third floor confirmed that Jack's father was indeed dead, and he had been carried outside to where they were laying the bodies for cremation, and it was there he would be found.

Mark broke the news to Jack and pointed to where he thought Jack's dad probably was.

"You're sure?" Jack asked.

"The nurse was sure. She said he was placed right there" Mark pointed again to the street, and that was confirmation enough for Jack. He didn't need to walk over there and start lifting sheets. He did not want to see his dad dead, because he would surely lose it.

"Jack…you said we needed antibiotics. They'd be in the pharmacy, right?" asked Mark.

Jack had almost forgotten why they had brought the bigger backpacks with them.

"Yes, they would be. Good thinking." Jack answered, so he wheeled his mother back around to walk back inside the annex heading straight for the pharmacy again.

They both took off their backpacks and opened them, hoping to fill them up with the supplies they needed.

"I'll go inside and grab my dad's PDR and look to see what we need. Stay out here with my mother" Jack said, as she had fallen asleep sitting up in the chair.

Jack knew exactly where Paul kept his Physicians Desk Reference (PDR), a large book containing information on drug names and their uses. He found it back in the break room next to the coffee maker and began to scan and write down the names of all the drugs he thought they would need, and then he began to painstakingly look for them on the shelves, both standing and not, and through the piles of spilled drug bottles on the floor.

Clindamycin…check, Erythromycin…check…penicillin…check, Cipro…check. It took him about forty-five minutes to find everything he was looking for and he filled both packs as he went. He also threw things in there he stumbled across, things he had not thought of and things he did, such as alcohol, cotton balls, big giant bottles of ibuprofen, and Tylenol, which were labeled APAP, bandages of all sorts, shapes, and sizes, and a variety of other things.

He spotted some bottles of morphine the robbing murderers must have missed, but he had no use for them. Ibuprofen and Tylenol would have to do for anyone in pain.

After almost filling both backpacks with every single bottle of antibiotics he could find, he tied them both shut and purposely avoided the sight of the blood on the wall and the coagulated blood on the floor below the blood-stained wall, toward the front counter as he exited the pharmacy, back to the front where Mark was tending to his Mom.

The packs had significant weight now combined with the bottles of water. Jack helped Mark with his pack on, and vice versa and the three made their way out of the building and off the hospital grounds toward Speer Blvd., retracing their steps to head home the way they came. It was close to noon now and the midday sun was beating down on them, different than the cool morning air they rode in earlier. Getting home would take a whole lot longer than getting here, as they were now on foot. They had roughly twelve miles to walk home, and if they were lucky to make it home, they would probably not get back until five or six, missing the President's address at 4:00 due to the two-hour time difference.

As they walked down Speer with Jack pushing his mother and Mark alongside him, Jack offered, "This wasn't supposed to happen Mark".

Mark didn't know what to say to him. What could he say, but speak he did.

"I know"

"No Mark...you don't know. Yesterday when we came upon that plane that crashed, I noticed a big plume of smoke coming from downtown, and I thought right then and there we should go to my parents at that time, but then I thought better of it. I thought we needed to get back to our families, me to my brother and my sister. Had we gone to the hospital then, my dad would still be alive" stated Jack. "It's my fault he's dead."

"You can't think like that. You don't know that to be true. What if we were still there with them for some reason and those guys came in and it happened the same way, only this time the guy that shot your Dad shoots and kills us too, and maybe your Mom? You're not responsible for any of this. Your parents decided to stay down there and help, and they probably would have done the same thing had we been there. This is not your fault Jack! It's just not." Mark replied while grabbing Jack's shoulder to massage it, but it didn't make Jack feel any better.

Jack would just have to work this out by himself, but if he ever brought it up again in front of Mark, which he undoubtedly would, Mark wouldn't hesitate to offer him the same consolation and common sense, however often Jack might need it.

The two of them took turns pushing Julie home and it was exhausting. Jack's mom had woken several times throughout the walk, sometimes weeping, then reversing course and letting them both know how much she appreciated being rescued by them.

They each had another sandwich in their packs and gave one to Julie and they split the other between themselves. She had eaten the sandwich in short order and the boys had wished they had not eaten the other one, but instead saved it for her.

They knew when they got home, Vivian would take over, cleaning her up, feeding her, consoling her, and then finally taking her across the street to lay her down in her bed.

It was a tiring, but uneventful walk back home, which was a welcome respite from the sadness preceding their trek.

They were now more than two-thirds of the way home and into the hottest part of the day, the second half of the afternoon. Julie had once again drifted off, so Jack started talking.

"I never imagined the world could be so cruel, at least not here in Denver. Maybe in the other big cities, but not here. The story your friend's dad told us this morning about the guy getting bum-rushed on his porch and stabbed to death, the other story that guy told us this morning about people beating and killing each other, those two homeless people yesterday robbing the dead at that plane crash, and now my Dad...a man that wouldn't hurt a fly...it makes you wonder if that kind of stuff is going on all across the city or other cities around the country. Is it happening in Mexico and Canada as well?" and then he asked something that sparked Mark to attention.

"Where is God? Why is he letting this happen?"

Mark thought about what he said for a moment, then answered with this...

"God is here with us Jack", and he pulled out his little Jesus from his pocket.

"I know that you're hurting and it's hard to see anything good that's happened today, but we *did* find your mom, and other than getting slapped, she was spared, and we found her. It could be so much worse, as bad as it is. We might be walking home alone or walking home with her wounded. We could have been wounded or killed today, but we were not. We made it down to the hospital easy enough and got out of there the same way...knock on wood.

The greatest gift God has ever given us, besides Christ dying on the cross for our sins, is free will. The freedom to make our own lives and do what we choose. With that freedom though comes a price, that's possibly being subjected to another man's free will that might be a detriment to us. God doesn't interfere, otherwise, our will wouldn't be free."

Mark then opened his hand and showed his little Jesus to Jack.

"See? He was with us all along today."

Jack pondered Mark's words and thought about them intently for the next mile.

Mark's words were so profound. He only wished he understood them.

Though Jack was attending a Catholic college, he was not as well versed in the Lord as he wished he was. His family went to church every Sunday just like Mark's did. He did believe there was a God because it didn't make any sense to him for there not to be, but he never felt his presence in the same way that Mark did by the way Mark spoke of him. Maybe it was worldly things that blocked his vision or just a basic lack of understanding regarding Jesus as the true Son of God. Either way, his vision had always been blocked. He had always felt disconnected from God and never really connected with the Lord, or his place in Jack's life, even during all the times in prayer he sat through at the dinner table throughout his growing up.

Though he spoke a decent prayer over the dead at the crash site the day before, he was just trying to distract Mark, while giving him some comfort at the same time.

Jack was more of a Humanist than a Christian, and he had always believed more in the goodness of mankind until now.

His attendance at the very Catholic Benedictine College was as much a wish to make a connection with a God he could not see, touch, or know, as it was to get a great education.

Mark, on the other hand, was a natural believer in Christ and all that comes with it.

Mark was raised a devout Catholic from the time he was days old, being baptized at the altar by the family's priest, to the time he took his first communion, then leading to his confirmation.

Mark went to Catechism twice a week and served the Church as an Altar Boy on Sundays and religious holidays.

Mark even received the Ad Altair Dei medal, the Catholic religious medal for Boy Scouts, which he was equally as proud of as his Eagle Scout rank.

Ironically, Mark's wish was to also attend Benedictine College like Jack, but for vastly different reasons.

After hours of pushing that wheelchair, they finally entered Cherry Knolls, making the final stretch toward home. Jack's mom would be home now, but his dad would never be coming home again, and another emotional hurdle would have to be dealt with regarding Kate and Rocky...and he was dreading having to experience it.

Mark was excited to be back in the neighborhood, and he had no desire to ever make that trek again. His body was tired and aching, and all three of them were slightly overheated from the heat of the day.

Finally, they had made it home. As Jack helped his Mom up from the wheelchair in the Jenkins' front yard, Vivian opened the front door and rushed outside to greet the three of them. Julie immediately started bawling her eyes out at the sight of Vivian, harder than she had at any other time during the day, and naturally, this made Viv cry right along with her.

"Come on inside. Your kids have been eating here with us and so will you. I'm making dinner right now" Viv said to Julie. "We'll get you all cleaned up inside."

Realizing that Paul was not with Julie, Vivian imagined the worst and she was sure she would get the full story later.

Vivian put her head under one of Julie's arms, put her arm around Julie's waist, and walked her up to the door and inside of the house.

And just as predicted, Mark's mom came to the rescue right in the nick of time, just as the boys were about to drop from exhaustion.

As Mark and Jack lay in the grass, Mark played back the events of the day in his head, looking over at Jack and wondering how terrible it must feel what Jack was feeling at that moment.

He was also intrigued by the possibility that Jack could be on a spiritual quest to find God and that he might be a witness to it.

SIX

Week Two

Seven days had gone by and life as they knew it had come to an abrupt halt. The neighborhood had changed, and not for the better. The smell of death had permeated the air, even though the dead were mostly in their homes. If there was a window open, the smell of rotting flesh wafted out into the street, filling the nostrils of those who walked by. It was also a sign of invitation to those searching for what they needed to survive, so for the truly desperate seeking water, food, medicines, or paper products, the smell was an indicator to those aggressive enough that the home was unoccupied, permitting them to enter that home, brave the nauseating odor, and search for whatever they needed.

Unfortunately, they almost certainly came up empty for what was needed the most, such as food and water. Sometimes a neighbor would find a hidden case of water here and there, or maybe a can of chili, but for the most part, the best they could hope for was some pain relievers of some kind or a roll or two of toilet paper.

Contributing to the smell of the dead were people defecating in their backyards. If you have enough people doing that outside, eventually the air becomes putrid with it. Some would go in grocery bags in the house and throw them out in the back, whereas others had no choice but to drop their drawers in their backyard and make a new pile.

There was also the smell of urine…and it was everywhere.

Finally, you had the overflowing trash cans, filled with every kind of trash imaginable, creating a smorgasbord for the local wildlife, such as rats and raccoons. The rats were also attracted to the feces and they would eat it, thereby creating a huge rat problem in the neighborhood where previously one did not exist.

Throw in copious amounts of dog shit piles and emptied litter boxes, and you end up with a world-class stinkhole rivaled only by the city dump.

There was talk a couple of homes had resorted to eating their cats and dogs, as horrifying a thought that is.

People were no longer staying in their homes, but canvassing the neighborhood for what they needed, either by asking, begging, or even stealing.

Some had become so desperate, hungry, and even angry, that they would take by force anything you had that you were not willing to share, even if your sharing meant taking food away from your family.

The night before, gunshots were heard a half-mile away at the other end of the neighborhood, close to Colorado Blvd. Though the neighbors close by to that side might know the whole truth behind those gunshots, word had not yet traveled to the west side, which would have disclosed that a neighbor next door to someone hoarding food and water had broken down their back door, armed with an AR-15, then shot the family dead, followed by them ransacking the house of all their supplies.

Word had it that they were now living high on the hog.

Only the immediate neighbors know for sure what happened over there, but nobody had seen the family since the day before, and those behind the victim's house were sure to have seen something, but no one was talking, and no one was going to jail.

In just a week, Centennial had turned into a lawless town right out of the wild west, and the middle-class neighborhood of Cherry Knolls, where home values soared anywhere between 500 to 800 thousand dollars per home, was no different.

When most people become hungry enough, no matter who they are, they become brazen and will do anything to feed themselves and their family...even kill thy neighbor.

None of the manicured lawns were being watered and were now becoming dry, brown, and unruly. Flowers were wilting and vegetable gardens had already been picked before they succumbed to the same fate as the flowers, either by their owners, wildlife, or invading night marauders from a few streets over.

Things got busiest in the dead of night. When normal people were usually sleeping, the desperate were on the prowl looking for their next score or evidence of greener pastures.

There were three supermarkets within walking distance...the King Soopers down University at Dry Creek Blvd, the Whole Foods in The Streets of Southglenn, and the other King Soopers on Arapahoe, half a mile past Newton Middle School.

All three supermarkets had already been picked through and looted and were bare bone empty three days after they lost power. As long as there were things there to be taken, the community was fairly safe from house robbers invading during the wee hours of the morning, but once the store inventory was gone, the only place for these brand-new criminals to shop was within the neighborhood's pantries, and the pickings were getting mighty slim there as well.

Several people were shot at all three markets, people fighting over things like canned goods, water, and toilet paper.

It's amazing what people will do and to what lengths they will go to wipe their asses.

Vivian was short on flour and thought it was worth it to take a chance on stepping into the Whole Foods Market at noon, located at

The Streets of Southglenn, a local outdoor shopping mall closest to the house. She discussed it with everyone and only Kate thought it was a good idea. Even so, she decided to go but was only allowed if Mark or Jack accompanied her.

Fair enough.

Mark was busy messing with the Ham radio, as he had been most of the week with no success, so Jack volunteered to escort her. There was no way she was going alone.

They made the less than a mile walk and entered the front door and were barely able to stand the smell of the rotting meat overlooked by the looters, but Viv was prepared.

She took out of her pocket a container of Vicks VapoRub, opened the cap, and put a generous dab of it under her nostrils, blocking the putrid smell trying to make its way in her nose, handing it to Jack and suggesting he do the same, which he did…thankfully.

The market was an absolute horror show, the aisles filled with garbage, empty food containers, and yes…feces.

She didn't usually shop here, but she knew what she was looking for and the section in it would be found.

Her wish had been granted and the shelf was stocked full of various brands and kinds of flour. Since there were not many people with gas stoves, no one other than her would be doing any sort of baking. The plan would be to bake some loaves of bread, and also some brownies if she could also find some sugar, which was only a few feet down from the flour.

Since she was here with Jack, she decided to take home more flour and sugar than she had originally come for since he would be able to carry half the load, so she doubled up, handing two bags of flour to Jack, then grabbing two bags of sugar for her to carry herself.

"Jack, go up to the checkout and see if there are any of those expensive canvas grocery bags that we can use to carry this stuff home while I find some cocoa, will you?" she asked.

Jack set the flour down and sauntered up the aisle. The baking section was in the back of the door, so he had to walk back to the front to checkout.

"Back in a minute" he answered.

"Thank you Hun" she replied.

Just as she found the cocoa and bent over to pick up a can of it, she heard a voice say "Nice". She was startled and almost dropped the can, turning to see a man in his late twenties, holding a very large knife, and eyeballing her like she was a roast chicken, and he hadn't eaten in a week.

Before she could yell or say anything, the man was right up against her with his knife at the underside of her chin, and that is when she dropped the cocoa.

"If you make one sound or try to resist, I'm going to shove this knife through your chin and up into your brain...you got me?" he said.

She could barely speak but managed to stutter the words "I'm not alone."

He replied "I told you. Don't make a peep. I'm not worried about him. I've got someone up in front of the store taking care of him. Now, you do as I say. You're pretty good lookin' for an old lady. I want you to slowly take off your pants, then get down on your hands and knees, and spread your legs as wide as you can. I'm going to give you something and you are going to take it. All of it."

Vivian almost lost consciousness right then and there, and her heart was beating literally out of her chest. This man had not shaven for at least a week, and probably had not bathed for longer than that, but what she noticed the most was the disgusting odor coming out of the man's mouth, similar to if he had just eaten a shit sandwich coated in vomit, which is what she almost did at the smell of it.

"Why don't *you* get down on *your* knees cocksucker?" said the Arapahoe County Sherriff's Deputy as he held his Glock 17 9mm extended clip against the back of the man's head.

"Drop the knife" the deputy ordered.

Now it was the attempted rapist's turn to be frightened.

"If you don't drop that knife, I'm going to canoe your skull and watch your brains scatter all over this store. You've got one second!" the deputy offered again, and just like that, the knife hit the floor.

The deputy then turned the man to face him by the scruff of his neck, then smashed the man's face in with his weapon, so violently that the man's nose and mouth immediately exploded into a fountain of blood, shooting out of the man's nose and mouth simultaneously as he fell like a sack of potatoes into the shelving, slumping unconscious onto the aisle floor.

"You all right Ma'am?" the deputy asked.

She couldn't speak. Not a word. At least not for a few seconds, but she did once she got her composure.

"Where did you come from? Thank you...thank you...oh God, thank you so much" she stuttered as she leaned herself up against the very shelving that kept the man on the floor from catapulting into the next aisle from the severity of the blow he had just taken to his face.

"I'm an Arapahoe County Sheriff's Deputy. My name is Officer Tipton, and my partner is Officer Engleart. He's up in front of the store taking care of the other guy that was with this piece of crap. Me and my partner were sitting out in my cruiser in the parking lot when we saw you and a young man enter the store, then about thirty seconds after you were inside, we both noticed a couple of guys, this guy being one of them, follow you in, and I recognized him almost immediately. I've had plenty of dealings with him in the past and he's not one of the good guys, as you can see for yourself. We knew these guys were up to no good, so we followed them in, and then, well…this happened" said the Deputy "I'm just glad we got to you in time."

Just then, Officer Engleart had the other guy in cuffs walking up the aisle, followed by Jack, holding the canvas bags that Vivian had sent him up to the front to get.

"Nighty night creep" chuckled Engleart as he waved at the unconscious thug sleeping soundly in the aisle. "Wonder what he did to deserve that?"

"I'll tell you about it later, but trust me, he deserved it" answered Tipton.

Officer Engleart then uncuffed the other guy, kicked him in the ass, and told him to run like hell out of there, which he did.

"You're not going to arrest him?" asked Jack.

"And take him where?" replied Engleart. "There's nowhere to take him. The jail is shut down the same as everything else. Besides, we are off duty. Not taking Sleeping Beauty anywhere either. Just going to leave him here, and when he wakes up, he's going to be in a world of hurt. Good luck on him getting his broken nose and jaw tended to."

"Why don't you and the young man let us drive you home?" offered Officer Tipton.

"Drive us home? You have a car that's working?" asked Jack in disbelief.

"Yep. Put the stuff you came in here for in the bags you're carrying and let's get the two of you home".

Vivian was a little bit in shock still, mostly from her encounter, but also from the news they were going to be *driven* home in a *working car*.

They both bent down to pick up the flour, sugar, and cocoa, then stuffed them in the canvas bags and walked out of the store with the two officers that had saved the day.

As they walked out the door to the police cruiser, Tipton offered, "Our cruiser just happened to be parked in the garage underneath the Sheriff's office, so nothing happened to it. There are also two other cruisers out there that made it without any damage. Our problem is finding fuel. We are currently at less than half a tank because we had just filled up and we haven't gone anywhere but here in this parking lot for the last week. Neither of us wanted to sit at home, so we come out here to help if we're needed, and today it turns out we were."

It was kind of a shock to hear an actual engine running as they turned out of the parking lot, then turned onto Easter Ave. at the direction of Viv as she steered the cruiser to its destination.

"Now that we know where you live, we will come by from time to time when we're in the area to check in on you. Be safe" Tipton said as they drove away.

Viv had pretty much been in a cloud ever since her rescue, but she was now coming out of it as the two of them carried their bags up the walk to the front door of the house, and that's when she asked Jack to promise that he would never speak of this to anyone…ever, and he agreed.

He handed his bag of flour to Viv, then said goodbye as he was going to walk across the street to his house and check in on his mom.

Something had happened, had happened to Jack…something good.

In his mind, a miracle had just taken place. By all rights, he should be dead, and God only knows what would have happened to Mrs. Jenkins.

The potential rapist's partner was sneaking up behind Jack as he was preoccupied at the canvas bag rack looking for the biggest bags he could find when suddenly he heard a loud crash behind him. He looked back to see a police officer on top of some guy's back while handcuffing him.

Turns out the guy was seconds away from shoving a twelve-inch hunting knife in Jack's back, which would surely have killed him, then afterward would join his partner in the back of the store to take turns on Mrs. Jenkins. Then out of nowhere, like angels sent from God, they prevented anything bad happening to either of them by stopping these assailants before they could do them any harm.

What if these cops had not been in the parking lot? Or see these guys come in behind us? What were the chances they would be there at that exact time they chose to arrive? In a working police car?

These questions dumbfounded Jack to his very core, but the miracle was not lost on him.

All he knew was that he should not be breathing, yet he was here and dodged the biggest bullet of his life.

The question he had asked Mark almost a week ago had just been answered.

Where was God?

Today he was there in the store with us.

It was God, most definitely.

Maybe throughout his life, Jack had just not been paying close enough attention for the miracle. It was Jack's epiphany...the one he had been searching for.

He would be paying much closer attention from now on.

Sadly, he could not share it with Mark, because that would break the promise he made to Mark's mom.

Mark, above anyone else, would appreciate what had just happened with Jack's awakening and recognition of it.

Something had happened to Vivian as well. She wanted nothing more than to lock herself in her bathroom and have a good cry…a loud bawling cry, but she couldn't.

She had to hold this one in for the sake of her family.

She came so close to having something taken from her that she had only shared with one man, and that was her husband.

God, I miss him so, she thought.

That's when Mr. Parsons's shotgun came into her thoughts.

In just a short week, the neighborhood and surrounding areas were not safe anymore and they needed to protect themselves.

What if it were pedophiles that had cornered Brian and Rocky at the park and the same thing that happened to her happened to them? Or to Katie?

What if those same kind of men come into the neighborhood and break into one of their homes, trying their luck with Viv again, or Julie, or Katie?

She couldn't even bear the thought of such a heinous thing, but she was awake to the possibility now, which was more than she was before.

In all honesty, she would have shot that man right in the face had she had a gun, and she wouldn't have felt bad about it afterward. Not one bit.

She was never anti-gun. She just didn't want them around her curious babies, but they were not babies anymore.

She was going to do something she would not have even dreamed of, even as early as this morning. She knew Mr. Parsons kept a loaded shotgun in the coat closet behind his front door from talking with him in the past.

She was going to ask Mark to go get it and bring it over here.

It wouldn't protect her away from the house, but it would certainly be a deterrent here <u>in</u> the house.

She'd rather have a pistol of some sort, but a shotgun would do.

It would do just fine.

The day after they came home with Julie, Jack and Mark went over to take Mr. Parsons's body out of the house to lay him in his lawnmower shed, with the intent to bury him in his backyard if no family had come by looking for him. They didn't want to bury him, only to have to dig him up for a family member should they show up, so they wrapped him up from head to toe in several blankets they found in the house, then carried him out to the shed, making sure to shut the doors, keeping any wildlife out that might disturb his body.

He was just beginning to ripen when the boys showed up, so they got him out of there before he left his stench in the house, so asking Mark to go over there would not be too big of a favor to ask.

She thought, more than anything, Mark would be amazed, confused, and puzzled why his mom suddenly wanted a weapon in the house, especially a gun, after all these years of refusing to have one.

Not only was she concerned about strangers coming in from outside the neighborhood, but she was also spooked by some of the people in the neighborhood that were becoming desperate and willing to do anything they felt they needed to stay alive, even if it meant forcibly taking what was yours.

Viv was deep down a kind soul that would do anything for just about anyone, even a perfect stranger, but they could not give away what they have to survive, even to someone crying and begging for it at her door, no matter how much her heart broke for someone in need of help.

Frankly, she could not remember ever turning someone away that came to her door, in a parking lot, or even at an intersection that was asking for food or money.

There was one guy, in particular, an old guy, that used to park himself on the island at the intersection of Dry Creek and University. He was always there with his sign, day and night, asking for money because he was homeless and a senior citizen, and she could never drive by him without slipping him a buck or two. That was just who she was, but things were different now. Their food and water supplies were instantly cut in half because they were now taking care of their friends across the street. The most concerning thing to her was how quickly the water supply was shrinking, but that was mostly because all seven of them were using the water to bathe, wash their clothes, or clean dishes.

She had already been thinking about what uses to curb the water with.

They started with 500 cases of water and had already gone through twenty cases in one week. At that rate of usage, the water would run out in four to six months, whereas it should last a full year, even with the extra mouths to feed.

The harsh reality for Viv to learn, and she was just beginning, was that charity truly does begin at home.

She also knew it wouldn't be long before other close-by neighbors got hip to their food and water supply. After all, they would be the only ones not scouring the neighborhood for Assistance. Soon the natural gas would dry up and they'd be having to cook everything outside on the grill or over an open flame fire pit in the backyard.

There may come a day when that shotgun might have to be pointed at one of their neighbors to keep them at bay. It would be a day she dreaded, but it would have to be done if things went sour.

Her husband would be proud of her. That much she knew.

It had been eight days since she had spoken to Bill, and she hoped he was alive.

Sitting on the edge of her bed, she flashed back to the President's short address she listened to before the boys had come home with Julie.

It was the antithesis of hope, as it was nothing but bad news.

He stated that after further analysis, it was determined that the infrastructure of America would not be coming back any time soon, no earlier than twelve, to possibly eighteen months, maybe even two years, and that would only be the major cities coming online first. This was due to pivotal transformers having to be built, which would come from several allied countries around the world, and it would take time to have them constructed, delivered, and installed, especially the number of them that the U.S. required. He also said that if you lived in a major coastal area, to be on the lookout for British, French, and Japanese military trucks distributing MREs, water, and medical supplies. He told us to hang on and that we were basically on our own.

The more she thought about what he said, the angrier she became. Damnit! They've been talking about the possibility of something like this happening for years! Why didn't they harden the system to prevent this from happening? They could spend trillions of dollars on things that made no sense, but they couldn't spend a fraction of that to protect us from this?

Ninety percent of us will be dead before the first cities are even online. Why?

Down the hallway past her bedroom door, Mark walked by, heading toward his bedroom. "Mark Honey, I need you to do something for me" she shouted down the hallway.

"Have you ever shot a shotgun?" she asked.

SEVEN

Fourth of July

T he real and ever-present feeling of isolation was something every human being living in North America was experiencing, no matter how many people were in their immediate living space, and Cherry Knolls was no exception. For the majority, people were not leaving their homes, even going outside, at least in their front yards, for a variety of reasons.

The main reason was that cannibalism had taken hold.

There were no more food sources anywhere to be found and the dead, as long as they had not begun to rot, were being eaten and those not dead but close to it, were being killed for their flesh. It was easier to kill someone on their death bed than to hunt someone down like game.

The first thing to go were the animals in the neighborhood, such as dogs and cats.

Even the squirrels were being hunted…along with the rats showing up to eat the feces in the back yard of the homes in the neighborhood.

Two significant events had happened in the line of sight of the Jenkins home, one witnessed by Vivian and the rest of her kids, the other only by her in the wee hours of the morning.

Two weeks ago in the early afternoon, all watched in horror as a man, followed by his sons, were chasing someone's cat down the street, all carrying metal rakes. The cat had been cornered in Vivian's front yard and was killed, but not instantly, by one of the boys as he brought his rake down on the back of the cat, immobilizing the poor cat until the father came to it, then smashed its head with his foot, killing the poor animal.

Vivian screamed and ran out the front door, chastising the man for his horrible deed, but hunger has no morality, and the starving man and his boys picked up the cat and threw it into a plastic shopping bag without saying a word. The man looked up at her as she stood on the front porch with her boys behind her. He acknowledged her presence with his eyes but showed no remorse for what he had just done, then calmly picked up the family's dinner for the evening and began walking down the street with his three boys behind him.

Sitting at the end of the windowsill was Whiskers…horrified at what he had just witnessed. When one of the boys saw the cat in the window, probably taking mental notes where their next meal might be found, the cat hissed at him, then ran away and up the stairs down the hall.

A week prior, Viv had sent all of the boys on a trek down University to the local PetSmart to retrieve the biggest bag of cat food they could find, as Whiskers was running seriously low from the bag Mark had retrieved from Mr. Parsons's house.

The next best thing to killing pets and people was eating the food that they ate, so it was slim pickings for animal food in any of the supermarkets. When they arrived at the PetSmart, everything had been taken, except for a fifty pound bag of specialty cat food hiding in the back of the store on a pallet. The bag was torn a little, but no food had spilled out of it, so they gingerly picked it up and gratefully loaded it into a shopping cart, then trucked it back home, fending off a few people on the way. This would prove to feed Whiskers for possibly six or seven months…maybe more. What he would eat after that was anyone's guess.

Maybe they would have to begin feeding him whatever they were eating.

God help him if they had run out of food, possibly making him the main course.

Two days prior, the starvation game elevated its intensity.

It was 5:30 in the morning and Vivian was sipping a cup of coffee at the kitchen table when she heard a loud woman's scream in front of the house, so she jumped up to run to the living room window to see a heavyset woman fall on the asphalt, then pick herself up and continued running to the best of her ability. She was being chased down by four men, one of them carrying a rifle and another carrying what looked to be an old military stretcher. As she passed Vivian's front yard, a shot rang out and the woman fell onto the street.

The man with the rifle had just shot her down.

When he came to where her body lay, he pulled out a pistol from his waistband and shot her again, this time in the head to make sure she was dead.

The man carrying the stretcher laid it down next to her, and all four men rolled her onto it. Once she was securely on, they each grabbed an end of a pole attached to the canvas, picked up the stretcher, then reversed course, walking back the way they had come.

Horrified, Vivian watched this hunting expedition take place right before her eyes…and she didn't make a sound. Either this woman had done something awful to warrant this vigilante punishment, or she had just become several days' worth of meals for her killers.

What was worse was that she thought she recognized one of the men from driving past his house two blocks over, many times on her way to or from home before all of this began.

This was a game-changer and now the stakes had just been raised. She had heard from her sons that people were eating other people in the neighborhood, but there was no mention of people killing other human beings.

As she stood back far enough from the window not to be seen, Mark, Brian, and Rocky, who had spent the night with Brian, rolled out into the living room just as the men were carrying their hunt out of view.

They heard the gunshots, but not the screaming beforehand.

The boys had not seen any of what had just transpired outside her living room window, but Vivian made no bones about the boys staying very close to home from that point on, explaining what she had just witnessed.

This is why she sent Mark over to Mr. Parsons's house to retrieve his shotgun and however many shells he could find.

The scenario she had seen would not be happening here if she had anything to say about it, and the shotgun behind the front door would be doing all the talking.

It was the morning of July 4…six weeks since the bright light and the big swoosh.

True to their word, the Sheriff's Deputies had come by to check in on them, at least two or three times a week. They had not been by the house since the execution of the woman out front, but they would be sure to be informed about it the next time they swung by, which would probably be that day.

It had been decided that Julie and her three kids would begin staying with Viv and her two boys the day that the woman was killed. It was just too risky to have them sleeping across the street, vulnerable to predators, mostly humans.

Viv would share her king-size bed with Julie, Brian would give up his bedroom for Kate, and Jack would sleep on the living room sofa, while Mark stayed in his room. Brian and Rocky would camp out on the living room floor.

Whiskers would sleep wherever he wanted, but he seemed to prefer sleeping at the feet of Mark in his bedroom.

It only made sense that they would stay there with Viv. They were already taking their meals and water there and using the latrine in the backyard.

Viv had gotten the food and water supply pretty much under control and began to severely limit what the water would be used for. Water would only be used for drinking and cooking the freeze-dried food they were eating. There would be no more washing of hands or even bathing, so everyone had become fairly ripe, especially the boys.

Mark and Jack started dry shaving, but when their razors became useless, they each started growing a beard.

The same holds for Viv, Julie, and Kate. Shaving their legs and underarms without water or shaving cream caused serious chafing for them, which they endured, but when their razors became useless as well, they too started to sprout hair on their underarms and legs, causing embarrassment in the beginning.

Viv and Julie tried to cover their arms and legs by wearing pants and long shirts, but in the heat of summer, that proved to not be very practical, so they learned to live with it.

Kate didn't much care.

At least it was easier since neither of them had their husbands around, although they would have gladly traded the embarrassment for them to be there with them.

The days had become scorchers and spending as little time in the house during the day had become a must, no matter how dangerous it was to be outside.

The only way they could sleep at night was to open all the windows to let the house air out, letting the soft breeze blow, which also kept them from choking on their body odors.

In the morning, they had to close all the windows to prevent the smell of cooking from reaching outside, alerting the neighborhood that there was food to be had there. Fortunately, the natural gas was still available through the gas stove, so they had not yet had to resort to cooking outside, which probably saved them from a confrontation or two from hungry neighbors.

That dynamic would come soon enough, as the gas running out could come any day.

Viv and Julie spent most of their time on the back porch, drinking coffee or tea.

Though the smell was terrible outside, it wasn't as bad in Viv's backyard as it was in the rest of the neighborhood.

One of the smartest and best things that had been done was the digging of the latrine.

Since the tent was sixteen feet long, Mark would just dig another hole next to the one previously dug that was filled up with dirt and waste. He created a system. After doing your business, you would take a cup of dirt from the hole that was dug, then sprinkle it over what you left in the hole. This kept the smell down and the flies somewhat at bay.

They were now on their third hole dug, which put the toilet seat close to the middle of the tent. That left room for two to three more holes left to dig, and when all holes were dug and filled, they would just move the tent to another part of the yard and start all over again.

The biggest concern was toilet paper.

They started with 200 double rolls that were kept down in the basement, which was part of the survival plan, but after six weeks and seven butts to wipe, they were almost down to one-third of their original supply. Soon, Viv would have to come up with a plan to ration the toilet paper to make it last as long as she could.

Whiskers' litter box was being changed once a week, but instead of cat litter that had run out a couple of weeks after they took him in, they had begun using sand from an old sandbox behind the garage that Bill had built for Brian many years ago.

When the litter box became full, they dumped it outside along the back fence, keeping the smell as far away as possible.

Cat litter was something the boys completely spaced out on when getting cat food from PetSmart, but fortunately, with the sandbox, it did not need to be high on the priority list.

Julie had been in a despondent daze ever since Paul had been killed and struggled to keep her chin up and best face forward, but because of her children, she managed to brave through it.

She had been doing half of the cooking, which was nothing more than boiling water, then adding dehydrated food to the water, covering the pot for a few minutes, and then dishing out the food. She also wasn't sleeping very well, but no one else was---to be honest about it.

They all slept with the potential of waking up to marauders trying to break into their home, taking what they needed to survive, and killing everyone in the process.

This caused many nights of unrest, especially with the women in the house.

Viv did all the bread and brownie baking. It was her self-appointed job since she knew her oven best. Baking in a gas oven was a little bit different than baking in an electric oven, so she decided to solely take on this task with no argument from Julie.

Viv was also having a hard time, not being able to talk to Bill, not knowing if he was safe, hurt, or even alive and had no way of knowing.

Viv and the others had no contact with everyday friends or family.

The isolation was destroying her psyche nearly as much as the absence of her husband.

She had not spoken to anyone in her church since this had begun, nor any of her friends or family. She had no clue as to their situation. The only friend she had close by was Julie. All the rest lived at least a couple of miles away. Her mom and dad were still in Rifle, a small community in the Rocky Mountains where she grew up, over a hundred miles away, which might as well have been as far as the moon. She didn't know if her parents were even alive. She feared the worst, after all this time, because they were in their eighties, and her dad was reliant on oxygen because he suffered from COPD.

She suspected he was one of the first casualties of the power outage, leaving her mom to fend for herself at the end of a dirt road outside of town. Viv could only hope that she was being cared for by neighbors down the road from her, otherwise, she knew that her mom had most likely passed away shortly after her father.

She also had a sister in Breckenridge living with her husband; there was no telling if they were alive or dead. Although they were much closer to her parents, they too were many miles away.

Bill's parents had lived in Sandusky, Ohio where he had grown up, but they had long since passed away years earlier. Bill was an only child, so other than an aunt somewhere in New Jersey, he was the only remaining member of his family to carry the torch, other than his two boys.

After several cups of coffee with Julie at the kitchen table, she heard a knock on the door. When she looked out the window to see who it was, she let out a sigh of relief because it was Officers Tipton and Engleart standing at the door.

"Hello Fellas" she greeted them, holding the door open for them to come in.

"Mornin' Mrs. Jenkins," they both said as they walked into the living room. "Morning Mrs. Price. We heard you might have had some commotion here a few days ago", queried Officer Tipton.

They had no idea what, and they both would be floored when she filled them in.

After giving them the play-by-play, Viv's voice was followed by a long pregnant pause of silence.

"I'll be right back," said Officer Tipton, as he got up from the kitchen table and walked outside to his police cruiser.

He came back in a minute later carrying something wrapped in a cloth, accompanied by a box, then handed both to Viv.

"This is my other pistol and a box of shells I carry with me," he said as she unwrapped the gun from the cloth it was wrapped in. "Under normal circumstances, I'm breaking several laws and department protocols by giving this to you, but these aren't normal circumstances."

Officer Tipton then took the gun out of her hand and began instructing her how it was to be used, such as how to eject the clip from the gun, how to re-load the clip and insert it back into the gun, how to hold the gun, aim it, how the safety worked, and most importantly, how to fire it.

"We can't be here to protect you. That's a fact but giving you this weapon gives you the advantage." Tipton said. "I wish we could go to a gun range where I could give you a crash course on how to properly use this weapon, but that's just not possible. Gasoline is hard to find, and when we do, we usually have to siphon it out of a car stuck on the road somewhere, so we are severely limiting our driving."

Tipton then handed her back the gun, carefully placing it in the palm of her hand, making sure the safety was in its correct position.

"I'm speechless," she said. "Won't you get in trouble for this?" Viv asked.

"As I said, this probably breaks all kinds of laws, but who is going to enforce them? Even though we are employed as Deputies, there is no Sheriff's Department up and running at this time. We are not getting a paycheck, nor do we answer to anyone. We pretty much are making our own rules at this time, so my rule states that I can give you this weapon in hopes that it will protect you from the criminal element. God knows you need it" he replied. "What happened in front of your house, I'm sorry to say, is an all-too-common tale these days. This is happening in virtually every neighborhood, and yours is no exception. I imagine this sort of thing is happening all across the United States. I can tell you that we are seeing a whole lot fewer people, not only in this neighborhood but across town as well. If I had to guess, I would say at least half the population around here is deceased due to starvation, lack of water, or being outright killed and eaten. People have lost their minds and there is not much we can do about it. There is no police protection for the general public anymore. Other than us, there are maybe two or three patrol cars out there, and those are in the neighborhoods where those particular officers live. Engleart and I both live less than a mile from here on the other side of Arapahoe High School, which is why we were in the parking lot that day we first met, otherwise we may have never crossed paths, which I'm very glad that we did.

Arapahoe County jurisdiction stretches from the west end of Centennial out past Aurora, so you've got maybe three to four total police cruisers covering the entire 200 square mile area."

"Thank you," she said, then proceeded to embrace them both, giving them each a big hug, followed by Julie following suit.

"I've got something for both of you."

She reached over to the counter and lifted two paper plates filled with beef stroganoff, home-baked bread, and a brownie each…all from the night before, handing them each a foil-covered plate.

"This is the least we could do for you men. We are so blessed to have you checking in on us and we feel so much safer because of it, and now this" Viv said as she held up the weapon gratefully, once again wrapped in the cloth that Tipton had it wrapped in.

The officers appreciatively accepted the gift of food from Viv, said their thanks and goodbyes with a promise to return soon, then exited the front door.

"Happy Fourth of July" both men expressed as they stepped into their police cruiser.

Once inside the car, they headed down Cook Way to exit the neighborhood.

Everyone else in the house was still asleep.

Viv and Julie were always the first ones up. The kids seemed to get their best sleep in those early morning hours, knowing there was a warning sign that would be alerting them should an emergency pop up.

Viv took the cloth-wrapped gun and the box of shells down to her bedroom and placed them both under her underwear, kept in the top drawer of her dresser.

Her prayers had been answered with the gift of the gun given to her by Officer Tipton.

She now felt much more secure leaving the house. It enabled her to go somewhere if she truly needed to leave her home.

Later that morning, everyone arose from their slumber. They meandered throughout the house and backyard just like any other day. It was overcast that morning, and it looked as though they may get a welcome thunderstorm sometime in either late morning or early afternoon, which would be typical for a Fourth of July if past weather was any indicator.

It had been an unusually hot summer with less precipitation than in previous years, with only a smattering of short, late afternoon outbursts of rain lasting ten to fifteen minutes.

The one bad thing about the rain is it would dampen all the feces, trash, and dead bodies strewn throughout the neighborhood, reinvigorating the smell to a new intensity, stinking up the hood for hours on end.

All had become accustomed to the smell but became reacquainted with it once the rainstorms stopped and the source of the odors exploded in the heat of the re-emerging sunshine.

And just as the sky portended, the clouds above began to violently thunder, creating crackling lightning, filling the sky with its sounds of fury.

Colorado thunderstorms were something to behold and to be feared.

Maybe being closer to the heavens, being a mile above sea level, made it feel as if you could reach up and touch the clouds and possibly touch God himself.

This storm would not disappoint if it was torrential rain that you were looking for, accompanied by deafening thunder, causing Whiskers to hide under Mark's bed until the frightening display passed overhead. As the rain came down, everyone in the house sat at various windows, taking in the cool moist air wafting in that permeated the house and everything inside, and for the first time in what seemed a lifetime, no one could smell the distinct body odor of anyone else in what was once the exceptionally clean and beautiful home of Vivian Jenkins.

Outside, most of the living stood in front of their homes and danced in the street, mouths open, catching those succulent raindrops as if they were manna from heaven, others placing pots, pans, buckets…anything that could capture the rain, outside to be emptied into their stomachs once the rain stopped.

There was no telling when they would have this opportunity again.

The rain lasted this time for a couple of hours, causing flooding in the gutters, partly because a body had washed away from the side of a house and into the gutter on the street. It then floated away, arriving at the opening down below the street into the sewer, thereby blocking the water's passage and causing the streets to flood.

While the rain poured, the air smelled clean, fresh, and beautiful. It was a smell that eluded the inhabitants of Cherry Knolls for far too long, and it was welcome to those still alive to breathe it in and enjoy it.

But then the rain stopped, and the sun came out.

And that is when the smell of death was worse than any time ever remembered.

It was stifling and could not be escaped.

All the windows remained open to cool everything down inside, so there was no way to avoid it.

Eventually, everything would dry up and return to normal. The horrible smells would subside to a manageable stench that everyone could live with.

"Mom, what would you think about lighting off some mortars when the sun goes down," asked Mark, hoping for a positive response.

It would be dark soon, as the sun was setting over the not-too-distant Rocky Mountains.

She pondered his question for a moment, then she answered him.

"You do realize that if we do that, it could put us on the neighborhood's map, right"

Up until that evening, they had been careful and lucky enough not to attract any undue attention to themselves. They cooked inside, not flashing their bounty to the outside world.

"I think you may have a point, but I don't think a few fireworks are going to tell people we are blessed with food and water. I think if we do it quickly, most in the neighborhood aren't going to know where they are coming from exactly, so we could do it and not suffer any consequences, don't you think?" Mark replied.

"People? Thoughts? Ideas?" Viv shot back, putting it out to the group to see what they were thinking.

"I say we do it!" chimed in Brian.

"Yeah," said Rocky. "Let's do it. It's the Fourth of July!"

Everyone else pretty much agreed, with very little rebuttal.

Even Julie had nothing to say against it, but she had nothing to say *for* it either.

Half an hour later, Mark retrieved the fireworks from the garage. Both Mark and Jack lined up five mortars in the street outside in front of the house, and they were joined by everyone else inside the house except Julie, who stayed inside, preferring to look out of the living room window.

Up the street where it curved, Jack noticed the body blocking the drain to the gutter but chose to say nothing, as he did not want to spoil the moment. In a couple of minutes, it would be too dark for anyone else to see it anyway.

Mark then lit the first mortar, exploding into the sky with brilliant reds, blues, and other assorted colors, and its boom reverberated between the houses in the neighborhood. He then lit the next one, and the next one after that, followed by the last two of the line.

The last remaining people alive on their street emptied of their homes and looked to the sky, gasping in glee and wonderment.

Jack then set up another five in a row. This time he lit them off, repeating the order that Mark had established, and all with the same response from the neighbors.

Mark set up the last five mortars in a row, but this time Brian, Rocky, and even Kate wanted to get in on the act. He gave each of them a wooden match and decided they would each light a mortar at the same time. The neighborhood had more people watching now. Shortly after they lit the mortars, they all exploded in unison while the neighbors all clapped and cheered.

As the mortars exploded above, you could spot the body up the street momentarily.

For the first time in a long time, it felt good to feel normal again.

EIGHT

Darkness on the Edge of Town

B ill had almost driven himself crazy over these last nine weeks, constantly thinking about how his family was holding up, or even if they were alive. It was July 29th, sixty four days since the bright light had hit the U.S, stopping life as everyone knew it. Canada was almost in as bad of shape as we were, with Mexico making its recovery ahead of everyone else.

Mexico City was spared as they were under the "light line", but the border towns such as Juarez, Mexicali, and Tijuana were completely wiped out. They suffered the effects the same way the U.S. had.

Alaska and Hawaii were both spared, but the effects on banking were at first catastrophic. Everything had shut down for several days until the world determined and decided that America still had an economic infrastructure. All assets were temporarily seized and monitored by China, ironically; the country that had incurred most of America's debt.

A lot was going on in D.C. and it was exciting to watch. A few transformers had been replaced in the city close to the Capital. Some electric cable had been replaced, making it possible for a few signal and streetlights to come back online. Progress was being made, albeit slowly.

Fortunately, because of his position in the government, Bill had been getting plenty of bottled water to drink and MREs to eat. There was some discussion about Bill being allowed to be taken to Mt. Weather, an underground facility located in the Blue Ridge Mountains in Virginia, also known as "High Point".

Mt. Weather was a secure facility twenty stories underground with the capacity to hold up to 2000 people, designed and constructed for all members of congress and their families, the president, vice president, the president's cabinet, Joint Chiefs of Staff, and other critical members of society that were integral to the rebuilding and re-tooling of America, providing food in several dining facilities, sleeping quarters, an underground lake and shopping mall, and plenty of fresh water. Private sleeping quarters were only available for the president,

However, the spaces allotted to the vice president, Joint Chiefs of Staff, and all nine Justices of the Supreme Court, would be vacant on account all had died on the day of the Bright Light.

The president, head of Homeland Security, and the director of FEMA had all set up shop within the facility and were conducting their daily operations, such as ordering new transformers to be delivered to east and west coast ports, Texas, Florida, and Alabama ports, and through to the northern cities, such as Detroit and Chicago by way of the Great Lakes.

Relief ships from England, Spain, China, Japan, Argentina, Russia, India, Brazil, Argentina, New Zealand, and Australia had all been delivering meals, bottled water, medical supplies, and fuel to these same ports, but unfortunately, not even a small dent had been made in providing relief and aid to the tens of millions affected.

Many millions of Americans had already succumbed to death, and the hardest hit was the middle of America, from the Rocky Mountains to the Mississippi River, due to their hard-to-reach inland status.

Bill had heard of Mt. Weather but didn't know much more about it than the average citizen.

He had a friend in the White House, and that's how he found out he was being considered a high-level asset to be moved there.

Once America was open for business again, so much would have to be done...enough to boggle the mind. Livestock, automobiles, trucks, computers, phones, and factory equipment would have to be shipped in and the seed would have to be planted...it would take close to twenty years by all liberal estimates before the United States of America would even be a player on the world stage, and it was highly doubtful that America would ever be a true economic superpower again.

In nine months, it was estimated that America would lose roughly 307 million of its 350 million citizen population.

Since Bill was a statistician for the Department of Agriculture, his skill and assessment abilities would be crucial to the rebuilding of America's agricultural infrastructure.

Bill was sitting on the steps outside his apartment building, waiting for the military vehicle that would bring him his next day's supply of food and water, containing one case of bottled water and four MREs, along with paper products, such as toilet paper and napkins.

Each month he would get other things like mouthwash, toothpaste, disposable razors, shaving cream, and liquid hand soap.

Even if he had not been expecting a delivery, he would still be out on the stoop.

It was a stifling 102 in the shade, with the humidity index at ninety percent, and his apartment had to be at least ten degrees warmer, even at six in the evening.

The dog days of summer had arrived.

D.C. had experienced an incredibly hot and humid summer, and even though this was his fifth summer there, it had not gotten any easier for him to bear.

Around the corner came a black government vehicle and pulled up front to where Bill was sitting. Exiting from the back seat was his friend from the White House.

"Just got the word, Bill. Get your personal items, briefcase, and five changes of clothes, dirty or not, and come with me. You're going to Mt. Weather!" the friend ordered. "Hurry up partner…you have five minutes. We have to stop at your office to pick up anything you'll need before we get there. You'll be there for a while and we won't be coming back to get anything you forgot."

Bill didn't even have time to think, but without any hesitation, he ran up the steps to his building, up to the second floor, down the hallway, and into his apartment.

He grabbed his duffel bag out of the hall closet and started filling it with shirts, socks, pants, and underwear, all dirty, along with toiletry items, framed photos of his wife and kids, passport, wallet, keys, and anything else he thought he would need.

He also had a clean suit still in its protective cellophane bag, hanging on a hangar in his bedroom closet, which he threw on top of everything else, then zipped the duffel shut and headed out the door, locking it behind him.

He figured he'd be meeting with the President, so he would need a suit if he wanted to look the part, and after a brief stop at his office, on his way he went, heading across the state line of Virginia and over to the Blue Ridge Mountains.

❧❧❧

Mark had been fiddling with the HAM radio ever since the day after they brought Jack's mom home. He hooked up the coaxial cable to the radio and the power cord to the big Interstate car battery, switching to different frequencies while sitting at the table by the back door, but his hopes of talking to his dad were dashed after learning the farthest his signal would reach was eighteen miles, maybe twenty tops, due to the antenna.

He had established contact with a few other HAMs in the Denver Metro Area…other preppers in Northglenn, Aurora, a couple of people in Centennial, Lakewood, and Highlands Ranch, and on one night close to 11 p.m., he was able to talk to a guy up in the mountains in Evergreen for a good twenty minutes.

All had shared similar stories of cannibalism and murder.

Some had seen a car or truck on a road traveling somewhere unknown, mostly during the day, but once at night.

If nothing else, it was comforting to know that there were others out there going through the same things his family was going through.

As far as real-time national information, the best source for that was the NOAA frequency on the hand crank emergency radio.

One of the HAMs told him a story that chilled him to his bones.

He had been walking his dog as he had done every night around 10:00 p.m. on West Colfax Avenue when suddenly he came upon a very large group of people covered in black robes with hoods. He was walking around the corner of a Walmart at the corner of Wadsworth and Colfax, when he stopped dead in his tracks at the sight of about thirty to forty people wearing black robes with hoods, all standing in a large circle in the parking lot in front of the store. He immediately backed himself and his dog up so he could peek around the corner of the store, and what he told Mark took his breath away.

All of them were chanting around a pentagram painted on the asphalt while holding huge sticks with flames burning from the top of them, and he could hear the screaming and crying of a child. He couldn't tell if it was a boy or a girl at first, but then he caught sight of the child and it was a baby girl around three or four years old, and she had been stripped butt naked.

She had been thrown into the center of the circle by one of them, when one of them took out a very long sword from under his robe and cut her in half, killing her instantly, all to the delight of the crowd.

As bad as that was, what he was told next was the chilling part.

After the baby girl dropped onto the asphalt into two pieces, they all ran to her and started ripping her apart, cutting her into pieces with knives and eating her raw flesh, until what was left was entrails, a head with hair on it, and pieces of bone with shards of meat attached to them, leaving her unrecognizable as a human being.

The man became so overwhelmed with fear that he almost screamed, but he managed to stay silent and ran all the way home crying, and he hasn't walked his dog since at night, but only now in the daytime.

Normally a story like this would have been hard for Mark to swallow.

How would it have been possible for the murder of a little girl at the hands of a group of people out in the open, on a major thoroughfare, to take place in such a public way?

But these were different times they were living in.

Mark's mother had told Mark and Jack what transpired in front of the house before the Fourth of July, the story of the woman that had been hunted down and murdered in front of their home. She told them because she wanted them to know that the same thing could happen to them. She explained to Mark in particular why she wanted a gun in the house, because of things like that happening. Those things were the reason why she didn't want the younger kids playing out front anymore, and why she insisted that Brian and Rocky didn't go to the park to play ball anymore without both Mark and Jack accompanying them, preferably with the handgun given to her by Officer Tipton.

The neighborhood had become a danger zone, a hunting area.

Later on, Mark had gotten the full story of what that woman's murder was all about.

He had been talking to someone that lived a couple of streets over that knew more about what had happened.

People were starving to death two streets over and they were dropping like flies.

A conversation had started between two men, commiserating on their hunger, with one telling the other that he was so hungry, he was willing to try eating one of the dead people on their street., with the other one open to the idea. They were both watching their families dying in front of them and they were willing to do anything to feed themselves and their families, so that night before it got dark, they had gone to a few homes on their street to look for people that had recently died, and after entering some homes of the dead and attempting to pick a body to take home to eat, they could not get past the smell, as they were all people dead for some time in various stages of decay.

They finally found a body that had probably died a day or two before, and it had not started to smell yet, so they stretchered it out of there and carried it to the back yard of one of them to be butchered and barbequed.

Even though the body had only been dead for a short period compared to the other bodies they had seen, butchering the body wasn't a pleasant experience for them and the meat tasted sour to them after cooking it. All the members of both families tried eating the meat, several times, but they just couldn't bring themselves to eat it, even burning the meat was unpalatable...not because it was immoral, but because the meat just did not taste good to them, but after trying it several times, they did acquire a taste for human flesh, and all agreed they could eat a human if the meat were fresher and had not been dead for so long. They decided to be hyper-vigilant on their street and butcher someone as soon as they died.

This went on for a couple of days and hunger overtook their better selves, so they decided that the only way they would be able to survive would be to kill someone still alive on their street, but it had to be someone that deserved to die to feed the others.

Since there were not many people still alive on their street, this left few for them to choose from, except this one woman that lived six doors down from the two families. She originally lived with her widowed father, but her dad passed away a couple of days after the power went out, as his oxygen machine stopped producing oxygen. That, combined with the heat, caused him to stroke out and die in his bedroom.

The only thing she could do was cover him up with blankets and close the bedroom door, then try to seal the bottom by stuffing clothes under the door, which worked for a few days until the odor of his rotting body began to creep under the door. Eventually, she acclimated herself to the smell and learned to live with it.

Though her father had not eaten much anyway, it left more food for her. In their basement, there was a king-size supply of canned goods that he had collected and stored over the years, enough to last someone at least a year or more.

The one thing she didn't have was fresh water.

At the time of the power going out, she had a load in the washer that was in the rinse cycle, so even though the water had soapy residue to it, she had to drink it once she had emptied all the toilet tanks and bowls in the house. Her only source of liquid was now in the canned fruit she was eating. Fortunately for her, there were hundreds of those cans still in the basement.

This woman stood out to the cannibals because they hated her to begin with, and she also had some meat on her. She was heavyset but had lost some of her fat since this all started

She would sit on her front porch to escape the heat and could be seen eating cans of chili, peaches, and whatever else she had down in the basement.

People were starving to death and some would ask her for food, but she never helped anyone unless they had water to trade for. She just kept tormenting her neighbors like this until most of them died from starvation.

One guy came up onto her porch threatening her, but she just went inside and barricaded herself in. She became the person everyone loved to hate, and that is how she became the first target for the cannibal hunting party.

The families decided that she was the one that most definitely deserved to die, and she was the obvious choice to be the first one eaten at their dinner tables, so they hastily crafted their plan to abduct this woman and introduce her to their Weber gas grill.

The morning before Fourth of July, the two heads of the households, one of them with a hunting rifle strapped over his shoulder, along with their oldest sons, silently crept down the street in the pitch blackness before the sun came up, with the intent to enter her home by quiet force. They would then wake her and convince her to come with them at gunpoint, walk her down the street and into one of their basements, then kill her. They still had some shame about what they were doing, so they wanted to keep this on the down-low as much as possible. Besides, they didn't want to tip off the neighborhood that one of them could be next. One of the boys had brought an old army stretcher with him, just in case things didn't go according to plan and they had to kill her right then and there.

When they approached her front yard, they didn't expect her to be on the front porch, but there she was, sitting in a rocking chair, eating out of a can of pears. The heat in the house was unbearable and she couldn't sleep, so she got up earlier than she normally would have, and thinking it would be safe to be outside at that time of the morning, she left the confines of the inside of her home and tiptoed on to her front porch, can of pears in hand, where she could cool off.

Upon seeing the hunting party, she immediately ran toward the front door, then stopped when she heard one of the men shout "Stop or I will shoot you dead".

She dropped her can of fruit and stopped dead in her tracks, then turned to the group with a man pointing his rifle at her, then saying to them "What in the bloody hell do you want?"

They had not spent much time thinking out their plan ahead of time, and all of them waited for one of the others to say something.

"*Well*? What do you want?"

After a long pause, the other man said "Lady…you've been eating food out here in front of the rest of everybody while your neighbors are starving to death. We want some of your food. Not all of it, but some of it!"

Then the man with the rifle said "You are going to come with us, and we are going to look in your house for some food. Now you be quiet and come down off that porch, or I'm going to shoot you dead, and then we'll take <u>all</u> of your food. Now, what's it going to be?"

She stepped down off the porch, thinking the only way out of that situation was to let them go inside and take what they wanted. After all, what choice did she have?

The man with the rifle then got between her and the porch, still pointing the rifle at her, and told her to start following the two boys walking down the street, so they all walked.

"I thought you wanted food. Why aren't you in my house taking it? Where are we going?" she asked.

"You just be quiet" he whispered. "Keep walking"

Something wasn't right and she knew it.

Why were they walking her away from the house and the food, not taking any of it? Two days earlier she saw these same two men go into the house across the street and carry the man who lived there, and who had just died, out of his house and down the street to their houses at the end of the block. Shortly thereafter, she saw smoke from a BBQ grill down in that same direction.

She knew damn well those same two guys were cooking that poor bastard.

After passing five or six houses, it was starting to become light out, and she could see their faces in the dawn's early light, and these were faces that had the look of men about to do something terrible.

She suddenly turned around and pushed the man pointing the rifle at her to the ground, then began running down the street away from the group of men, screaming at the top of her lungs, loud enough to wake the dead.

She was barefoot and wearing nothing more than a pair of shorts and a halter top, so she was unequipped to outrun them for long as they made chase. The man with the rifle had a couple of opportunities to take aim and fire at her, shooting her dead, but he did not want to do that on their street, waking up their neighbors and having them see what could soon lay in store for them.

She was heavyset, so he let her run herself out because he knew she wouldn't last long, but when you're being chased by a man with a gun that wants to kill you, it's amazing how much farther you can go than you thought you could.

When she got to the end of the street, she rounded the corner with the boys and men half-heartedly chasing after her. It was better to let her get off their street and on to another one. After passing the next cross street, she rounded the corner of the next one after that, and that is when the man took aim and shot her down, right next to Mark's house.

After Mark had been told the details of what had happened in front of their house that morning, he shared it with Jack, but not his mother. There was no need for her to be told, he thought, so he never did.

Jack had been on a personal quest to know God ever since the incident at Whole Foods, and the story Mark told him just furthered his separation from his previously thought belief that mankind was inherently good, that mankind could be relied upon to save the day.

On the contrary. He now believed that man was inherently evil because he saw it all around him.

As August had arrived, Mark and Jack had gotten into the habit of sitting on top of their second-story roof so they could monitor what was happening in the neighborhood, but they would only do this at night, so as not to be seen, alerting others of their presence.

Night after night, they sat up on the roof in the darkness, scouring the streets of Cherry Knolls with a couple of pairs of high-powered binoculars belonging to Jack from his bird-watching days. They had a clear view of the backyard of one of the suspected killers of the woman that had been mowed down out front, and the things they saw go on there only confirmed that the stories were true; that they were eating people because human arms and legs were being brought out from the back door of the house and thrown on to the Weber BBQ grill, as could be seen from the firelight of the flaming grill.

Somewhere in that house, probably in the basement, there had to be a blood-soaked killing floor akin to a slaughterhouse.

To an extent and unbeknownst to the two of them, Mark and Jack had become hardened to the inhumanity of what they had seen over the past two and a half months, and they knew that eventually, these people would be coming to their street, probably sooner than they had hoped.

There are only so many times you could witness a human being cooked over an open fire that, before long, the newness begins to wear off on you. As disgusting as it was, this is what was happening to these two young men.

Never could either of them have ever imagined it would come to this.

These are people that a few short months ago were laughing, eating, drinking, living life, and enjoying the company of other people, and now they were enjoying the taste of them.

One night up on the roof, Jack turned to Mark and said "I've been thinking about the words you said to me on the way home from the hospital, about God. I really envy you, Mark. You believe so strongly, and I want to believe the same way you do. I've tried to read the Bible many times throughout my life, but I can never get past Genesis… never could."

Mark looked at Jack intently and asked, "What is it about Genesis that keeps you from going on?"

"It just seems so unbelievable, that all of these men could live to be hundreds of years old. It makes no sense to me and sounds more like a fairy tale." Jack replied.

"You're starting in the wrong place Jack" Mark answered.

"Huh? When you read a book, you always start from the beginning" stated Jack.

"Yeah, I know, but not with this book. You need to start with the Gospels" said Mark. "That's where you begin."

"The Gospels?" Jack queried.

"Yes…Matthew, Mark, Luke, and John…in the New Testament. Where you are starting is the Old Testament, which talks about the coming of Christ, a collection of stories about his arrival. The New Testament is about Christ after he arrives. It talks about his life, his death, and his resurrection. It also talks about what is to come.

The four Gospels are books written by four of his disciples. These books speak about their interaction with him and the miracles they saw him perform, the things Christ told them, but most importantly they talk about his death and his coming back to life.

That is where you need to start because that is where you will find Jesus and know him the way I do. Genesis can be very confusing, and I can see why you've struggled with it. Trust me. If you start with the Gospels, Genesis will be easier to get through and it will make more sense. Before you do this though, you need to ask God for understanding. Pray to him to help you through it. If you ask, he will answer."

Jack thought long and hard about what Mark had just said. Nothing he had done in his life had brought him any closer to understanding and knowing God, and he desperately wanted to.

There was never a time in his life when he needed to know Jesus more than that moment. The insanity of what the world was becoming was more than he could bear. He knew that if he could not have what Mark had, there was no way for him to continue this life filled with terror, emptiness, and so little regard for human life.

Both were very afraid for their younger siblings and their mothers. They were both on constant guard for their families, in a new world full of things they were not prepared for.

What man could be?

"Jesus was the sacrificial lamb for *all* of us," Mark said. "That's why he is called the Lamb of God. He did not just die for those that believe in him…he died for all of us, so we could be welcomed into God's Kingdom. You are now on the Hunt for the Lamb of God, and I know if you truly seek him, Jack, you will find him. He is waiting…waiting for you." Mark finished.

And with that final thought, the two made their way off the roof and into the back door of the house, locking the door behind them.

NINE

The Underground Rail System

V iv was worried.

Supplies were dwindling, and she knew they would not make it until America had begun to recover.

It was simple mathematics.

There was only a couple of months' worth of food left, maybe a couple of weeks of water after that, and the toilet paper could run out as soon as next week, prompting thoughts of using books, magazines, and even clothing to wipe with.

Then what would they do?

They had done everything they could do to conserve what they had, making it last longer than she ever would have thought possible with the extra mouths to feed, but alas, soon the day would come when they would meet the same fate as the other neighbors in the hood that had run out of food and water.

Would they become the hunted or the hunters?

The latter would be something they could never do, no matter how hungry they became.

The thought of killing someone that wasn't trying to kill them first was abhorrent to her.

The thought of eating someone was beyond abhorrent...it was an abomination to Christ!

Somehow, someway, they would have to think of something, somehow to survive this and continue for her children, and Julie's children.

She had resigned herself to the fact as she knew it, her husband was not going to be coming home to save them from this wretched end; however, they would have to figure it out.

Viv was dying for clean clothes to wear and to be able to take a bath.

Down by Cherry Knolls Park was a creek where some were washing their clothes, but it was just too much of a risk. Some were even bathing in it, which seemed even riskier.

Besides, leaving the house would put their house at risk of being robbed and the last of their supplies stolen.

The natural gas had run out and they were now cooking their food on the gas grill in the backyard. The saving grace was they were not grilling meat, but instead boiling water and dumping the freeze-dried contents of the cans into the pot, then covering the pot with a lid so the food would be hydrated and stay hot at the same time, thereby keeping the aromas from spilling out into the neighborhood.

Still, even that seemed to be much riskier than doing everything in the house.

Most of the surrounding neighbors had died, some recently, creating new odors circulating through the air of the neighborhood.

Though the neighbors still alive were suffering greatly due to malnutrition and dehydration, they managed to survive by pailing out water from the creek, catching frogs, and catching an occasional squirrel that had managed not to be killed yet.

The suburbs, along with the cities, had the worst of it.

At least in the outskirts, there were deer to hunt and lakes to drink from.

Not so in the suburbs, such as Centennial, Littleton, and Lakewood, which saw more than their share of murder and mayhem.

‿‿✦‿‿

Bill had been at Mt. Weather now for over a week and was getting the lay of the land. It was an enormous complex of buildings, a lake, meeting rooms, endless hallways leading to massive rooms serving as dormitories and eating halls…even a shopping mall with stores giving away clothing and whatever else you might need that was not immediately provided to you when you got there, and all underground.

He had been rubbing elbows with a lot of Senators and Representatives he'd seen on TV but had never met until then.

Privacy was at a premium at Mt. Weather, which could only be had in a toilet stall. Even the showers were of group design, so it would not be uncommon to be standing next to a Senator buck naked washing his balls; a sight you wish you had not seen, wishing for some drain cleaner to scrub your eyes out with.

His friend from the White House was there as well, and the two of them would sup together whenever possible.

The most humbling was meeting the President for the first time, which took four days to happen after he had arrived. Bill had made sure to put his suit on, but mismatched with his tennis shoes, as he had forgotten to pack some dress shoes.

As luck would have it, the President was wearing Dockers and a polo shirt, leaving Bill a bit overdressed, but he was still glad he had worn his suit. All the rest of his clothes had not been laundered yet, which would have made for a stinky first impression.

His first meeting with the President was in a large meeting room with the biggest conference table he had ever sat at. The table had to be at least fifty feet long and six feet wide, with exactly fifteen chairs on each side and two chairs at each end; exactly because he counted them. The President was sitting in the middle of one of the sides, and Bill was in one of the end chairs.

Had the table been any longer, they would have needed microphones run through a PA system for each person, so everyone would be able to hear each other.

Around the table was an outer circle of chairs for spillover.

Every seat was full in the meeting and the subject matter was the topic of getting New York City, Washington D.C., and Los Angeles up and running, which lasted approximately forty-five minutes on updates on their progress.

Halfway through, Bill was wondering why he was even in that meeting since there would be no discussion on that day regarding anything germane to his expertise.

Later, he was informed by his friend Philip that President Biden wanted Bill to be brought up to speed on everything being done regarding America's rebuild, plus it would be a good opportunity for Bill to meet the President.

After the meeting, Bill and the President were introduced, which was when the President joked with Bill about him wearing a suit to an orgy.

He wouldn't make that mistake again, he thought to himself.

After the intro, Philip and Bill retreated to the dining hall where the President, Senators, and Representatives took their meals, and they discussed his figures and estimates on the completion of equipping certain farmers with machinery needed, and a timeline from planting seed to harvest.

They also discussed their families.

Philip had his wife and two kids there with him in the facility, as most of the people there did. Unfortunately for Bill, he hadn't seen his family since March and had no idea if they were dead or alive, and it was like dying a slow death not knowing.

After they finished their meal consisting of roast chicken, mashed potatoes, carrots, salad, and a strawberry parfait for dessert, they exited the dining hall and sat in a couple of high-back leather lounge chairs along the main corridor, directly across the entrance to a hallway he seldom saw used.

Philip then pulled out a flask from his vest pocket and handed it to Bill.

"Nice. What is this...and where the hell did you get it?" asked Bill.

"Being on the President's staff has its perks. It's Jack Daniels." Philip answered.

Bill cracked it open and put the flask to his lips, taking a generous swig.

"Ahhh...so nice. It's been a while, my friend." Bill thankfully offered, then took another and handed it back to him, feeling the warm glow of the whiskey. He then saw something at the end of the hall they were opposite that intrigued him.

At the very end of the hallway was a big black steel elevator door, which suddenly opened, and out of it walked six or seven military men. These were not high-ranking officials, such as Joint Chiefs of Staff, but ordinary soldiers, enlisted men, walking past them and into a smaller dining area reserved for the different staff and military that worked inside running the facility.

"Where does that Elevator door lead to?" asked Bill.

Philip answered his question by asking Bill a question of his own.

"How much do you know about Mt. Weather Bill?"

"Not much really. Just what I've read. Built in the 1950s…houses FEMA and Homeland Security. Escape hatch for our government to continue running…. built really with a nuclear attack in mind. That's about it really" Bill said. "I will tell you this. I am very impressed with how they dug this out and reinforced it. I sure as hell never imagined I'd see the inside of it"

"Aha…this place is so much more than that….so much more than what you can see" offered Philip. "That door leads to the train station."

"What would you say if I told you there is a rail system connecting every major city and military installation in the United States?" asked Philip.

"I'm listening," said Bill.

"Back in the '50s, The Rand Corporation was contracted by the United States to construct boring machines to dig facilities like this all across the U.S., and you should see these things. I have. They reach about five to six stories tall, and they can dig through anything.

In the old days, they used an auger, only it was a forty-foot auger. As they dug, they had a conveyor belt that ran the earth that had been dug out behind it, leaving it for tractors to scoop out, then remove from the area it had just dug, then came along the '60s.

Now, instead of auguring through, they upped their game and invented something called a nuclear subterranean. It's run by nuclear power and instead of auguring, it melts its way through anything, including stone, and instead of having a conveyor belt pushing the dirt out behind it, it melts the rock, leaving a glass wall following behind it. It changed everything.

In the '60s, they began constructing tunnels connecting most major cities and military installations, all about 8000 feet below the Earth's surface and it's strictly military.

These places are connected by tunnels because the government built an electric rail system that transports people and equipment wherever they or it is needed; *it* being equipment.

These trains don't even touch the tracks, but they instead hover… and these things can fly man! They go about 250 miles per hour, and they're as smooth as sitting in your Lazy Boy back home.

Say you left here at 7 a.m.…you'd be in Denver by 1 p.m., losing two hours to the time change of course!"

Bill sat upright at attention with ears perked up.

"Go on…tell me more" demanded Bill.

"Not much more to tell. That's about it." Philip stated. "It is definitely a game-changer for sure."

"What *about* Denver?" Bill asked.

Suddenly it dawned on Philip that he might have said too much.

"Where does this train stop in Denver?' Bill asked with an edge to his voice.

"NORAD and DIA" Philip whispered.

"Are you fucking kidding me, Phil?" Bill said, now with a little more intensity in his tone. All this time I've been telling you about my family and you haven't said anything? I've been telling you that I'm worried sick about them."

"Wait, wait, wait a minute. Hold on…just, just hold on Bill."

Philip was now more nervous than a long tail cat in a room full of rocking chairs.

"I've got to get on that train, Phil. Simple as that. You've got to get me on it!"

"I can't Bill, at least not now." Philip knew he fucked up big time.

"If not now, then when?" Bill asked, sounding borderline demanding.

"I would have to get permission from President Biden himself. He's the only one that could authorize you to be on that train."

Philip was emphatic on this point.

"Bill, you are here because you are needed *here*! I can talk to him, but I must figure out how to approach it. He's a compassionate man and might understand your need, but he also will have to take into consideration your value to him, which is why you're here in the first place." Phil explained.

He mentally kicked himself squarely in the ass because he knew he screwed the pooch, but there was no getting out of it now.

"What do you plan to do? Are you going to stay there, because if that's the case, I already know what he will say? He won't allow it. He needs you here for this integral part of the rebuild."

"I won't stay, but I will want to bring them back with me, just like the families that are here now," Bill replied. "I have to make sure they are OK."

Philip agreed to speak with the President about it first thing in the morning and gave Bill his word that he would, which was all Bill could ask of him. Philip excused himself and said he needed to spend time with his family before he gave Bill a wink and shook his hand, assuring him he would not only speak to the President but would speak on Bill's behalf.

"Thanks for the whiskey," said Bill.

Bill's brain was exploding with hope, anxiety, joy…just about every emotion under the sun. He was also worried about what he might find if he were allowed to go but that wouldn't stop him. If he had not been in that place surrounded by so many people, he would have jumped for joy at the prospect of reuniting with his family. Be that as it may, he stayed subdued and said a silent prayer to himself instead.

"Thank you Jesus for the opportunity presented before me and my willingness and ability to be aggressive with Philip to possibly make this happen."

Jack had been awakened by a noise outside. He lifted his head off the arm of the living room couch he was sleeping on and peeked out the window. Standing outside in the street were several men, being extremely quiet, other than the man that coughed waking Jack, and all were illuminated by the pale moonlight. One of them lit a match and fired up a cigarette, slowly inhaling the toxic smoke as if it was life-giving air, then exhaling it out. The flame from the match lit up his bearded face. All men had beards now.

One of the men was carrying something over his shoulder, which looked to be a rifle, and another man was holding on to what looked to be a stretcher of some sort. Upon focusing on them further, Jack could hear them whispering, but couldn't make out what they were saying.

Everyone else in the house was sound asleep except for Jack. Had the window not been open, Jack would still be asleep as well.

This looked to be a hunting party looking for their next kill and Jack wondered if they were finally being targeted. There weren't many people left alive in the neighborhood except them and those who chose to eat human flesh, so at this point in the summer, chances were the hunters were looking to disrupt Jack and Company from their slumber.

What were they waiting for? Jack was asking himself.

Viv had made her way down the hallway from her bedroom and was standing in the darkness a few feet from Jack behind the front door, looking out of the door's peephole. Jack knew she was there but couldn't see her. What he couldn't see was the pistol she was holding, and the terrified look on her face.

The whispering outside continued, and it seemed there was a discussion of disagreement going on, and God only knows what the disagreement was about.

The only thing that Jack was fairly confident of was their disagreement involving the occupants of the house that Jack was currently in.

Viv crawled over to where Jack was on the couch, and he could now see her in the moonlight coming in through the window, and the gun.

She then whispered up to Jack "Oh my God. Do you think they are here for us?"

"Yes," he whispered back.

"Well…are we just going to wait for them to come in? I don't want us to end like this. We've come too far" she said.

"What were you planning to do with that gun?" he asked. "I think we should fire a warning shot at them. That will make them go away," said Jack. "What do you think?"

Their conversation was then interrupted by the sound of the invader's footsteps creeping up in the tall grass of the front yard, a yard that hadn't been mowed in months.

Viv then handed the gun to Jack.

"You do it. My hands are shaking too badly. I can't," she said with a quavering voice.

Jack's hands were shaking too, but not as badly as Vivian's.

Brian and Rocky were now wide awake on the living room floor but had been motioned by Viv to not make a sound, and they remained silent but attentive.

Jack then stood up and tiptoed to the front door, gun in hand. He checked the safety on the gun to make sure it was off, and it wasn't. He turned the safety off, quietly turned the deadbolt on the front door, then opened the door and squeezed off a round that cut through the silence of the neighborhood. He then shut the door immediately behind him and relocked the living room door, then ran back to the couch to look out the window.

With the ringing sound of the gunshot, Mark, Julie, and Kate all leaped out of their beds and ran to the living room, bumping into each other in the hallway, then stood at the edge of the living room trying to figure out what was happening. Seeing them standing there, Vivian motioned them to get down on the floor.

No one was standing up outside and all hit the deck with the sound of the gun going off, then Jack yelled out the window. "We're armed in here and we will shoot you dead if you try to come in here!"

Stunned silence. Jack and Viv could then see several of them jump up from their prone positions and start running down the street at breakneck speed, making a speedy escape while leaving the others behind. There were still four of them lying in the tall grass, and one of them crawled over to the man lying next to him.

Suddenly one of them could be heard saying "Jerry's dead. Bring that stretcher up here."

He then said loud enough to be heard, "Hold your fire! You shot one of us. Let us get to him and we'll leave. I promise."

Jack's heart sank at the sound of what he had just heard. He never meant to hit anyone, let alone kill one of them. He put his face in his hands and sunk below the couch onto the living room floor.

"Go ahead. We won't shoot. Get the hell out of here and don't come back, because there's more where that came from!" Viv shouted back out the window, surprisingly forcefully.

"YEAH" shouted Rocky, to his mother Julie's consternation.

Then in the moonlight, Viv could see two more men come into full view, one carrying the stretcher. They rolled the man that had been shot onto the stretcher, then a man each grabbed a front pole. The remaining man laid his rifle across the dead body on the stretcher, grabbed the two poles in the back, and all got up and started running down the street carrying the stretcher, going in the same direction the others had gone.

Viv sat on the couch behind Jack, who was sitting on the floor in front of her, and she could see how upset Jack was, so she tried to comfort him.

Viv touched his shoulder and said, "You saved our lives."

"Yes Jackie" said his mother. "Don't beat yourself up. You saved us."

Mark then sat next to Jack at his mother's feet and put his arm around him.

"They won't be coming around here anymore," Mark said to Jack.

"They'll be back" Jack answered him, sending a chill down the spines of everyone else in the room. "They are starving, and they'll be back. As soon as they finish eating their friend, they will come back to this house because they know there are people in here. They will just be careful next time and try to ambush us differently but make no mistake about it…they're coming back for sure."

Stone-faced in the dark; they all nodded their heads in agreement.

One of the casualties of this dystopian nightmare was the innocence lost of the children, never to return, and now Jack needed to find Jesus more than ever.

TEN

Permission Granted

B ill Jenkins had been called to a meeting with Philip and President
Biden in the President's office, three days after Bill and Philip
initially discussed Bill's trip to Denver on the train.

Philip had kept his word after all, and Bill was more than grateful.
No matter how the meeting turned out, Bill would forever be in Phil's
debt for keeping his word by creating an opportunity to meet with the
President and try to convince him to let Bill go to Denver to collect
his family.

As Bill was being escorted down the long hallway to the President's
office, he played the conversation he was about to have in his mind,
crafting rebuttals and reasons why it would be prudent to allow him
this train ride. All he could do is make his case the best he could and
let the chips fall where they may.

This time around, Bill was wearing sweats and a T-shirt for his
second meeting with the President, and as luck would have it, the
President was formally dressed in a suit and tie.

Nuts! He thought to himself, as he stepped through the door. He
just couldn't win.

"Good morning Bill," said President Biden." I see you dressed for
the occasion."

Humor. A good sign. Things were already looking up.

"Just following your lead Sir! Good morning!" Bill answered the President.

"Have a seat Fella's" Biden offered.

Phil was standing next to the President at the side of his desk, and Bill acknowledged him with a handshake, then shook the President's hand. They all sat down, with Phil sitting next to Bill across from the President.

"Phil tells me you have your family in Denver, is that right?" the President asked.

"Yes, Sir" Bill answered. "My wife and two boys."

"And you want to go out there and bring them out here?"

"Yes, I do Sir...in the worst way"

"It's August the fourth. We've got several briefings happening in the next few weeks, and I will need you in on them. After that, I could stand to lose your presence for the following two weeks, but after that, I will need you here because you and your knowledge will be critical to our rebuilding."

Biden relented, looking Bill dead in his eyes.

"Bill, I understand the need to have your family here with you and out of harm's way, but," he proceeded with caution, "have you considered that they might not be alive? I know that sounds harsh, but the reports we've been getting regarding the Midwest are not encouraging, especially in Denver. Colorado as a whole has done well, but the cities, such as Ft. Collins, Colorado Springs, Pueblo, and *especially* Denver, have had widespread murder. Most of those still alive there have resorted to cannibalism to survive. What do you really think the chances are that your family hasn't fallen victim to this?" the President asked.

At the mention of cannibalism, Bill's stomach turned inside out. Bill knew there were no firearms in the house, as was family policy, and had no idea the condition of his family, but could only hope for the best. He could not even entertain the possibility of his loved ones being eaten.

"Sir, I can tell you this…" Bill did not wait for his permission, "I am a prepper of sorts, with two resourceful boys, and I left them 500 cases of water and a year's supply of freeze-dried emergency food. They certainly have enough food and water to sustain themselves, but I can't speak about them being alive or not, because I just don't know. Those things you mentioned are concerning to me for sure, but if anyone could survive this, it would be them. My oldest son is an Eagle Scout and he's a really smart kid, and he's a big kid…plays football for his high school as an offensive lineman. I don't see anyone pushing him around or taking advantage of him. The same holds for my wife and my youngest. None of 'em take any shit, so if anyone could live through this, I suspect it would be them."

After a long pause the president said "I'm going to authorize your trip, but I'm sending two soldiers with you. They will be with you every step of the way to make sure nothing happens to you, and to make sure you come back here, family or not. You are not authorized to stay there, no matter what. We've got room for your family here, so you can bring them back with you…no excuses. Do we understand each other?"

Bill was about to burst with joy and almost leaped over the President's desk to embrace him, but thought better of it, and instead shook his hand vigorously.

"Yes Sir…Yes Indeed!"

Bill could hardly contain himself.

"There will be a train leaving for DIA and NORAD on the 25th of August at 5 a.m.. I expect you back here no later than September 5th… now get out of here and I'll see you at our next briefing." the President said enthusiastically and followed with "Can't wait to meet your family!"

Bill was on cloud nine as he was leaving the President's office, turning down the hallway leading back to the main area, but his joy and excitement were tempered with fear and trepidation.

The wishing and wondering would soon be over.

Too bad he couldn't let Viv know he was coming home.

❧

Satan had found his opening to the population through starving men and women, known prior to themselves and their neighbors as decent God-fearing folk, but they now had resorted to becoming nothing more than beasts of the field, feeding on human flesh and possessing empty souls. The light had died in them, with not even so much as a flicker of goodness left in their eyes, and the only thing that could satiate their desires was the thrill of the hunt...hunting human beings like big game in the woods; hence, they would be called the "hunters."

They were not human anymore and possessed none of the qualities that human beings have innately. Soon they would change physically, into something so ugly that the most hardened would look upon them to be shunned, yet now they accounted for the majority of life that walked on two legs in North America and could not be concerned less about their appearance or their taste for human flesh.

It was how they were wired now.

They traveled in packs, mostly in the darkness of night, and the more human flesh they consumed, the more of a taste for it they acquired. It was an addiction they could not shake even if they wanted to, and they didn't want to.

They were disciples of the darkness and would stop at nothing to kill anything or anyone if it meant feasting until their appetites had been filled.

And this is how Officers Tipton and Engleart had met their fate.

Outside of Macy's on the west side of the mall, the two of them sat in their police cruiser when Tipton noticed a man and a woman sitting by one of the doors of the store, looking at the two officers as if they wanted to come up and speak to them, but was too scared or shy.

Finally, Tipton rolled down his window and called to them.

"Hey…you two doing okay over there?" he asked.

"Doing fine Officer" the man answered back.

Tipton recognized the man, calling out to him.

"Tom! Is that you? Come over here!"

It was Tom. Tom Dorsey. He lived over in Cherry Knolls, a subdivision to the east of the mall. He hadn't seen him since before the blast, but as Tom got closer to the cruiser, he noticed something different about him. Besides being filthy, he had a bizarre look about him, and Engleart noticed it too.

"That fucking guy is looking at you like you're a blue plate special, a chicken dinner with all the trimmings," said Engleart. "I'd be careful with him if I were you."

"Nah…I've known this guy since we were kids in high school. He's ok…he's just a little dirty." Tipton retorted.

Tom stopped about three feet from the cruiser but was close enough for Tipton to get a whiff of him. "Man Tom, I'm glad to see you've made it this far. A lot of people we know haven't."

"Yeah…I know. It's a shame what's happened to this town."

And just like Quick Draw McGraw, Tom reached around to his back waistband and pulled out a semi-automatic pistol and pointed it directly at Tipton's chin.

They both were caught completely off guard and neither had gotten close to their service revolvers.

"Don't think about it boys. You'll never live to tell the tale." Said Tom.

"What in the hell do you----"

Just like that, Tom blasted Tipton right in the face and shot Engleart in the neck, exploding his carotid artery all over the right side of Tipton.

Both were dead instantly.

Following the untimely deaths of the two officers, the woman that was still sitting by the doors of the store jumped up and ran over to the scene of the crime, screaming wildly and jumping up and down.

"We finally have a car!" she proclaimed.

Out from behind some vehicles in the parking lot emerged other men and women, celebrating just like the woman with Tom. They were part of the plan and happy about their newly gained bounty.

"Dinner time" said one of the men.

They opened both doors of the cruiser and lifted the officers out, then opened the back doors and threw them inside on top of each other. Tom got behind the wheel and the woman rode shotgun, blood be damned.

"I'm driving these fellas over to take them down into the basement. Everybody should meet me over there and help me cut these fuckers up so we can put 'em on the grill. Let's eat!" Tom shouted to his friends, and away he went, leaving the others walking in the same direction as the car, hungry as hell because it had been a few days since they had eaten.

The pack of hunters had their eyes on the two officers for quite some time, and this hunt was planned well in advance. It was true that Tipton and Tom had gone to school together, so they knew each other well enough for Tom to be able to get close enough to pull this off.

Having a vehicle was a game-changer for them. Now they would be able to travel to different neighborhoods to find new food sources, be able to drive the victims back to Tom's house for grilling, and even fill up water jugs at the creek and drive them home without having to carry them.

This was how Tipton and Engleart had helped Vivian Jenkins and company more than anything else they had done in the past.

These were the same ones that had crept up in their yard that night and were very reticent to go back and try their luck again. They certainly would have if they had to, but now they didn't.

As the sacrificial lambs that they were, they provided a much-needed distraction away from the Jenkins house, because Jack was right, they would have come back again, regardless of the risk.

Both officers would not be going home that night, and their families would be left to fend for themselves from that day on, never knowing what happened to them.

Tensions were high in Viv's home ever since they foiled the ambush from Tom and his fellow hunters from two blocks away, and they would never know the sacrifice given for them, although unwillingly for sure.

No one slept from that point on without one eye open, and the lack of sleep started to show in their attitudes and behaviors.

Tempers started to become short, and the two youngest boys began arguing a lot with each other, or they would team up on Kate.

Jack had taken Mark's advice and started reading the Bible again, only this time he began with the Gospels as suggested, always praying for God's help in understanding, which proved to make all the difference in the world to him. It was important for Jack to read his dad's Bible, so he went across the street and pulled it out of his dad's nightstand, which made Julie cry at the sight of it every time he cracked it open, reminding her of her sweet dead husband.

For Jack, his reaction was the opposite. It made him feel close to his dad as if his dad was sitting on the couch next to him, with both of them reading it together, giving him a great source of comfort.

Viv thought it was possible the household would end up killing each other before the supplies ran out.

Mark was the stoic one, always keeping his composure, trying to keep himself busy.

The tent had already been moved twice, as latrine holes kept filling up. They had run out of toilet paper a week ago and were now using old rags and socks to wipe with. The women would have to drip dry.

Life had truly started to feel like a struggle, and no one knew how this would all end up...or end in general.

Though none would ever speak it or admit it, all of them in their way began to doubt God's presence in their lives, as all they could see around them was evil...all of them except Mark, and surprisingly enough, Jack.

Mark was stronger in his faith now more than ever, partly because he saw Jack coming around to the Lord in a very profound way, and because he had convinced himself that a miracle was right around the corner.

He could feel it. He had no idea how it would manifest, but he knew it was coming.

It was Viv who spotted the cruiser drive by the house as she was looking out the living room window, something she had been doing a lot since that night of the hunters. Tipton and Engleart were driving awful fast, and not stopping at the house like they always did, when they were in the neighborhood, so unlike them.

Had they been going a little slower, she would have noticed it wasn't Tipton driving at all, but instead, it was the guy that had been in her front yard that night with the rifle. She might have also noticed the bodies of the two cops lying dead in their backseat.

"Very strange" she whispered to herself, walking back to her bedroom to take a late afternoon nap.

It had rained earlier and cooled things down a bit, so with the window in her bedroom open and a cool breeze blowing in, she thought she'd take advantage and make up for some lost sleep from the past few nights.

~~~

Being at Mt. Weather had allowed Bill to take a reset and think more clearly than he had for quite some time. Instead of the sweltering hot apartment he had been sleeping in, he was now in air conditioning, making for much better sleep, even though he was now stretching out in a bottom bunk set in an enormous dormitory-style situation, together with hundreds of other people, strangers he did not know, but all in all, it was a much better style of living than before. His clothes were now clean and so was his body, making full use of the laundry and shower facilities.

The tradeoff was the lack of privacy and the noise. The one thing that he appreciated was the lack of sound in the city. What was once a cacophonous din became crickets overnight. No more traffic, fewer people making noise, no music or television blaring through his window. It was quiet and he liked it, even though he hated what it represented.

Bill had talked to Philip about his adventure several times in the last couple of weeks and got well versed on the protocol of his departure and arrival in Denver, what was expected of him, and how this rescue operation, which was what they were calling it, was going to go down.

The first thing Philip wanted to do was prepare Bill for what he was about to see when he got on the train, then when he arrived in Denver. Bill would be met by Philip in the dining hall at 4:30 in the morning, then be escorted by Philip down the elevator and into the station.

At that time, Bill would be given a folder containing clearances he would need to board the train on both trips; on the way there for himself and on the way back, which was the most critical, clearance for his family to board with him. He would also be given clearance to enter the facility once getting off the train, and then clearance for him and his family to re-enter the DIA/Base 12 facility once returning to the airport.

Once arriving at DIA/Base 12, he would be greeted by the General that oversaw operations on the base, then he would be escorted by the two soldiers accompanying him on the trip to his home and back.

Philip had stressed to Bill that he may see things in the Denver base that he's never seen before and to not be taken aback, and to remind him that anything he sees there would be classified information.

Since the dining hall would not be open until 6:00 a.m. the morning he was leaving, he would not have to worry about breakfast because he would be served on the train…and lunch.

There would be an enlisted person that works train detail, who would be there specifically to take care of any needs he might have.

What Philip wanted to convey to Bill more than anything else was that he was being given 11 days to find his family and get back there to Mt. Weather. In a perfect situation, he would find his family the same day he arrives, then get back to Base 12 with them, and board the train the next day, then return.

The President understands that this is not a perfect world and things happen, and you might have to spend more time there to locate them in case they've moved from their location, so he the President believes he's given Bill all the time he needs to find them, and also because Bill would be going into possibly hostile territory.

Bill needed to be prepared for the worst. The Denver area, more than any territory in the lower forty eight, except maybe New York

City, was the most hostile area they had reports on. The city had been completely overrun by cannibalism and methamphetamine use, with untold casualties being reported daily.

This was sobering news to hear and made Bill even more anxious to get out there. He'd leave right then and there if he could, but the twenty fifth was still five days away and he would have to grit his teeth and bite his lip until then.

Then the conversation turned to the recovery of America.

Philip told Bill that the situation was a lot worse than President Biden was making it out to be, because after all, the President, as everyone knew him to be, was the eternal optimist.

At the moment, the country was concentrating its rebuilding efforts in New York City, Washington D.C., and somewhat Los Angeles, but the effort was like threading a needle.

The truth of the matter was these cities would never be what they once were, nor would the country. Estimates were that America had already lost at least half of its population, with many more to die in the coming months. The hardest hit were the cities and suburbs because they had the densest populations with the least number of natural resources, so the only way of survival for them was to turn to cannibalism.

He also stressed to Bill that the only way for America to come back would be through agriculture and oil.

The only ones that were prepared for something like this were the super-rich and the government/military, but being prepared to survive versus being prepared to make a full recovery were two different things entirely.

Truth be told, America was looking at the minimum of at least twenty, thirty, maybe even fifty years before they would truly get on their feet again.

In the meantime, you have states like Iran and North Korea, who have now been confirmed as the players behind the EMP, teetering dangerously close to starting a full-scale war.

Now that America was out of the way, Iran could be looking at taking Israel out for good. Israel, on the other hand, could make a pre-emptive strike, and Philip wasn't talking about taking out some nuclear sites but instead wiping Iran off the map entirely.

The problem with Iran, as crazy as they are, they believe in their crazy ideology and will die to promote what they believe in, whereas Kim Jong Un is a wild card that doesn't believe in anything except protecting himself and his country, which makes them less of a threat.

The only reason one of our allies has not taken North Korea out yet is China, plain and simple.

The reason Phil gave all of this information to Bill was to stress the importance of his role to play in the rebuilding back of America, and that is why it was so important for him to not only return, but to return *safely*. He wanted Bill to not take any chances unnecessarily.

The soldiers that would be accompanying Bill would be Army Rangers at the top of their game, and their sole purpose would be to provide cover for Bill and keep him alive.

If Bill had not appreciated what President Biden was co-signing him to do, he certainly did after his conversation with Philip.

ELEVEN

By the Grace of God

"Have you considered that we might have to leave here?" Julie asked Vivian as they both lie in bed in the wee hours of the morning.

They were now using pages of books to wipe with. Pages in books were softer and more absorbent than pages out of a magazine.

They had run out of propane on the gas grill and were now burning lumber stacked up out back by the garden shed, creating a bigger risk of being exposed to the hunters.

Curiously enough, they had not come back, giving all of them a false sense of security, but not enough to let their guards down.

They would soon be out of the water, maybe a month or two tops, depending on how they conserved it, and the food would run out shortly thereafter.

"And to where Julie? Where would we go?' Viv asked.

"Don't you think eventually we will have to? If these bastards don't come back and eat us first, we will die here anyway once everything is gone." Julie answered.

She had slowly digressed all through the summer, looking for a reason to live without her husband, and digressed to the point of despondence. Her children were not enough to keep her alive, and at one point during the summer, she seriously considered taking her life, but after the incident with the hunters, she realized she didn't want to die as much as she didn't want to live, where living to her in this time meant being in constant fear of what lay in wait for her around the corner, so she trudged on looking for reasons to stay alive, sometimes day to day, and sometimes down to the minute.

All she knew was that the man she loved, the one she depended on, the only man she had ever been with, was forever gone. She just wanted the dull, aching, never-ending pain to stop, and she could not understand why God had let this horrible dream begin with no end.

Thus was the faith lost in Julie and it would take a miracle for her to get it back.

Having a conversation with her was like pulling teeth, and the more you tried, the less headway you made because nothing interested her anymore.

Both women were now on their sides on the bed facing each other and it was obvious to Viv that it would take a long time for Julie to find peace.

"You know…I've been waiting all summer for Bill to come walking in through that front door, and he never comes," said Viv. "I miss him so much. I don't even know if he's alive. It's like he's dead. He might as well be."

"At least you have hope, Vivian. I wish I had hope. I wish my Paul were here with me, but he's not, and I know he won't be coming back, where you can still have hope, I can't" Julie responded in a somber tone.

"Yes, but at least you know where you stand and what you can count on now," Viv said, but immediately felt a twinge of guilt saying such a thing to her as if it sounded heartless. "I'm sorry Julie. I didn't mean it to sound like that…Look…I know you're afraid and I am too. Deathly afraid. I never told you this or anyone else for that matter. Do you remember when Officer Tipton and Officer Engleart gave me and Jack a ride home that day from Whole Foods?"

"Yes?" said Julie.

"They rescued both Jack and me. I was about to be raped by a meth addict...I'm assuming he was a meth addict. His teeth were all rotted and his breath smelled like a toilet. He snuck up on me and put a knife to my throat and told me to take my pants off and get down on the ground. Jack was upfront in the store getting bags to put the flour in. And then, out of nowhere, there was Officer Tipton pointing a gun to his head. He stopped it from happening. Had he not been there, God knows what would have happened," she said with a long off stare.

"Officer Engleart stopped another guy from sneaking up on Jack that was getting ready to stab him in his back. We were both saved that day, and it was like God was there to stop it from happening. By the grace of God, we are still here today," she looked back at her friend and was greeted by a set of wide eyes and a dropped jaw.

"I made Jack swear not to tell any of you. I didn't want any of you more worried than you already were." Viv told her, almost whispering.

After a long pause, giving Julie time to think of something to say, she finally said "Thank you...thank you for not telling me. Hearing that would have put me over the edge for sure. I've been having thoughts Viv...bad thoughts." said Julie.

"I know you have Julie. I've been worried about you. I can see it in your eyes. Jack, Kate, they've all been worried about you, for you. I know this has been so hard for you, but you're still here, even when we've been surrounded by so much evil outside.

We are all in this together and we will get through it the same way. No matter what happens, we will all be together" Viv said calmly. "Because we have to."

As Viv said those words, she thought to herself that they must have sounded hollow…untrue, because deep down, she did not believe them herself. Her husband was never going to walk through that door because he would have already done so.

There was nothing more she wanted than for that to happen. She'd been waiting so long…so goddamn long.

She was sure he was either dead, or it was physically impossible for him to reach them.

Whiskers jumped onto the bed between the two women and purred, looking for someone to give him some love, to pet him and rub his head. He loved a good head rub. The only one in the house that seemed to still have a good food supply was Whiskers. That big ol' bag of cat food was only half gone, so he had a way to go before he would be in trouble.

The summer would be gone soon, and even if they were to make it past the hunters, they would have to deal with the winter, and without any natural gas to provide fuel for the furnace, they all would surely freeze to death before Christmas.

Viv didn't want to admit to herself or anyone else that she too had lost her faith, not only in her husband coming to save them but in Christ as well.

She couldn't remember the last time she looked at herself in the mirror.

She was afraid to.

She stared at her Bible sitting on her nightstand, collecting dust, and possibly a candidate for the latrine. The books in the house had taken a hit for sure, and the thought of the soft pages of her Bible would be a welcome change from the chafing that came from Mark's school books, but the thought of crapping on Jesus seemed so sacrilegious.

And so, it sat, collecting more dust.

She heard stirring coming from Mark's bedroom, then he walked past heading out to the tent for his morning constitutional.

People were getting up and it would be another day of trying to stay alive.

One more day…in a long line of one more days.

They were down to their last can of freeze-dried bacon and eggs, so after Mark came out of the tent, she would have him light a fire in the gas grill-turned wood pit so she could boil some water. She sure missed her stove.

※ ∧ ↗

It was August 24, the night before Bill would board the train for Denver. His duffel was packed with several changes of clothes and toiletry items. Everything else would stay behind, as he was planning on returning with his wife and boys in tow. He would have to find another area within the dorm room that had four beds close together so they would not be all spread apart.

He played this out in his mind so many times that he could have recited scenarios by heart in his sleep, all concerning his options if they were not in the house, but no evidence if his family were dead.

He also tried looking into the future, what a life could look like for the four of them in the new America, especially after envisioning the grim picture Philip had painted for him.

How long would they have to stay in Mt. Weather?

Where would they live in D.C., assuming that is where he would go back to?

Would there be a college for Mark to go to once he graduated after his senior year in high school, wherever that would be?

Would he ever again accept a position that separated him from his family?

These were just some of the things ruminating in his brain as he lay on his bunk, waiting for the lights to go out at ten. His alarm was set for 3 a.m., giving him enough time to shower, dress, and swallow down a few cups of coffee before meeting with Philip at 4:30 a.m. to be escorted through the black doors of the elevator, dropping close to a mile and a half into the train station beneath Mt. Weather.

The longest elevator ride he had ever taken was back in the late '80s when in the Sears Tower in Chicago. He remembered quite vividly how the car seemed to sway underneath his feet as it zoomed up to the top, then how he could feel the whole building move once up on the observation deck.

To him, it was uncomfortable and somewhat frightening. He did not do all that well when it came to small, confined spaces.

The same held for flying. He had to have an aisle seat, otherwise, he would be borderline unruly and extremely uncomfortable to be around, as his family could attest to.

He had turned down the last middle seat on a flight he had to be on, thereby missing a meeting in Philadelphia, which eventually cost him the job he had at the time.

He was hoping the train would not be cramped and confining, especially for an eight-hour ride, but this was one ride he would not refuse. No matter the comfortable conditions, he would have to make the best of it and suffer if he must. There would be nothing stopping him from getting on that train.

The lights had just gone out in the dorm, so now he could shut his eyes and go to sleep, as long as the two men a bunk away would shut their mouths and stop talking to each other. He thought he might have to go over there and stuff a sock in their mouths.

☙❧

Tom spit the mouthful of gas onto the pavement, gas that was being siphoned out of the minivan stalled halfway onto the street, with the front end still in the gas station as it was exiting. This was a good source for a fill-up, as it was obvious that the minivan had just gotten gas before the bright light hit.

He noticed a pack of hungry feral dogs eyeballing him as if he were a nice juicy steak, but they were keeping their distance for the moment. Before Tom Dorsey had acquired a taste for people, he would have shot as many of those dogs as he could, then take them back to his house to be thrown onto his BBQ grill.

Now, the thought of eating anything but a barbequed human being made him nauseous.

That night would be the first long trip he and the neighbor across the way from him would take in his newly acquired police cruiser.

As soon as they took the bodies out of the back seat a few days ago and brought them into the house, they wiped off the blood as best they could, at least in the front seats.

They took the cruiser down to the creek, and with some creek, a little 409, and some elbow grease, they were able to remove just about all the blood from the windows and front seats. They weren't that concerned with the back seats because more bodies would be thrown in on them, kind of defeating the purpose of cleaning them.

After filling the five gallon gas drum, he siphoned it off into the police cruiser, and while that was filling the tank, he started another can on the minivan with another gas drum and hose.

He figured it should take at least four full cans to fill up the cruiser and he was currently on his second can, so it would be a while before he finished up.

It was still amazing to him how his life had changed so drastically in such a short period. three months ago he was the manager/mechanic at the Raceway Garage doing oil changes…barely making his house payment and bills, and feeding his family.

Now he was unemployed but without bills. In a sense, life had become a whole lot easier. The biggest difference was the lack of running water…and his diet. Another difference was not having to go to the store for food, but instead, he hunted it, which they were preparing to do that night.

Besides the awesome acquisition of the vehicle, they also came into possession of two service revolvers with ammo, plus a nice shotgun with ammo as well, although he never wanted to use the shotgun when on a hunt. There wasn't much more he hated than having to spit out BBs while he was eating.

Sometimes he had a momentary thought concerning his newfound diet and the morality behind it, then as quickly as the thought entered his brain, it left as quickly as it came.

Tom Dorsey never believed in God, and never subscribed to the "do unto others as you would have them do unto you" life.

The way he saw it, everyone was out to get you, and some were better at it than others, so if the chance came your way to better your station in life, you had better take it, or shame on you.

It didn't matter to Tom if someone else got hurt, because the way he saw it, it was better them than him.

Because Tom raised his boys with the same mindset, it was pretty clear he would never be awarded a trophy for the parent of the year, but that's how he did it and he had no reservations about it.

His boys were quick to get their first taste of human, whereas his wife was reticent, even though she was starving to death when she had her first bite, but eventually, she came around to like the taste and soon would have nothing else. To her and the rest of the family, it tasted like pork, and she always *loved* pork.

The boys were in Tom's camp immediately and were being groomed to become man killers.

The night they attempted the attack on the Jenkins household, his brother had been the one that got shot dead in the front yard.

They stretchered the body out of there, and like everyone else they stretchered home, they butchered him, but not Tom. Tom couldn't do it, and he certainly could not eat him. He refused to have any part in it, because after all...he was his brother...so the neighbor across the way had to do it, and they ate on him for close to a week.

Needless to say, Tom was itching to go hunting again after that, because they were close to starving to death by the time they made their next kill; hence, Tipton and Engleart.

They were still eating on those two, but it was time for another hunt, so that night with a full tank of gas, they would make the drive to Highlands Ranch and scour the neighborhoods looking for their next meal.

Tom's neighbor knew of a guy named Bill Sigler, a heavyset guy close to 280 pounds, that if he were still alive, would make some tasty steaks out of his hind quarters alone.

They both decided that he would be their first stop.

This was the curious thing about cannibalism.

The first thought would be only out of necessity, and not a diet choice, and for most people, that would most likely be true, but not for those that had a true yearning for nothing else than human.

These people might as well have been zombies because their appetites were the same, although zombies might prefer brains, whereas Tom had no desire to open someone's skull and eat their brain. A leg or ass portion was simply fine with him.

After Tom had finished filling the gas cans and transferring them into the cruiser, he started it up and headed over to the neighborhood to pick up his neighbor and head out for the hunt.

When they pulled close to the Sigler home, they stopped far enough away to not be seen and pulled over to the side. Tom whipped out his binoculars and there he was, on the front porch of his home, barbequing something up on the grill; probably a deer they had been able to shoot not far from home.

Highlands Ranch was on the outskirts of the suburbs and bordered lots of open territories favorable to deer, mountain lions, and other small animals.

This guy was everything his neighbor said he was. Had to be about six foot two inches and weighed at least 280 to 300 pounds. Obviously, this new life was agreeing with him because it didn't look like he was missing many meals if any.

"Damn dude, this is a big ol' boy. We're going to have to cut him up before putting him in the car. There's no way we pick him up and just throw him in the back seat." said Tom.

Tom reached into the back seat, pulled out a hand saw, and a large hunting knife to be ready when needed.

They both decided to make their way up the street slowly and quietly behind some cars where they wouldn't be seen. The sun had gone down. It was now becoming twilight, which tactically worked to their advantage. Before long, they were in the yard behind the big man, about ten feet back, with Tom pointing his hunting rifle at him and the other with the service revolver taken from one of the sheriff's deputies, aiming directly at the big man's noggin.

As the big man was turning a human leg on the grill with a pair of oven mitts, he blurted out, "I can see you guys behind me".

Up by the front door, there was a big mirror propped up to the side that pointed out to the street, enabling him to see anything behind him.

How fitting it was…cannibals getting ready to kill other cannibals, so they would be eating people that ate other people, making them wonder how the meat would taste, but these hunters would never get that opportunity, because around the corner of the garage came the big man's adult son, armed with a Ruger pistol, and he began firing rounds at the two assailants, dropping them both to the ground.

Bill Sigler then turned to the fallen men, walked over to them, pulled a pistol from his chest holster that they couldn't have seen, and nonchalantly squeezed off a round in each one of their skulls, killing Tom instantly, as he was not hit with a kill shot by the big man's son. The other man was already dead because his aim on him was true.

"Nice when dinner comes to you, isn't it?" he asked his son Will. His son nodded, smiling in agreement. "Tend to that leg for me, will you son?"

He then picked both men up one at a time, just like they were stuffed animals, throwing each one onto a giant cart covered in blood that had been used to transport his kills to his grill.

And that was that.

The hunters became the prey, and the Siglers would put off the killing of one of their neighbors for a day or two.

Tom would no longer torment Cherry Knolls, and all could breathe a sigh of relief if they only knew, and that would be the last of the police cruiser seen passing by the Jenkins home, causing Vivian to always wonder why she had not seen the police officers anymore.

By the grace of God.

TWELVE

Lamb of God

Bill was up and at 'em at 3 a.m. sharp, in the shower, shaved, dressed, and in the dining room with his duffel bag by 4 a.m., drinking his K cup of coffee and waiting for Philip to arrive.

In just a few hours, he hoped to see his family and give his sweet wife a big hug and a kiss. Bill was not a devout Catholic like his wife, but he had spent a lot of time on his knees in the chapel, rosary in hand, praying for her and the boy's safety, and just as hard for their reunion.

He tried to imagine him and the two soldiers driving to his house, capturing all kinds of scenarios in his brain, spanning from a quick and easy drive from DIA into the neighborhood, down to firefights with blood thirst cannibals all the way there.

He also tried to imagine what was under Denver International Airport which caused Philip to remind him that what he sees there remains there and not out on the wire.

Soon he would know.

Just as Bill finished his first cup of coffee, two high ranking military men walked into the dining room, walking directly to the K cup machine Bill had just used and was ready to use again, so he got up from his seat and followed them, acknowledged their presence, used the machine after them, then walked back to his seat, acknowledging them again as he walked by them sitting a distance away from where he was sitting.

Hmmm, he thought to himself. They must be taking the train and wondered if they were going to DIA or NORAD.

Right on time, Philip walked into the dining room and straight to the K cup machine, acknowledging Bill while passing where he was sitting.

Coffee in hand, he sat across from Bill at the table.

"Man, I hate getting up this early," he said to Bill.

"I'm pretty much use to it" Bill replied. "Old habit. I've always been an early riser, and fortunately for me, I don't require much sleep. Sleep is highly overrated anyway."

After a little small talk and going over the bullet points of what they had talked about previously, Philip handed Bill the folder containing all the paperwork he would need, and then got up and headed down the hallway that led toward the elevator.

This was not your normal elevator. It required a key card.

After swiping the card, the doors opened and both men walked into the elevator, the door closing behind them, then suddenly it felt like the floor dropped out from under their feet.

"Sorry...I should have warned you" Philip said jokingly.

"Thanks, Pal" Bill answered with a laugh.

After a minute, the car slowed down to a stop, then the doors opened into a small room.

"Bill gasped "What the hell?"

Philip then walked to another set of doors, swiped his key again, the door opened, and inside they went. This would continue three more times until they reached their final destination, one and a half miles below where they started.

The doors opened with Phil motioning Bill to exit the car, while Philip stayed inside.

"This is as far as I go, Bill. Godspeed my friend. See you in eleven days at the latest", and with that, the doors closed.

Bill, with duffel in hand, looked around at what you could only describe as surreal, which was the train station. To his left, there was an enlisted man behind a glass window sitting in a chair, looking at a huge monitor displaying an image of the United States with lines and dots covering it; which were the train lines and stations around the country.

There were also lines and dots extending outside of the U.S. into Mexico and Canada.

The soldier behind the glass motioned for Bill to come to him, then spoke in a microphone into a speaker built into the glass.

"Good morning Mr. Jenkins. I understand you are boarding for DIA/Base 12?" the soldier asked.

"Yes. At 0500 sharp." Bill answered.

"You should have a boarding pass for me sir."

Bill looked in his folder and there it was on top of the pile of papers, and pulled it out, holding it up to the glass.

"Yes Sir…that's it. Can you please put it in the drawer in front of you and slide it toward me?

Bill put it in the drawer, then slid it toward him. The soldier looked it over.

"Very good sir. Everything is in order, and you are good to go. You are in Passenger One car." The soldier then slid out his boarding pass through the drawer. Bill looked it over, then said "There's no seat number on this. What seat do I sit in?"

"There is no seat number Mr. Jenkins. There are twenty seats in the Passenger One car, all high-back leather seats, very comfortable. You will like them. Just pick any seat available…any seat to your liking." the soldier answered.

"Please walk through the double doors across from you and open them when you hear the buzzer. Have a great trip!"

Bill turned and walked to the doors, and when he heard the buzzer, he opened the doors and walked into what could only be described as something out of a science fiction novel. He found himself on a long boarding deck with six long train cars sitting there waiting for him. The deck had to be at least as long as a football field, with illuminated signs on the cement floor, designating each car for what it was…Passenger One, Passenger Two, Freight One, Freight Two, and Special Freight Three. The sixth car was in the front and contained the Engineer.

The train was waiting to be boarded and would be leaving in approximately ten minutes and it looked more like the Monorail at Disneyland than an actual train. What also amazed Bill were the walls and ceiling, as he scanned the whole area. The glass must be the glass walls left behind the nuclear subterranean that Philip was talking about, and they were beautiful.

The lighting was subdued, but functional.

Looking behind him, he could see a placard over the double doors he had just walked through to enter. The placard said, "MT. WEATHER/ VIRGINIA".

Looking down the tunnel up ahead of the train were not two rails, but only one in the center, and upon closer inspection, the train was not sitting on the rail, but hovering above it.

As Bill was about to board Passenger One, several military men came through the double doors behind him, two of which were the men he saw in the dining room, and they turned to the left and boarded Passenger Two, not acknowledging Bill at all, as if he were not even there.

When Bill stepped into the car, he was taken aback just a bit, because it was unlike anything he was expecting. There were twenty seats in an exceptionally long car just like the soldier had told him, but this was like first-class for the super-rich. The seats were all very plush, roomy, and soft…all made of very expensive leather and were spaced apart along the length of the car with ten seats on each side.

The seats resembled Lazy Boys more than your typical train or airline seats.

He stuffed his duffel overhead of a seat halfway down the car, and then sat down, sinking into the cushion, just like the softest pillow he had ever felt.

Wow! he thought to himself. So, *this* is how the rich live.

Through a door at the front end of the car walked out a woman soldier dressed in standard-issue army fatigues, who then approached Bill.

"May I have your boarding pass please?" she asked Bill.

Bill reached into his shirt pocket and handed it to her.

"Mr. Jenkins! My name is Lieutenant Lucinda Banks, and I will be taking care of all your needs on this trip. Can I get you something before we leave the station?" she asked.

"No thank you. I've had all the coffee I'm going to drink today but thank you!" he replied.

"We are not expecting any other passengers to join you this morning. We will be leaving at 5:00 sharp, approximately five minutes from now. Your expected arrival time will be 11:14 a.m. Mountain Standard Time. We will lose a couple of hours due to time zone changes, but you will be onboard for approximately eight hours and fourteen minutes. I see you are leaving us at DIA/Base 12. Is that correct?" she asked.

"Yes ma'am. DIA," he answered her.

"During your trip, should you need anything…anything at all, I will assist you. I will be in the room behind the door I came out of. All you have to do is push the blue button on the wall next to you, and I will come out. Fifteen minutes after we get started, I will be serving you breakfast. How does a bacon and cheese omelet with rye toast sound to you, along with some OJ?"

"Wow...sounds great...thank you Lieutenant" he answered.

She then turned around and returned through the door she came out of.

A few minutes later, the train doors closed and immediately began to move, but curiously enough, Bill could not feel movement like a normal train would have felt. He could tell by looking out the window that the train was moving, and then it accelerated to such a high speed that looking out the window became slightly uncomfortable for him.

Curiously enough, there was no feeling of acceleration or movement. It was as if the train was still sitting still at the boarding dock, except for a low humming sound and a slight vibration...not noticeable unless you were looking for it.

As promised, Lieutenant Banks came out of the room holding a silver tray containing a large plate with one of the biggest omelets he'd ever seen, accompanied by fried potatoes on the side, a small plate containing buttered toast, a small glass of OJ, with napkins and real silverware.

"If you would pull the table down from the wall next to you, I will set this down," she said. Bill hadn't noticed the table next to the blue button, but there it was. He unlatched it from the wall, and it slowly descended before him.

"Enjoy," she said after setting the tray down.

The omelet was very tasty, tastier than anything he'd had on a commercial airline or train anytime in his past, eating every bit of it.

Half an hour later she retrieved the tray, then came back out and asked him if he'd like his feet up. Saying yes, she reached to the side of the seat and out extended his legs from underneath a footrest.

"Can I get you a cocktail?" she asked.

Damn, Bill thought to himself. Government work is good if you can get it.

"Yes…scotch…rocks…*please*," he answered.

He couldn't remember the last time he'd had a cocktail served to him.

After bringing out his cocktail and serving it to him, he thanked her, then leaned back in the seat, drank his drink, and slowly drifted off into slumberland with the aid of the alcohol and the soft vibration of the moving train at 250 miles per hour.

Next stop, Denver.

⁓⁓⁓

Jack had woken with the dawn on August 25th and reached for his father's Bible.

The light before sunrise was creeping in through the living room window, and this was the time he most liked to read. True to what Mark had told him, reading the Gospels first was the way to go. Reading the accounts of the four disciples was what he had to do to understand everything else he would read in that book. He became inspired, so much so, that his high point during each day would be in the beginning. That is when he would read.

He opened the book and would go to Exodus, after the day before finishing Genesis, where he came to understand God's creation and his relationship to mankind.

It was then he had not seen what had always been there.

At the very beginning of the Bible was a page he had never turned to in the very front, what was once a blank page that had writing in it, and it was addressed to Jack.

"To Jack, my oldest son, whom I love very much."

And it continued.

"You are reading this book now after I am gone. I want you to know how proud I am of you. I have had this Bible since before I was the age that you are now. Please do not mourn me, as I am in a much better place now. Though at the time I am writing this to you, I can't possibly describe what it is like in heaven, but I know that it will be beautiful. When you are sitting on the couch reading this Bible, know that I am sitting there next to you, reading along with you. You are going to do great things, Jack...I just know it. Please take care of your sister and your brother, and especially your mother, and know that I love you with all my heart and always will. Love, your Dad."

The tears started to roll down Jack's cheeks in the early morning light, sitting on the couch, with Rocky and Brian fast asleep on the living room floor. Holding his hand over his mouth, he began to bawl like a little boy, being careful not to wake anyone.

How could he have known I'd be reading his Bible on the couch and feeling him next to me? How could he have known that? This was the thought in Jack's brain.

And then Jack felt an arm across his back and over his shoulders.

He turned to look at his father, Paul Price, sitting next to him, feeling his embrace as if he had never left.

Paul then whispered in his son's ear.

"I can only do this once Jackie. I can't return. The next time you will see me, you will be with me. It is beautiful here son. This is just the beginning. I know you have been struggling with your faith but struggle no more. Jesus is alive and he is the living, breathing son of God, and he is with you too, watching over all of you. No harm will come to you. I love you, Jackie. Take care of your mother and tell her that I love her."

And just like that, Paul Price was gone.

Jack wasn't asleep and this wasn't a dream, because this felt more real to him than anything else he had ever known.

This was the Holy Grail that Jack had been looking for,

In a flash, Jack was a true believer in all the things he had never believed in before.

He had felt the presence of Christ.

His hunt for the Lamb of God had ended, and he could not wait to share it with Mark.

Everything changed for Jack at that moment.

He was no longer afraid of the evil outside, nor did he feel guilt over the death at his hand, because he knew he had been forgiven.

He had been lost at sea but had been thrown a life preserver.

Inside, he now knew that they would all survive this nightmare because he knew they were under the protection of the Lord.

Though it seemed to him it had taken forever, he got down on his knees over the couch, and thanked Jesus with all the gratitude in the world, professing his love for him and promising that he would do anything asked of him…anything for the Lamb of God.

※※

After dozing off for what seemed a few minutes, Bill awoke from his slumber that lasted a full two hours, and he was surprised at how refreshed he was feeling. He looked at his watch and it showed 8:15 on the dial.

His drink glass had been removed from his tray table and the table had been put back into position, likely from Lieutenant Banks while he slept.

He looked around at an empty car other than himself, the same way he started.

He pressed the blue button, and out from the door came Lieutenant Banks, smiling at Bill, then asked, "Yes Mr. Jenkins. What can I do for you?"

"Is there a bathroom in this car?"

"Yes…toward the back. See that door?' she said as she pointed to the back of the rail car.

"Go through that door and you will find everything you will need," she pointed. "Will that be all?" she asked.

"Yes, thank you so much for everything you are doing for me. This has been a very pleasurable ride…exceptionally smooth. It's like we are not even moving!" he replied.

"No problem sir. In a couple of hours, I will bring a menu out to you for lunch."

She then turned away again and walked back through the door she came out of as Bill got up from his seat and walked to the bathroom door.

Even the bathroom was first class with cloth towels instead of paper.

Sitting back down, he suddenly realized how lucky he was to be in the situation he found himself in. So many people suffered such great tragedy in America these last few months, some quickly and others a prolonged and agonizing struggle to survive, only to succumb to the forces of evil surrounding them.

His only hope could be that his family did not struggle too much, were still alive, healthy, and still in the house where he and Viv had raised their two boys.

Soon he would have answers to all of his questions.

The big surprise for him would be to find out his family had now grown to double in size, including one furry friend named Whiskers.

THIRTEEN

DIA/Base 12

Bill's lunch was every bit as good as his breakfast, consisting of Chicken Kyiv, rice pilaf, and asparagus. With two more hours left on the train before it arrived in Denver, he opted to have another drink, so he summoned Lieutenant Banks once more.

He asked her for another, and when she brought it out to him, he asked her if she wouldn't mind sitting down and chatting with him for a while. She sat down in a seat across from him.

"So, lieutenant...how long have you been in the army?" he asked.

"Three years this October. I went to OCS and came in as a Second Lieutenant. I've been at that rank ever since."

"How long have you had this current detail, being on this train?"

"Close to a year. It's been interesting, believe it not. I haven't seen the sunlight for a few days, and it will be like that at times. Sometimes I'll go up to a month before I get out on top, but the tradeoff is worth it. I've met some very interesting people. I've met President Trump a few times because he used to utilize the train a lot during his Presidency. Very nice man. A lot nicer than people would think he is. I've yet to meet President Biden, but from what I understand, he will be riding with us shortly."

"How many facilities are there underground that this train stops at?"

"I can't tell you that sir. That's classified information, but I can tell you there are many, many stops along its route."

"How long is that?"

"I can't tell you that either. Sorry."

"Can you tell me anything about where I'm going?"

"I suppose since you are going there, I could speak a bit on that. What would you like to know?"

"Hell, anything you feel good speaking to, I imagine."

"I can tell you it's our largest underground facility. FEMA has their central base of operations there."

Then she leaned over to him and whispered, "To be honest with you, that fucking place spooks me!"

"Really? Why?"

"You'll see when you get there. You won't be able to miss it. As soon as you get off the train and go through the double doors, you'll see a cavernous room to your left. When I say cavernous, I'm not kidding. Far as the eye can see. No joke and there are aircraft in there I've never seen before in my life. I don't want to say any more about them, but you'll see what I'm talking about.

Then there are the H units, but I call them robots. They are all around the place there. They look exactly like humans and move like them, but if you get close enough to them and happen to look in their eyes, you'll see they are not human...oh, and they don't speak, but they do listen. Like I said...spooky."

"Wow...food for thought' Bill said.

"I have to prepare some documentation for this trip. Is there anything else I can tell you...that I can *speak* to?" she asked.

"No. I think I'm good. Thank you"

"Sure thing sir. We'll be arriving in about an hour and forty-five minutes."

Bill was now very curious about his arrival, and in deep thought, as he sipped his scotch, then he dozed off again.

The train had slowed for its approach to Base 12, and Bill was now wide awake.

The only reason he knew it was approaching the station was because of what he was seeing out of his window. The wall of the tunnel was now becoming more visible in definition, and the vibration of the train had changed. When it had come to a complete stop, the doors opened, and in walked a high-ranking military official, accompanied by two enlisted military soldiers dressed in full battle fatigues.

"Mr. Jenkins? Bill Jenkins?' said the officer.

"Yes," Bill replied.

"You have some paperwork for me, sir?"

"I do indeed" and Bill reached into his briefcase before he handed him the paper folder containing what he had been given by Philip.

After inspecting what Bill had handed to him, the officer handed Bill back the paperwork he did not need.

"You will need this to get back into the facility and reboard the train sir."

"Ahhh…thank you."

"I suggest that you fold that up and put it in your pocket. You don't want to lose that." said the officer. "My name is Colonel Jack Horne, and with me are Sergeant Sanchez and Halliday. They will be escorting you to pick up your family."

These soldiers both looked as though they could rip the tongue out of an adult male grizzly bear and send it down the trail crying for its mother.

"Please Mr. Jenkins. Follow me," instructed Colonel Horne.

Bill grabbed his duffel out of the overhead bin and followed the

Colonel and his two Sergeants out of the car and onto the boarding deck of DIA/Base 12.

This is where the adventure began, and Lieutenant Banks had not done her description justice.

Before exiting through the double doors, she had told him about, he noticed a huge placard overhead, saying "Welcome to DIA/Base 12".

As they walked through the double doors, he immediately looked to his left, and he saw something so fantastic that he would be hard-pressed to put into words.

In a room far beyond cavernous, he saw two black triangular craft hovering at least twenty feet above the flight deck floor, with no suspension wires or apparatus holding the aircraft up.

These were not airplanes, but instead something that had to be alien in nature.

The room itself had to be at a bare minimum of 150 to 200 feet from the floor to the ceiling and the size of at least ten to twelve Bronco Mile High football stadiums in size, spanning as far as Bill's eye could see, but farther than that.

It was, without a doubt, the most amazing thing Bill had ever seen in his entire life.

From the bottom of both crafts, a boarding ladder descended to the floor from the middle of each craft, with servicemen scurrying about, going in and out of the crafts carrying various packages inside, then exiting the crafts empty-handed, going back for more packages to fill the crafts with.

The speed that these men were walking was almost mind-boggling, almost inhuman.

Bill took all of this in within a matter of seconds as he stood there behind the Colonel and his men, waiting for direction from them.

He scoured the topside of the crafts, looking for guy wires holding the ships up, with none to be seen. They were hovering above the floor…motionless.

It became obvious to Bill that whatever was going on here, it was not anything the general population knew about. This was something out of science fiction, more apropos to Star Wars than Popular Mechanics, or even Popular Science. He felt as though he had stepped into a world, he was unprepared to deal with, and for a moment, was a little scared.

"You've been briefed on what goes on here, correct?" said Colonel Horne.

After a long pause, Bill said softly "Not really. I can't believe what I'm seeing. What I *was* briefed on is everything I see here is classified. That's all I was told."

"Yes. Classified." barked Horne. "We're on the same page then, right Mr. Jenkins?"

"Absolutely Colonel" replied Bill. "We're on the same page. Most definitely"

Even if Bill wanted to say something about what he had seen, he wouldn't even know where to begin.

When Denver International Airport began construction around the turn of the century, there was a whole lot of speculation about why there was a need for a new airport. The previous one, Stapleton Airport, had served the city well and was very functional, plus it was a lot closer to downtown.

The city annexed the DIA property, which was thirty miles east of town out in the middle of nowhere, and began building, creating a whole new part of Denver, a subdivision called Green Valley Ranch.

There was no need for a new airport, leaving many scratching their heads.

The new airport was futuristic in its design, including an underground baggage conveyor belt system that was supposed to be state-of-the-art but became a dinosaur because of its complete and utter failure to work properly following its design, which delayed the opening of the airport for months.

Some said it was intentional and became a cover for something else going on out there, but those were just rumors being whispered by conspiracy nuts.

The property of the airport is also much bigger than needed, which also confused some critics of the project, and on the outskirts of the land, miles away from the terminal where there is nothing but prairie dogs, air vents are popping out of the ground that was not there before the project started, for no apparent reason, leading some down the conspiracy rabbit hole that underneath the grounds of the airport, there was a secret underground government base.

No one knows for sure except the military what goes on there, but if the truth were known, it would blow the socks off anyone that found out, which is kind of how Bill was feeling after seeing those craft hovering a mile under the airport.

How in the hell did those things get down there, and the more pressing question is, how do they get out?

"Why don't you follow Sergeants Sanchez and Halliday to the chow hall, get something to eat, and then we will meet up at zero fifteen hundred hours in the meeting room next to the chow hall. Sound like a plan?" General Horne suggested.

"Right as rain sir" Bill replied, then he saluted the General, which made the General chuckle.

"You don't have to salute me, Mr. Jenkins. You are a civilian." said the General.

It felt obscene to Bill that he was getting ready to eat another meal and it wasn't even noon yet when people outside had died of starvation.

"I'll pass on the food. I ate on the train just before I got here. Is there someplace I can stow my gear General?" asked Bill.

"Sergeant Sanchez will show you to your room. You can stow it there."

"My room? Aren't we heading to my home?" asked Bill.

"You will be heading out at zero six hundred hours tomorrow morning. Way too late in the day to begin a mission. See you in the meeting room" replied the General.

The last place Bill wanted to stay overnight was there. It had been giving him the heebie-jeebies ever since he got off the train, and he couldn't wait to get out of there, but it looked like he had no say in the matter, so it was best to just go with the flow.

"Right sir," said Bill.

After Sergeant Sanchez showed Bill to his quarters, the Army Ranger headed to the chow hall to join Halladay, then Bill shut the door and stretched out on the bed in his room. He had been hoping to meet up with his family that day but told himself another day wouldn't matter.

He would have Vivian in his arms soon enough.

Bill's room was just down the main corridor from the chow hall, so he figured it would be no problem to find the meeting room. He got up from his bed at 2:45 p.m. and started heading that way, and once he got down there, he saw Sanchez and Halliday walk through a door and elected to follow them.

Inside the meeting room, an image shown on the wall was of his neighborhood, with his house plain to see. Next to that image was a map of the Denver Metro Area, for determining the route they would take the following morning. Right behind Bill was General Horne.

The sergeants then got up from their seats and saluted the General.

"Everybody take a seat" commanded General Horne. "On the left screen, you can see your home, in a subdivision called Cherry Knolls, located in Centennial. Is that correct Mr. Jenkins?" asked the General.

"Yes sir…it is."

"So, we need to figure out the best way to get there. Normally we would take Pena Blvd. to I-70, to I-225, then get off at Belleview, take it to University, and into your neighborhood." said the General, standing in front of the image and pointing out the route with a pointer stick.

"I don't know how much you've been briefed on what it's like out there, so I will assume you haven't been. It's a world-class shitshow out there Mr. Jenkins. The Denver area, from what I understand, is one of the worst city populations existing in America right now. It is the wild west meets the zombies. Something very strange is happening out there…people are eating each other, and not because they have no other options. People are eating each other by choice.

A couple of weeks ago we had four military trucks from France go into the downtown area on a relief mission sanctioned by us, and they were fully loaded with pallets of bottled water and MREs, with more on the way, to distribute to as many people that they could find that was still alive, and do you know what they found? They found resistance to their being there. The trucks were surrounded by hundreds of men and women who were only interested in the water, not the meals. The French soldiers didn't know what to do, so they passed out the water until it was gone. When they began to pass out the MREs there were no takers… none, and if the soldiers had not been armed, they believed their lives would have been in jeopardy. When they returned here from downtown, they briefed us on what they had encountered." He stiffened in the back.

"There has been a complete and total breakdown out there. There is no law enforcement whatsoever." He looked squarely at Bill.

The reason I'm telling you this Mr. Jenkins is because you need to know that this isn't going to be a joyride into your neighbor to pick up your family. No, not at all, and if your family is still alive and has not become cannibals like almost everyone out there still alive, that would certainly be the exception, rather than the rule." The colonel's tone was flat.

"Tomorrow morning you will go topside with Sergeant Halliday and Sergeant Sanchez. You will then leave here in a fully armored vehicle big enough to hold the three of you and your family, then you will get the hell out of there as fast and carefully as you can and get back to Base 12. No matter which route you end up taking, it will be hours at best each way. Normally a trip to your home from here would take thirty five to forty minutes tops, but with all the obstructions along the way, it's estimated to take much longer. That's why you are leaving in the morning instead of now."

Bill understood completely now why he would have to spend the night there, and the dangers that awaited him.

They decided on taking surface streets instead of the freeways to get there, assuming there could be exits jammed up by disabled vehicles.

"You'll be getting up at zero four hundred hours, giving you time to shower, take care of your business, eat, then the three of you will head out.

If you are not back on base by eighteen hundred hours, we're sending the cavalry out after you.

Any questions?"

Bill felt pretty good about the advance planning and was looking forward to getting his family out of that hellhole. He could only imagine what it looked like out there, and he was thankful they would not have to negotiate the downtown area, as they would be driving around it and not through it.

After Jack had told Mark about what had happened that morning on the couch in the living room, Mark jumped from his bed and put his arms around Jack, hugging him tightly while thanking Jack for sharing the miracle with him.

Jack had waited a couple of hours after his visit with his dad before creeping into Mark's bedroom to wake him, Bible in hand.

Mark now had a brother in Christ and could not have been happier.

"Somehow, someway, we are going to get through this nightmare over to the other side, whatever that means. No way this happens, and we don't make it. As your Dad said, he is expecting great things from you." expressed Mark. "Did you see any sign of the hunters this morning?"

"Nothing. Not so much as a blade of grass moved out there, at least not that I could see.

All I know is that I never want to have to shoot that gun again, but if I have to, I will. I'm just glad they haven't been back. Probably because they know we are armed and will defend ourselves. I certainly don't want to end up on their dinner plates." said Jack.

"Nope. Me neither." returned Mark.

They couldn't know that the hunters would not be returning. Not ever.

Mark was starting to be concerned for his mom. She had been the rock of the household ever since the whole thing started, but it looked to him as if she were in the beginning stages of a breakdown. Soon they would be out of food and water, and he had no ideas or plans on what they would do next. One thing he did know is they would probably have to uproot themselves from the house and go elsewhere to find greener pastures.

But the question concerning his mother was what to do about her. How could he shore her up and bring her survival spirit back to the forefront?

Then there was the situation with Kate. No one had become aware of it, but he and Kate had started to become close...very close.

She was a couple of years younger than Mark, but he had always been sweet on her in his own very private way, and how ironic it was that tragedy that brought them together. Eventually, they would have to come to terms with their feelings for each other and announce to the rest of the house what the future held for the two of them, making things more complicated, as if things weren't complicated enough already.

Time was not on their side. The conversation would have to be had now to decide what they were going to do when the time came.

Viv peeked her head into Mark's room.

"Good...you are up. Can I get you to start a fire out there so I can make breakfast?" she asked.

"Sure thing Mom" Mark replied.

Viv then looked in her bedroom and saw Julie lying wide awake and staring at the ceiling.

"Come on Hun. Get up and have some coffee with me. Mark is going to start a fire and we can have a cup," she said to Julie.

Though that time of the month had long since passed for the women, it was in full bloom for Kate. After waking herself, she discovered the telltale signs that Flo was on her way into town, so she jumped out of her bed and ran to the living room, almost bumping into Vivian, while looking for Jack. When he wasn't there, she ran back to Mark's room and was surprised to see Jack in there talking to Mark. She then stood next to him.

"Would you go across the street to retrieve some tampons from the hall closet?" Kate whispered in Jack's ear.

She then looked sheepishly at Mark.

"Good morning." she said as she left the room, heading back to her bedroom.

"Gotta go across the street for a minute. Do me a favor and stand at the door and provide cover for me if I need it, ok?" asked Jack. "Kate needs me to get something for her."

"I can do that, then I have to start a fire for Mom" Mark replied.

Jack walked outside into the fresh air, then trudged through the tall dead grass, making his way across the street and into his house.

The morning air was crisp and a nice change from the stifling heat of the summer, and it looked like fall might make an early appearance.

Mark stood on the front porch with a loaded shotgun in hand, ready to fire if so needed.

He noticed the fresh morning air as well and thought to himself that it was good not to smell the horrible stench of rotting bodies anymore. Things were looking up.

Brian and Rocky were still on the living room floor. They had woken but were playing Uno. Nothing seemed to faze those two. They just kept rolling with the punches, especially lately with the absence of the hunters.

One thing the combined families had been doing a lot of lately had been praying together on the living room floor. Even though their faiths had been taking a hit, they were not yet to the point of giving up on God, especially with Jack on his quest to know God better.

And the prayers were helping, at least with their fears.

Even Julie was hanging in there more than she had been. There were times when she came close to ending it all, but decided against it, not only for her kids but also because she'd be taking a chance of not going to heaven to be with her husband. That was the upbringing in her. She was raised to believe that it was the one sin you could not ask forgiveness for, and as bad as things had been, it was nothing compared to being denied admittance to heaven, spending eternity in purgatory, or worse, hell.

So, she trudged on, getting through each day, sometimes by the skin of her teeth.

Bill spent that evening mostly in the recreation room, provided mostly for the grunts, but it was also used by officers, and sometimes guests, such as Bill. Most of his time was spent on the pool tables, playing with anyone that could keep up with him.

In college he was known as a pool shark, so his game was pretty good. Though those days were long past and he hadn't played nearly as much pool as he used to, it all came back to him.

Toward the end of the evening, before he retired, he managed to play a couple of games with Sergeant Halliday, who looked different out of uniform.

"So…what are you expecting tomorrow?" asked Bill.

Halliday looked at him, took his shot which sunk the nine ball, then answered.

"To be honest with you sir, I have no freaking idea. I know we are taking an MRAP (Mine-Resistant Ambush Protected Vehicle) out there, so whoever makes these decisions thinks we could run into some serious trouble. You heard what the General said today. I sure hope your family is there when we get there, otherwise, this will be a horseshit mission. However it turns out though, we've got your back, and nothing is going to happen to you. You can count on that!" replied Halliday.

"I appreciate it, soldier. I really do." Bill answered.

The last thought on Bill's mind before falling asleep that night was the moment, he opened the front door to see the look on Viv's face.

FOURTEEN

The Gauntlet/Homecoming

B ill was going up the elevator with his two accompanying soldiers, dressed in full-out combat gear, ready to take care of business.

Instead of a series of elevators, as he took at Mt. Weather, this was one elevator making the trip all 8000 feet to the topside, and when it began to rise, the acceleration was so great it forced him down almost to the floor, taking him a minute to pull himself back up.

When the door finally opened, they walked out into a brightly lit room filled with jeeps, a few tanks, and a ton of MRAP vehicles, and they walked to the closest one.

Halliday was carrying a duffel full of bottled water and MREs for Bill and the soldiers, but also for his family. They had no way of knowing their condition, so they were prepared to feed and hydrate them upon their arrival so they could comfortably make the trip back to Base 12.

Sanchez then handed Bill a military-issue bulletproof vest, along with a combat helmet to wear.

"We need you protected almost more than us Mr. Jenkins. Our orders state you are precious cargo, so you need to be treated as such. Put these on!" ordered Sanchez.

The vest was cumbersome and the helmet heavier than it looked, but he put them on gladly.

They started the ignition on the MRAP and let it warm up before the three boarded it, with Sanchez driving, Halliday riding shotgun, and Bill in the back compartment. He wasn't isolated from them as the front cab and compartment were connected, but he still did not have the viewpoint the two soldiers had.

The vehicle began to move up to a metal pole, and Sanchez pushed a button on the pole, and suddenly the ceiling began to open, ushering in the rising of the dawn. As promised, they were leaving the facility with the rising dawn, getting a jump on the day, and if all went well, they would be back sometime in the afternoon.

When the ceiling was fully opened, the vehicle began to move up the ramp to the outside world, where the nightmare awaited them.

If you had not seen the giant overhead door there before, you would not have even noticed it was there. It was camouflaged with the natural grass and underbrush surrounding it.

The MRAP then moved along a dirt road for about half a mile until they came to a stop at a guard shack and a soldier inside of it, and a gate leading off the Denver International Airport property.

Where they were exiting was unfamiliar to Bill because you could not see the airport terminal or any of the three concourses in any direction you looked, which made sense since this was a top-secret facility.

After showing the guard their paperwork, the gate opened and they headed east on 88th Ave. to Hudson Rd, where they would begin their navigation on surface streets instead of the freeway, just as General Horne had said they would.

Other than the occasional car blocking a lane, the drive seemed almost normal, as they were on the very fringe between civilization on the very outskirts of the city and the Colorado prairie, so there were not nearly as many cars as there would have been had they been on the freeway. To all three, this seemed to be part of a very good plan that could get them to their destination ahead of schedule and back to base, possibly even on time for lunch.

What *was* abnormal was the total absence of human beings along the way. Even being out in the sticks, they would have already seen twenty to thirty cars drive by them and several people in their front yards, or on their porches.

What slowed them down the most were the stalled cars. As they started to approach the edge of the city of Aurora, a city to the east of Denver, the cars became much more prevalent along their route, and the worst were the intersections, with some of them being impassable, causing the MRAP to jump the curbs and drive around them.

It had already been an hour since they left Base 12, which was fifteen minutes more than it would have taken to get to Bill's house under normal circumstances, and they were still a good twenty five miles away, but all in all, it was smooth sailing, until they saw her.

As they were driving past the Southland Mall, there she was.

It was a woman in her mid to late twenties standing next to a big panel van on the side of the road, flagging them down while holding a small child next to her, and she looked desperate.

The MRAP didn't appear to be slowing down, so Bill barked at the Sergeants, "Hey you guys! Aren't you going to stop for her? She looks like she's in trouble!"

The sergeants looked at each other, with Halliday turning back to Bill and saying "Our orders are to stop for no one"

"Fuck that!" Bill yelled. "She's a goddamn American in trouble. Since when does the military not come to an American's aid in distress?"

The sergeants again looked at each other, then Sanchez slowly pulled to the side about ten feet from where she was standing and mumbled something about how they should not be doing this, with Halliday and his M4 Carbine strapped to his shoulder exiting the MRAP first.

"Are you ok Miss?" Halliday called over to her, then she walked to where Halliday was standing by his door.

Meanwhile, Bill reached into the duffel and pulled out a couple of bottles of water, one for her and the other for the child, then exited the vehicle through the back doors and walked around the side to the woman and handed her the two bottles.

It was then a shot rang out, just missing Halliday and hitting the side view mirror. Halliday immediately trained his rifle on the panel van, waiting for the man to pop out again so he could take his shot. Of course, the man stuck his head around the corner of the van and was immediately terminated with extreme prejudice, taking a bullet right between his eyeballs from Sanchez, who had jumped out from the driver's seat and taken aim over the MRAP's hood.

"Why in the hell did you do that?" Bill screamed at the woman as she still held the child up against her, but now crying. "You were setting us up and we were just trying to help you!"

The woman then became very defensive, but then admitted they needed their vehicle.

After checking the body to make sure he was dead, Halliday walked back over to the woman and said, "Whatever help you might have gotten from us, you just pissed that away".

She pleaded with the three men to take her and her child with them, that she was sorry, that her husband made her do it, but they were having none of it.

Both soldiers got back in their vehicle with Bill jumping in through the back where he had exited, then continued driving as the woman screamed and cried for them to stop and come back.

Sanchez turned and looked back at Bill…and angrily barked "That sir is why we don't stop! We never stop! Period! Never again!"

Bill, at that moment, felt like a complete and total idiot. His indignance almost got all of them killed and he knew it.

"I am very sorry fellas. Won't happen again. I promise" he offered, voice quavering.

"Damn skippy!" offered Halliday.

They continued their trek and turned west on Arapahoe Road, the last stretch of road leading to his neighborhood, but they were still a good twenty miles away.

Bill had no idea what to expect on the way home, but one of the things he didn't envision was how ugly everything looked to him. All the grass had not been watered or mowed for months in any direction he looked, and all of it was dead.

Even some of the trees looked like they were dying.

As they progressed westward, they began to approach his city of Centennial, and they began to see people here and there. He saw some tent cities set up on the south side of the boulevard just after passing Parker Road, and even saw an elk on a spit being roasted over a big open fire, which was a good sign. The people out there were far enough out of the city that the wildlife was abundant and could still be hunted, providing a source of food that prevented them from resorting to hunting their neighbors.

All of the people they passed began waving to them and cheering. It had been months since they had seen a moving vehicle, giving them false hope that help was on the way.

They were now making their approach to the I-25 bridge, which they would traverse underneath, but about half a mile away, Halliday spotted a logjam underneath the bridge through his binoculars, as he had been doing reconnaissance for Sanchez as he drove.

What he was seeing did not look promising, so he encouraged Sanchez to slow down way before the potential problem, then came to a complete stop about a quarter mile away.

"I don't know. It doesn't look good. I don't know if we can get through that or not. There are a lot of cars underneath that bridge, and the weird thing is the way they are situated. If I didn't know better, I'd say they had been pushed there to purposely block someone trying to get through, and it's that way on the oncoming side lanes as well. It's your call Sanchez." said Halliday.

"This MRAP will cut through those cars like a hot knife through butter. This vehicle was made for this. Let's drive up on it and see what we see." said the sergeant behind the wheel. "Roll your window up in case it's a trap. Don't want any of us taking a bullet."

Sanchez then put the MRAP in gear and slowly made his way to the gauntlet, and upon arriving at it, he stopped fifty feet away, and just sat there idling.

They sat there for a good ten minutes, and then it started.

First, it was one guy climbing on top of the hood of a Chevy with a rifle in hand, then another, and another. Soon there were close to fifty men and women on top of the cars, just staring at the MRAP like it was a showdown between two gunfighters on the streets of Laredo.

Then one of them pointed his rifle and fired off a shot, pinging off the bulletproof glass of the windshield. Then there was another, not even putting a chip in the glass.

"How many hits do you think that windshield can take before it loses its integrity?" asked Halliday.

"I don't know, but I sure don't want to find out" and he then put the MRAP in gear and headed straight for the roadblock. It hit the Chevy first, knocking the man off the hood and falling in between the front of the MRAP and the Chevy, turning the man into a meat and metal sandwich, crushing him as they pushed the Chevy aside, and then all hell broke loose with the firepower. Halliday and Sanchez both ducked down in their seats as they made their way through the firestorm of bullets pinging off every exposed surface, and true to form just like Sanchez said, the MRAP cut through that pile of vehicles like butter dripping off a hot biscuit.

At least four of the would-be killers had died under its wheels, but the MRAP continued on Arapahoe Road like nobody's business, leaving the mess and squalor behind them.

Bill loved it and was whooping it up in the back.

"What in the hell would possess them to do that? Any fool could see how mismatched they were to us." Bill shouted.

The answer to his question was that people were losing their minds with nothing to live for. That is how desperate their lives had become. For all they knew, help would never come, and to them, one vehicle was no sign of help, but instead an opportunity, though an opportunity lost.

For what purpose did these people, who were probably once law-abiding citizens, choose to fire on the first vehicle they had seen in months? For what gain?

Were they hungry cannibals looking to feed? Were they trying to take the vehicle, which wouldn't do much good for their situation? Or had they become cold-blooded killers, killing for the sake of killing? What was their motivation?

The answer resided in them, but there would be no telling of their reasons to anyone that cared. Not then. Not ever. They had turned their back on God just as sure as they opened fire on those that meant them no harm.

It was 11:30 in the morning on August 26 and fall was less than a month away.

New York City had become a haven for the dead. three minutes without air, three days without water, and thirty days without food… that was the number three rule.

Most of the city had died within the first month, dying from thirst.

Some had food, but no water, and then there were those that had water, but no food. Food sources could be compromised and altered, whereas water was straightforward.

Yes, it could be substituted for other liquids, such as pop and juice, but if you were not hydrating, you were dying.

The rats in the Big Apple thrived during this time, as they had an abundant food source in all the dead human beings, which they found in every imaginable place you could think of, and their water source was the sewer system.

The rats had become huge…almost as big as small dogs, and they ruled the streets of New York. There were also packs of feral dogs that had not yet resorted to eating the rats, but they were getting close because unlike the rats, they would not eat the rotting flesh they found, instead leaving that to the rats.

There were very few human beings left alive in the city, and those still breathing had stumbled upon a secret stash of water and food somewhere, otherwise, they would be hosting maggots as well.

The humans still alive were afraid of the rats, just as they were afraid of the dogs, and they did not move about much after it got dark, staying inside a locked room that could not be infiltrated.

For whatever reason, cannibalism never took hold in NYC the

way it did in other parts of the country, and it was anyone's guess as to why not.

The hunters were there, but nowhere near to the extent they were in cities like Los Angeles, Chicago, and Denver.

Officer Moretti spent five hours with the businessman, on top of the elevator car, until the man dozed off after crying on account of his misfortune.

Moretti pulled the ladder out of the car, careful not to wake the businessman, and set it back up to the open door above so he could climb out of the shaft, then walk hundreds of blocks home, across the bridge over to Queens, to get to his family that needed him there. He felt terrible about leaving the man, especially pulling the ladder, and leaving him no chance of escaping, but he had no choice, except to leave him or die there with him.

Days later the man died of thirst before he could die of hunger. If the man had a supply of water and the ladder was still there, he would have lost enough weight without any food, and he would have made it through the escape hatch on top of the elevator car, but such was not the case.

The rats had enough food sources wherever they went, other than the two rats that fell in the elevator and tormented the man, so the rest of the rats left the man alone and he was mummified in the elevator car along with the two unfortunate rats, with no one knowing he was in there, except for Officer Moretti.

After Moretti had left, no human footsteps walked on that floor ever again, and no matter how much the businessman screamed at the top of his lungs for help or pounded on the floor and walls of the elevator, he was never heard, and no one came for him.

The MRAP pulled into a parking lot that had a good vantage point of view with no one close by. The men had all held their bladders for quite some time, so it was time to stop the vehicle and relieve themselves, so they did, each of the Sergeants taking turns providing cover.

They decided that was also a good time to take a break to eat, hydrate, take a smoke break, and stretch their legs. They had been in the vehicle for hours.

Everything around Bill at this point looked familiar to him. They were in the final stretch, less than five miles from his home.

This rescue mission always had its risks, highlighted by the fact there would be no way to call for help should they need it. Because of the EMP destroying the satellites, their satellite radios were inoperable. That was why General Horne had told them if they were not back to base by a certain time, the cavalry would be sent out to find them.

Bill was now starting to become very nervous about what they would be walking in on when arriving at his home.

They were parked with the old Macaroni Grill in sight, a favorite of theirs to eat at.

He distinctly remembered a time a couple of years ago, after Brian had won a ballgame with his team, they all went out to eat there.

He then looked west to the Rocky Mountains, never tiring of that view, which was much more visible since there was no smog in the air to block his view.

The snow had melted off the mountaintops during the summer, but they would be covered in snow again soon, probably sooner than anyone thought.

"Where did you guys grow up? Where are you from". Bill asked the two men.

Sanchez answered first. "I am from Goodyear, Arizona. A little town outside of Phoenix. One of its suburbs!"

Halliday then spoke up, "I'm from Grosse Pointe. Do you know where that is?"

"Isn't that in Michigan?" Bill asked.

"Yes Sir. It's a suburb of Detroit…sitting on a lake. Nice town. Nice place to grow up. Sits on Lake St. Clair. I was hoping to raise a family there with my wife. Now, I don't even know if she is alive."

"Man, that's got to be tough," Bill said. "I'm originally from Ohio, but I went to college here and met my wife, and she's born and raised in Colorado. Her parents live up in the mountains. I imagine they're dead now. I don't see how they could have survived something like this. You'll meet my wife soon enough. Anyway, we got married and bought a small house not too far from where we live now, and when my oldest was born and we were starting a family, we bought this place and have been here ever since."

"That's similar to my story. I met my wife in high school, and we got married. She stayed with my parents while I went off to boot camp and she's still with them." Sergeant Halliday remarked. "If you were going to survive something like this, Grosse Point would be a good place to do it. There's obviously a great source of water with the lake being there, and there is plenty of deer to be hunted for food. This sure isn't the plan I had when I joined up, but it is what it is. I need to know that she's ok. I wish I could know."

The longing could be heard in his voice.

"How about you Sanchez? You got anybody out there?" asked Bill.

"No Sir. Not a soul. Well, that's not exactly true. I do have my sister and her husband. They both live in Mesa, another suburb of Phoenix, but no, I've got no one waiting for me, if that's what you're asking" Sanchez replied. "You know, neither Halliday nor myself have been topside since the day right after this happened, and everything sure is different now. It's quite shocking actually. I hope your family is ok when we get there."

"We're going to find out shortly," Bill said, almost solemnly, with a hint of worry in his voice.

After spending a good forty-five minutes outside of the MRAP, feeling refreshed and ready to get back on the road, they all re-boarded the vehicle and headed toward their destination.

After seeing hundreds of skeletons along the way, some with meat still on their bones, Bill was hoping things would be different in Cherry Knolls. As they turned onto Nobles Road, entering the subdivision, a once beautiful neighborhood, it now looked like a bomb had gone off and no one had lived there for years.

"When you get up to Cook Way, make a right" Bill told Sanchez.

The pool on the left had water in it still but was filthy. Still, it had been a water source for many in the neighborhood, contributing to the survival of many of its residents, more so than other places in town.

Bill had already counted five skeletons in the front yards, and some missing arms and legs, causing him to almost choke and catch his breath. His praying was nonstop, and his heart was racing so fast it felt like it would jump out of his chest.

They made their turn onto his street, and as they drove, he could see his house come into view.

"Ok men…this is it up on the right," Bill said. "Just pull up behind this Honda."

They stopped right where Bill had instructed them and he could see the garage door was closed, but he also could see part of the backyard and caught a glimpse of the corner of the tent Mark had set up as the latrine, and he could also see and smell smoke coming from the back yard.

Hmmm, he thought to himself.

Most of the family were out back, boiling water over the fire in the grill, and they heard the MRAP pull up to the house, the sound of a moving vehicle, a loud vehicle as the diesel engine roared. Being on alert for the hunters, they all went into the house locking the back door behind them and looked out the front window.

They were shocked and a little confused, until Mark recognized his dad lumbering out of the back of the MRAP, and he screamed," IT'S DAD!!!"

The front door then swung violently wide open, with Brian running out first, jumping up into his dad's arms and crying, almost uncontrollably.

Then Mark rolled out of the door screaming, followed by Jack, Kate, and Rocky, all whooping and hollering.

The soldiers just stared at each other, grinning from ear to ear, standing there outside the doors of the vehicle and happy to be witness to the joy of this homecoming.

Then Vivian appeared at the door, standing on the front step, and all she could do was put her face in her hands and bawl her eyes out that her prayers had been answered, that her strong, handsome, beautiful husband would come to rescue them, and there he was in all his glory.

There was so much joy and elation being displayed in the front yard, that no one noticed Julie not out there, but instead looking out the window on the couch with tears rolling down her face, wishing that she too could have this moment that Vivian was having, being able to see her husband arriving from wherever he had been, being together with him again.

Bill saw his wife on the front step crying, and he was crying too, looking in her sweet, beautiful eyes, looking up to the heavens and thanking God for that moment, and not even noticing that his sweet girl looked like she had been rode hard and put up wet, a survivor of their times, and the matriarch that got them to this point, where no one in either family could have made it without her.

No one also noticed the tears that were rolling down the two Sergeants' faces, as they felt the love that they so much missed in their lives and would have given anything in the world to have experienced.

In this place of shocking terror and loss of humanity, the love shined bright and filled Cook Way to the brim as Bill slowly walked to his wife, then putting his arms around her and telling her he loved her, with Viv requiting the same while having her head buried in her husband's chest.

Bill was stunned seeing the Price kids across the street there with his family but said nothing, and he accepted their love for him as well. He couldn't have known he was now their surrogate father, but instead was grateful for this reunion. All these months of hoping beyond hope, trying not to think the horrible things that crossed his brain every time he thought of them, were now behind him and not true.

They brought their celebration into the house, with the soldiers walking in behind them.

FIFTEEN

Change of Plans

With everyone in the living room and before making an announcement., Bill turned to Sanchez and asked, "How much time do we have to pack up personal belongings before we have to leave?"

"An hour if we want to get back before they send a detail out to look for us" Sanchez answered.

"Ok, everyone. We are not staying here. We are leaving. Everybody needs to pack a suitcase with their personal belongings, things you absolutely need, nothing else. We are going to an army base at the airport, then we will take a train to Washington D.C. We've got one hour to pack, so get busy!"

"We are leaving our homes, Bill?" Julie asked.

"Yes. There is nothing here for us now. Come on, let's get moving. Chop chop!" he replied.

Everyone scurried about, with Viv, Mark, and Brian walking back to their bedrooms as Rocky, Kate, and Julie, with the help of Jack, opened the front door and walked across the street to their home.

"Mr. Jenkins…who are those people that just left?" asked Halliday.

"Those are the neighbors across the street. They have been staying here to survive. They are coming with us."

"Uh, no sir. They are not coming with us. We only have orders for you and your family" he replied.

"What in the hell are you talking about? We can't just leave them here?" Bill sounded off.

"Sir. This is not negotiable. Our orders are very clear, and we cannot deviate from them.

Our orders are for four people...you, your wife, and your two sons. That is it. Even if we took them with us, they would not be admitted into the base, let alone get on the train. There was never any mention of other people other than your wife and sons."

"Can't you get authorization? Can't you call someone?" Bill asked while becoming visibly upset. "Look...we can't leave them here. They will die."

"We don't have any way of contacting the base. Our satellite phones are not working, probably due to the EMP. Even if we took them, we would have to leave them outside the gate. I'm very sorry. Very sorry, but they have to stay here."

Bill then looked at Sanchez, hoping for some sympathy and understanding, and possibly an overruling, but got nothing from them.

"I'll be back," Bill said as he walked back to his wife in the bedroom and shut the door.

Viv had a suitcase on the bed and was undecided as to what she would put in the suitcase, staring at different clothes on hangars she had laid out on the bed.

Bill then walked over to her and grabbed her shoulders to get her attention, then sat her down on the bed next to him.

"Viv, they can't go with us." he said to her.

Viv jumped up from the bed, walked to the door, then turned to Bill.

"What? What do mean they can't go?" she responded in disbelief.

"Who can't go? Do you mean Julie and her kids? Do you have any idea what we've been through together? The day the power went out, they were stuck at the hospital and robbers came into the pharmacy and shot Paul dead right in front of her. She almost lost her mind over this, and they've been here with us ever since. I'll tell you something else. Mark and Kate are in love with each other. There is no way Mark will leave her behind, nor will I, for that matter. If they stay here, they'll die. There are packs of cannibals in the neighborhood and most of the people that are dead here have been hunted and eaten by these ghouls. I can guarantee you that within hours of us leaving them behind, they will be killed and eaten by our neighbors. One night they came into the yard and Jack shot and killed one of them, and if he hadn't done that, we would have been slaughtered right then and there, and now you're telling me that we get to live, and they have to die? I'm not doing it Bill, and if you can, you are not the man I've always thought you to be. I can't even believe you are in here saying this to me!"

"Jack shot somebody? Where did he get a gun? Paul would never have allowed a gun in his house." said Bill.

"He got it from me," she said as she walked to the bed, pulling the semi-automatic service weapon out from under the mattress.

"What in the hell? Where did you get this?" he asked in shock.

"An Arapahoe County Sherriff's deputy gave it to me after he saved me from being raped in Whole Foods. He wanted us to be safe. Times have changed and we've been living by different rules." Viv answered him.

"What?" he stammered in disbelief.

Bill couldn't believe what he was hearing. His family had been through holy hell these last few months, and it was starting to sink in.

He got up from the bed and put his hands on Vivian's shoulders, looked her dead in her eyes, and then said to her "Baby, I had no idea. I imagined the worst up until I got here. To be honest, I had no idea if all of you were alive or dead. Thank God you are alive. I don't know what I would have done if I had found all of you dead. It's too horrifying to even think about.

Out from under the bed came Whiskers, jumping onto the bed and looking up at Bill. The cat had hidden under the bed when all the commotion started in the living room, but he was now purring and acclimated to the new human in the room with them.

"And who is this? This looks like the cat from across the street... Whiskers, Mr. Parsons cat?" asked Bill.

"We rescued him. Mark found Mr. Parsons dead on his kitchen floor when the power went out. I sent Mark over there with a plate of food. Mark brought him here to stay with us. I'll bet we can't bring Whiskers with us either." she stated.

"Nope. Probably not" he replied. "You're right Viv. We can't leave them behind. I'm going out there to tell them if they cannot come with us, we can't go either. It's not going to be pleasant though. They have orders to bring me back no matter what. I promised the President I would be back. They may try to take me by force, so it could get ugly out there"

"The President?" she asked confused.

"Yeah. They decided I was instrumental in bringing the country back up online, so they took me from my apartment to this underground facility in Virginia where the President and both houses of Congress are staying, a place they have in case of national emergencies. I found out about a secret train that goes here to Denver, and I practically begged the President to let me come out here to get you guys. Part of the deal was that I had to come back, so he agreed and let me come. Now I'm going to have to break my word, but so be it.

I'm telling you, Viv, America is in a world of hurt right now, and I don't think it will ever be the same, not like it was before. The whole country, all the major cities, all of it is in the same shape as it is here. It's awful, horrifying. We saw dead people and skeletons all the way here. I can't imagine what it's like in Denver," he explained. "How's the food and water situation?" he asked.

"We ran out of toilet paper a while ago, and we will be out of food and water soon" she replied.

There was a knock on the door, and it was Mark.

Bill cracked the door open and whispered to him that they would be out in a minute.

Mark then whispered back "I heard what you guys were talking about in here. I've got your back Dad."

"Be out in a minute son" he said as he smiled and softly closed the bedroom door.

Bill looked at Viv, took a deep breath, then told her to stay in the room because he would handle this.

He then opened the door to see Mark standing there, waiting for him.

"Don't say a word, Mark. Let me do all the talking" Bill told his son, then began walking down the hall to the living room with Mark trailing behind.

"You guys said this was not negotiable. Well, I'm telling you it has to be. We are not leaving our friends behind. It will be a death sentence for them. There are cannibals in the neighborhood, and as soon as we leave, they will be killed and eaten! Don't you understand?" Bill asked the soldiers.

The soldiers looked at each other, with Halliday speaking first.

"Mr. Jenkins. I understand. We both understand. We have families and friends that we love too, but our orders are our orders, and we cannot deviate from them as I said to you earlier."

"Then gentlemen, I am not going. We are not going. You will have to leave here without me." Bill stated with all the stoicism he could muster up.

"No Sir. You are coming with us, whether your family comes or not, you are leaving here with us. Those are our orders" Sanchez exclaimed.

"Fuck your orders Sergeant. I just told you that I am not going with you" replied Bill.

"Sir, we will take you by force if we have to. Please don't make us do that" pleaded Halliday.

Mark had already gotten close to the front door while this exchange was going on between the three men. In the blink of an eye, he grabbed the shotgun leaning up against the wall behind the door, pumped a shell into the chamber, and pointed it at Halliday's head.

"My Dad told you he's not going with you" shouted Mark at the soldiers.

Both soldiers were shocked that Bill's son was pointing the shotgun at them, and he looked to mean business.

Sanchez's slid his hand down gently in position to grab his service pistol out of its holster, holding it above his gun, but making no move yet to grab it.

It was then Vivian's voice was heard as she stood in the hallway at the edge of the living room.

"Don't you touch that pistol Sergeant. I will shoot you right where you are standing. My husband said he's not going with you. We're not going with you." Viv affirmed as she stood there pointing the pistol point-blank at Sanchez's face, and her hands were not shaking one little bit. She was ready to fire without hesitation. This was *her* house, and she would be damned if anyone, government or not, would be coming in there and taking away her husband, and she was ready for anything to happen, no matter how it went down, which was perfectly obvious to both soldiers.

Had she been pointing the gun at his chest, he might have taken a chance and grabbed his gun since he was wearing a bulletproof vest under his fatigues, but knowing how good of a shot she was, he decided he could not take the risk of receiving a bullet to his face. He then moved his hand slowly away from his weapon, then put his trigger hand up, followed by his other hand up, both in an act of surrender.

"Ma'am...please put down your weapon. You too son." Sanchez implored.

"It's time for you both to leave my home," Viv said calmly. "Get your asses out of here now before we start shooting. I'm not kidding."

Stalemate. One of them had to acquiesce to the other, and on this day, it would be the soldiers.

"Yes ma'am," said Sanchez. "We will leave."

Mark stepped away from the front door so the soldiers could move toward it, with Halliday walking to it first with Sanchez right behind him. Halliday opened the door and walked outside and as Sanchez followed him. He turned to Bill and looked at him with the look of shame, as he had failed in his mission, The soldier turned back around and walked through the door. Mark shut the door behind them and immediately locked it.

All this time Bill had not said a word. As shocked as the soldiers were, Bill was even more shocked at his family's readiness to action.

"Who are you people?" Bill jokingly said to his two family members, especially directed toward Viv.

All three then looked out the window as Brian came out of his room and down the hall, oblivious to what had just happened in the living room.

As the soldiers entered the MRAP, Julie and her kids were all coming out of the front door to the house across the street with suitcases in hand. They stopped and stood on their lawn, dumbfounded as they watched the soldiers drive away from the house.

Bill went outside to greet them in the street.

"They won't be back," said Bill. "They were not going to allow you to go with us, so we told them to leave. It's just as well you packed your bags because we are going to leave here anyway. Take your bags up into the living room. We are going to have a meeting as soon as I figure out what we are going to do."

They all walked up to the house with suitcases in tow, and as Julie walked by Bill, she reached out to him to grab his face and pulled his face toward hers, and then kissed him on the cheek.

"Thank You," she said to him. "Thank you, Bill"

Sergeants Sanchez and Halliday slowly drove out of Cherry Knolls, knowing they had no choice but to leave without Bill Jenkins and his family.

They also knew if they were in his shoes, they would have done the same thing as he did. They too could not have left their friends to die, just as the two Sergeants asked Bill to do, and they wouldn't have done so had they had any other recourse.

This was not going to go over well with General Horne. They could only hope they would not suffer a punishment too severe. After all, what could they have done? What would the General have done? Possibly have shot and killed Mr. Jenkins and brought him back dead? Then what? And what purpose would that have served?

Driving back the way they came, they knew they had done the only thing they could have done.

SIXTEEN

Stick to the Plan

Everyone assembled in the living room, with Jack, Julie, and Vivian on the couch, Brian and Rocky in the armchairs, Mark and Kate sitting on the floor by the fireplace with folded legs, and Bill sitting on a chair he had brought in from the dining room.

"Well…it's good to be home with my family," Bill said as the room broke out in cheer.

"Things change and we adapt. As humans, we roll with the punches and change our plans as needed. First, I want to say I am truly impressed that all of you have made it this far. Your mother has been filling me in on what you have gone through and what you have done to survive. Truly remarkable," astonished pride covering his face.

"Everything that you've done up to this point has put us in the position we are in now, and it's not nearly as bad as you would think. I think what we need to do from this point on is treat our situation like a business, a business that is in the business of living. Sound like a plan?"

Everyone nodded their heads in agreement.

"Here is the one truth we all need to wrap our heads around right now, and I do mean *all* of us. We must leave here. We must leave our home, our cars, and most of our belongings behind us here, and the chances are excellent that we will never come back here, ever again. If we stay here, we will die here. When all of us can understand what that truly means and can accept the gravity of our decision, then and *only* then we can work as a team and move on to somewhere else where we can have a chance to live and breathe as free men and women, as God intended."

He made eye contact with each person, confirming they were all on the same page.

"Ok…everything we do, we do as a team, and as a team, we do for each other, and one of the things we need is to respect each other. Respect for me and your mother, respect for Mark, Katie, Julie, Jack, and even respect for you boys, Brian and Rocky. From now on, Katie, I will treat you as one of my children, which means I will not play favorites or treat you special because you are the little girl I've known since you were born who lives across the street, and that goes for you too Rocky. From this point on, I am going to treat you the same as I treat Brian, like my son."

They shared a smile.

I would be remiss if I also did not tell you, especially you Julie, that I am very saddened by the loss of Paul. I knew him well and he was a great friend, husband, and father. We will not forget him and we will carry his memory wherever we go."

Julie started to cry but stopped herself.

"I'm sorry. Go on Bill" she apologized.

"Now, where will we go? For us to survive, we need to be next to an unlimited supply of water, and from the way I see it, that leaves us with three options. There are three reservoirs within walking distance, that being Chatfield, Cherry Creek, and Aurora."

The room fell silent.

"I've thought about this and decided Aurora Reservoir would be too far of a walk. The closest reservoir to us is Cherry Creek, with Chatfield not that much farther. Both would be a good hike for us, and we could make both in a day. Thoughts?" Bill put it out there for discussion.

"What about food? We would also need to be close to hunting opportunities?" Mark stated.

"Yes. Another reason the reservoirs would be the optimum choice. I would think Chatfield would be better than Cherry Creek because of more elk with it being closer to the mountains. Being that close, however, also means a more severe winter experience, as opposed to Cherry Creek. At Chatfield, we would be more exposed, whereas at Cherry Creek there are many windbreaks with more trees there." Bill said. Our days of creature comforts are over. No more soft beds, at least for a while. We are going to be sleeping on the ground."

As the conversation went on, it started to become apparent that the obvious choice would be Cherry Creek Reservoir. It was also the closest in distance, and even though the hunting would probably be better at Chatfield, it would still be good at Cherry Creek.

As a group, they all decided on Cherry Creek.

"These next few years are not going to be easy, and when I say "-not going to be easy-", I mean our ability to adapt to this new life." We are going to have to boil all our drinking water, cook all of our meat on an open fire, and if we don't hunt and kill something, then dress the kill, we won't eat. It's that simple. We are now about to enter the days of the wild west, the frontier, and we will understand what our ancestors went through to survive, and if they could do it, we can do it. We will have our hardest time adapting to being outside in the cold, so we will have to prepare for that, but I know between the eight of us, we will figure it out."

He nodded his head, confirming to himself more than to his family.

"There is only so much we can take with us, even with something to transport our stuff with, and what we don't have with us when we get to where we are going, there are houses we can walk to and find what we need inside of them, I'm sure."

He then shared the list he was building inside his head.

"The one thing that can break us down is getting sick. We cannot get sick, no matter what. We especially cannot get an infection. Back before penicillin was invented, people died all the time from your basic simple infections" Bill warned.

"Dad, I think Jack has us covered," said Mark.

"What do you mean?" Bill asked.

Mark got up and walked back to his bedroom, then back out to the living room holding the two large backpacks both he and Jack had filled with antibiotics the day they rescued Julie.

Mark then opened the top of one of the packs and emptied its contents onto the floor at the feet of his dad.

"Jack went into his dad's pharmacy and took every single thing he could identify as an antibiotic and filled the packs with them. There's a PDR in the other pack!"

"Good Lord Jesus! You've got to be kidding me" exclaimed Bill as he picked up bottle after bottle of various antibiotics, both your standard-issue and your special strong medications for the worst infections, along with Ibuprofen, Tylenol, aspirin, bandages, and so much more. It was a mountain of drugs and medical supplies sitting at Bill's feet.

"The other backpack is filled with the same. When Jack and I rode to Denver General to get his parents, we brought these empty backpacks because I always remembered that you were nervous about not having these kinds of meds if something like this ever happened. You always told me they would be worth their weight in gold. Well… it looks like we are rich!" said Mark happily.

"Do you realize just how rich we are?" Bill shouted with excitement as he turned his attention to Jack on the couch.

"Jack, you've not only saved this family once but now countless other times in the future as well!

"This changes everything. This is an insurance policy. I can guarantee you there will be times in our lives when each of us will need these! Good work boys!" Bill said happily.

As Mark put the meds back in the backpack, Bill continued with his plans. "Can every one of us make the trip and do the walk? We have roughly thirteen miles pushing heavy carts and pulling a wagon. I'm not going to sugarcoat it. This is not going to be easy and will take every bit of stamina we have to get there, but it will be worth it."

"My knees are shot, Bill. There is no way I could make it. Someone would have to push me in the wheelchair." Julie offered.

"That's not going to be a problem. Jack can take care of that I presume. Right, Jack?" Bill asked.

"Got it" Jack answered.

"We're going to need something to put our belongings in to transport it over, along with basic stuff we'll need, like tents, sleeping bags, pillows, cooking supplies...stuff like that.

I believe we still have that big plastic little tyke wagon hanging in the garage, don't we?" Bill asked openly, welcoming anyone to respond.

Viv did with a resounding "YES!"

"We need to make a trip over to Whole Foods and grab a few of their best shopping carts. Those are what we will use." Bill added.

After taking a roll call of who could push a shopping cart full of stuff and who could pull the wagon, the only ones that couldn't be counted on were Julie and Jack, as they would be preoccupied with the wheelchair. That left Bill, Viv, Kate, Mark, Brian, and Rocky to push a cart or pull a wagon. With one on the wagon, that meant whatever they were going to bring with them had to go into five shopping carts and one big wagon, but the loads in each had to also be light and not cumbersome.

"Mark, Jack, Brian, and Rocky...I need you boys to walk with me to Whole Foods so we can pick up some decent carts. While we are there, we can also pick up anything we will need that we don't already have." Bill stated to the boys.

Mama, you can stay here with Julie and Kate. If you would be so kind as to let me have the pistol, you guys will have the shotgun here with you. We should be back inside of an hour, then maybe we can have some dinner? When we get back, we can eat, pack our belongings, and load the carts, then leave here first thing in the morning. Deal?" Bill asked.

The menfolk walked out the front door and made the trek out of the neighborhood to Whole Foods, pistol snugly in his pocket.

Viv was in heaven, as her prayers had been answered. Her precious Bill was back where he belonged, with his family. She had no idea what the future lay in store for them, but she knew that whatever it was, they would make it somehow because God was on their side.

Her faith had been restored and she felt like the weight of the world had been lifted off of her shoulders. No longer did she have to carry the burden alone. As much as she loved Julie, Julie had pretty much been useless these last few months while grieving the loss of her husband, leaving Viv to do all the cooking, cleaning, and running the overall show when it came to keeping them alive. As hoped for and expected, Bill had taken charge and was now the leader of this ragtag bunch of survivors destined for greater things.

Later in the afternoon, the men came back to the house with five shopping carts, all new and ready for the long trek the following morning.

After everyone had supper and had a chance to gather their belongings, they began to pack the carts and the wagon.

"The shortest distance between two points is a straight line," Bill said to the group.

"There are only two routes that fit that description. The first is walking Arapahoe Road, and the other is walking up Belleview to Yosemite, then turning right onto Union, which becomes Cherry Creek Dam Road, allowing us to survey the lake and see where we want to set up camp. I can tell all of you that Arapahoe Road would be a bad decision. On the way here, there were many people armed that fired upon me and the soldiers, and it would be hell getting through there, probably costing us our lives. I don't know if they were cannibals looking for a fresh kill, or if they were just looking to take the vehicle we were driving in. In any event, I believe it would be a costly mistake to take that route, a risk we shouldn't be willing to take." Bill offered.

"Whichever way we decide to go, it's critical that we stick to the plan. We have to stick to the plan…no matter what, we stick to the plan." Bill reminded them.

It was decided that Bill and Mark would push the heaviest carts, Brian would pull the wagon, and Kate, Viv, and Rocky would push the lightest carts. If needed, Brian and Rocky would alternate between the cart and the wagon.

The sun was beginning to set, so they had limited daylight to load the carts out in the back of the house.

They began with essentials, loading the first cart with cases of bottled water and freeze-dried food. They couldn't take all of what they had left, but they would have to make do. That filled the first cart, then the second cart was filled with two-man four-season tents to brave the elements, one for Bill and Viv, the second for Jack and Mark, the third for Julie and Kate, and the fourth for Brian and Rocky. Whiskers would have to alternate sleeping wherever he chose.

The second cart was packed with eight sleeping bags, which Bill had covered with a tarp.

One thing the Jenkins family was prepared for was camping, due to many of their past family campouts, and Mark's experience as a Boy Scout. It was decided that pillows were a luxury they could not afford due to room in the carts, so they would be left behind.

So far, they had food, water, and shelter covered.

To keep room for everything, they were instructed to only bring two changes of clothes and the clothes on their backs, plus a heavy winter coat, gloves, a cap, and heavy winter boots and socks if they had them.

"I'm thinking along the lines of taking an extended winter campout without cars to get us there. We just have to walk to get there," Bill explained.

Both Mark and Jack would walk with the backpacks of medicine on their backs.

Over the next hour, the Price family was across the street getting their personal items, as was the Jenkins family loading the carts.

Mark and Bill came out of the garage with a hand saw, hammer, a box of nails, a screwdriver, a box of screws, and three rolls of duct tape to be packed, along with the most critical things they would need-four fishing poles, Bill's tackle box, a bow, and a quiver of arrows.

One of Bill's hobbies throughout life was archery, and he was a damn good archer if he said so himself. He hoped to put those skills to good use for his family.

Viv came out of the house with the biggest pot she could find, a frying pan, assorted cooking utensils, to be added to eight plastic plates and flatware, along with four plastic bowls, complimented by a stack of plastic cups they had collected over the years from eating fast food.

She estimated that Whiskers probably had a month left of food in the bag, so the food and his food and water dish were added to one of the carts as well.

By the time they had everything loaded, the carts looked more like covered wagons traversing over the Colorado plains than the shopping carts they were, just like settlers did on the wild frontier.

Bill covered the rest of the carts with tarps he had in the garage, tying them down with a spool of twine, also a much-needed accessory for their trip. The tarps provided weather protection for the contents of the carts and wagon, but more so kept everything in place, and would be useful once they arrived at their destination.

They were able to finish the packing just as it became dark, with the aid of a flashlight, another thing going with them, along with the other flashlights and batteries that came out of the Faraday cage.

With everything completed and ready for the following morning's adventure, Bill called everyone into the house to go over an inventory list of what was packed.

"This is not going to be easy for several reasons," Bill reminded the group, "most of which are because of the dangers involved. It's not going to be easy at all, and sometimes it will be quite difficult to push these carts along the asphalt. Most of the time we should be able to walk on the sidewalks, but some of the time we will have to be on the roads."

He scanned their faces, looking for any adverse reactions.

"If everything were to go perfectly, we should get to where we are going by four or five tomorrow afternoon, but there are so many things that can go wrong along the way. There are things we will have forgotten to pack, as there always are, and things we would have wanted to take with us but didn't have room for.

The things we <u>did</u> pack are the bare essentials we will need for us to have a chance of survival. Once we get to where we are going, we will be dog-tired and only have enough energy to put up the tents, make dinner, and then go to bed," he assured them.

"Once we settle ourselves in and know what we have and what

we *don't* have, we can then make plans for scouting expeditions to complement our needs.

The things that have me concerned the most are the hunters.

We are leaving here tomorrow morning while it's still dark for two reasons:

One, to beat the heat of the day, and two, to draw the least attention to us on our walk."

He paused to let that caution settle in.

"I have no idea what we are going to run into along the way, but we do have a pistol and a shotgun, both with limited ammo, so if we can avoid engagement with any people, we will have more ammo to hunt with. We've got roughly four or five days of water and food depending on how we conserve it before we have to start boiling water and hunting for food.

I suggest we all lock hands and pray to the heavens above for guidance and protection," said Bill.

Just as Bill finished speaking, Jack asked if he could lead the prayer.

There were nods all around.

Everyone locked hands.

"Dear Lord Jesus," Jack began, "Thank you for the love you give us. Thank you for this life. Without you, nothing is possible Lord. As we embark on this dangerous trek in search of a new life, please blanket us with your protection and care. Please watch over us and keep us from evil and see us to our destination unharmed. Let us live to worship you and to love you and thank you for opening my eyes and my heart to you oh Lord. In Jesus' name, Amen."

"AMEN" followed the gang of eight.

With Bill back home, he was anxious to spend the night sleeping in a bed with his wife, Out of respect, Mark went out to the living room to sleep on the floor with Brian and Rocky, giving Julie his bed for the night.

It sure felt good to be home, Bill was thinking as he drifted off to slumber with Viv curled up beside him with her head on his chest and already fast asleep.

The last thought on his mind were the hunters.

SEVENTEEN

Much to be Thankful For

T he most important thing for Jack not to forget was his father's Bible, which he added to the backpack, full of the antibiotics he would carry.

Jack was sat up on the couch in the dark, wiped the sleep from his eyes, and guessed it was probably close to 4 a.m., judging by the faint light that barely approached the horizon through the living room window. Mark, Brian, and Rocky were still hard asleep on the living room floor, with Brian making cute little snoring sounds.

In the back bedroom, Bill lay wide awake with his arms folded across his chest and deep in thought. Thoughts about all of the things that could go wrong, and how he could circumvent any situation that arose filled him. Viv had long since rolled over to her side of the bed with her face buried in her pillow, still asleep.

In a few minutes, he would put his pants on and wake the boys in the living room first, getting them ready for the walk of their lives.

No plans had been made to eat breakfast. They would have to rely on a big box of Clif Bars Viv had stashed in the very back of her cupboard, forgetting about them until a week ago, when she stumbled upon them while looking for sugar to put in her oatmeal.

Bill would lead the caravan of shopping carts and take the heaviest one.

All would have a flashlight except Jack, who would be bringing up the rear with Julie in the wheelchair.

Part of Bill did not think they had a chance in hell of making it thirteen miles with so many handicaps to deal with, namely Julie, but the other part of him thought hope sprang eternal, and that was the part he most tried to concentrate on.

Whiskers was asleep on Bill's belly. How would *he* deal with this trip? Would he be constantly jumping out of whichever cart he was in, or would he be a good traveler and stick to the plan along with the rest of them?

How would they deal with the hunters if they came across their path? The questions kept running through Bill's mind.

The best thing about the route they were taking was that the homes along Belleview were exceptionally large, expensive homes, so they were farther apart, with lots of open spaces between them. They wouldn't have to cross into more densely populated areas until they passed under I-25. He hoped the same kind of gauntlet had not been set up under that freeway overpass, as it was on Arapahoe Road. Since Arapahoe Road was more of the main thoroughfare, he thought the chances were much less likely they would have to deal with something like that on Belleview. He could only hope.

Bill also remembered that there were lots of businesses, such as restaurants, and hotels in that area. *If memory served me right, there was a King Soopers right on the corner of Belleview and Yosemite, where we would be turning to make our final stretch to the reservoir.*

If they were really lucky, they might find something in the way of food or water still in the store, though he knew the chances of that were minimal, but it would still be worth a chance to look just the same.

Bill lifted himself off of the bed, taking care not to wake his girl.

Viv would need all the rest she could get before she pushed one of those carts the distance.

As Bill entered the living room, he could see Jack sitting up on the couch, illuminated by the pale moonlight filtering in the window through the sheer curtains.

"You ready for this?" asked Bill as he sat down on the couch next to Jack.

"I'd better be," whispered Jack. "I haven't had the chance to thank you for what you are doing for us, Bill. You and your family could have left us here, but you chose to stay with us. I don't think most people would have done what you did."

"I'd like to think they would have, but you're probably right and thank you, but what kind of people would we be if we left you behind? You guys have always been like family to us, and hell, now you are." he smiled.

"Who would have thought any of our neighbors could resort to doing the evil things they have done? I certainly wouldn't have predicted it. Now, with a little luck and with God's help, we will get the hell out of here and start somewhere fresh. I just hope and pray everyone is up for this. We won't get any second chances. If we cannot make this trip, we will die along the way, so we have to get there, and we have to get there today. I don't know if you've noticed, but fall is already in the air and I think it's going to come early. We need to get settled in and prepare for what could be a harsh winter, because it may come sooner than we think." Bill said.

"Agreed," said Jack.

"Morning," said Mark as he was awakened by the sound of his Dad's voice.

"Morning Mark. Up and at 'em" answered Bill.

Soon the whole house was up and getting dressed in the dark, as they made their preparation for the grueling walk ahead of them.

After everyone was dressed and had their fill of Clif Bars, they were each handed a flashlight by Bill. They all headed outside. He made sure the safety was on before he pushed the shotgun, barrel first, down into his cart, laid his flashlight on top of the tarp, and then put the pistol and box of shells into his pants pocket. He had solely decided that he would be the one to carry both weapons since he was leading the caravan.

Last to be loaded was Whiskers. He wasn't sure how the cat felt about sitting in the small part of Viv's cart, the part meant for kids to sit in and not cats. With a little encouragement, Whiskers managed just fine and did as he was told.

The last thing to be gotten, which they had forgotten to load the night before, were the binoculars and the emergency crank radio. Mark came out of the back door with them and handed the binoculars to his father, as he would be leading them. With backpacks on the backs of Jack and Mark, Bill accepted the binoculars gratefully, knowing they would come in handy to scout the road up ahead, and off they went in order, making a lot of noise from the wheels of the shopping carts and the steel sounds of the carts themselves. Unfortunately, the noise could not be avoided, and they would have to do the best they could.

Everyone was tense as they exited the neighborhood. They had no idea who was alive or dead, praying the hunters were nowhere near them as they made their way in the dark down Cook Way toward Arapahoe Road.

At first, the noise of the carts seemed louder than they were due to the group's hypersensitivity to sound. They constantly looked over their shoulders, continuing to push, finally arriving at Arapahoe Road and out of the neighborhood, giving them all a sigh of relief.

None of them could ever remember being outside of their homes this early in the morning, and other than their trip the day before to pick up grocery carts, most of them had not left the house since the Bright Light and the Big Swoosh happened, other than Viv and Jack's encounter at Whole Foods, or Brian and Rocky playing baseball at Cherry Knolls Park.

Pushing uphill on Arapahoe Road, taking them to University Blvd, was not met with any fanfare or enthusiasm by the caravan, but they slowly pushed on until they reached the crest of the hill with University Blvd. in sight.

They stopped for a moment to catch their breath, and the incredibility of being smack dab in the middle of the road was not lost on any of them. They would not be getting honked at or run over.

They were now the Kings of the Road.

Now at University, they would make their first major pivot toward their destination, heading north to Belleview.

﹌

Philip was tasked to give the bad news to President Biden, as he sat across from him at the lunch table in the dining hall.

"You're kidding me, right?" asked the President. "We never considered this as a possible scenario. I know it never crossed *my* mind. Never once did I imagine that Bill Jenkins and his family would opt to stay in that hostile environment instead of getting on the train and coming back here to safety.

Well…God help him, and God help his family and the people they are with."

The president vacillated between staring out into space and staring down at the plate of food in front of him.

"Looks like you are going to be our new Department of Agriculture's statistician Philip. How hard can it be?" President Biden jokingly asked Philip.

Philip was not amused.

"I'm sure he kept notes on what his plans were. We will check his locker to see what we can find" Philip answered.

Philip had briefed the president on everything that had been relayed to General Horne from the two escorting Sergeants that took Bill to his home, including the gauntlet they had gone through and the confrontation in the living room with an armed son and wife, leaving them no choice but to either risk a firefight in the home, or leave peacefully without Bill Jenkins in tow.

General Horne was trying to decide if the men would be punished, or maybe even demoted in rank.

"I'll tell you this. That Jenkins fellow is one hell of a resourceful man, along with his family. He's also a decent man. He could have easily left those people to fend for themselves, but he and his family chose to stick by them, thereby sacrificing their future. God love 'em." General Horne told Philip.

President Biden could appreciate the situation and would like to have thought he would have done the same if the shoes were on his feet.

❧

The sun was peeking up from the east and Bill was thanking God for the cool morning air. As good of shape he was still in, the grocery cart he was pushing was every bit as much weight as he could have borne, which was probably twice the weight as anyone else's.

Bringing up the rear, Jack was holding his own, pushing a good 120 pounds of his mom Julie, though the wheels on the chair were better suited for the distance they were traveling than he had thought.

As they came to the intersection of Orchard and University, they stopped to take their first real water break and to catch their breath; the first water break of many they would be taking throughout the day.

"How is everyone holding up?" Bill asked the travelers.

Each responded, either with an "OK, or "Good" or gave a thumbs up.

"Brady Bunch in the Wild Frontier!" Viv offered.

"We still have a long way to go. We haven't even hit Belleview yet, but when we get there, that will be a good chunk accomplished, and we're almost to Belleview, so good work gang" said Bill.

Rocky grabbed an old sock from the pseudo toilet paper supply and ran behind a car in the parking lot of Trader Joe's, located in the strip mall where they decided to take their break under a tree.

Their early departure caused an obvious delay for his morning constitutional.

Others had yet to bake their loaves of bread.

Suddenly they heard Rocky scream and then saw him run from the car he was behind with his pants still down around his ankles.

"Mr. Jenkins...there's a man over there!"

Bill grabbed the pistol out of his pants, then walked over to the car that Rocky was behind, and there he was. It was a man in his late thirties, crawling out from under the car Rocky was squatting behind, and he was in bad shape for sure. Bill put the pistol back in his pocket, as he could see there was no danger to be met with this man, because he was dying...dying of thirst.

"Viv...bring me a bottle of water, would you?" Bill asked.

Viv reached into the cart and grabbed a bottle of water, then brought it over to Bill. She knelt beside the man, putting the palm of her hand on his forehead.

"What is your name?" she asked the man.

He was delirious and could barely move his mouth to make a sound. Viv then grabbed the bottle of water back out of Bill's hand, opened it, then put it to his lips slowly. The man began to drink the water, then started coughing because some went down the wrong pipe. He was trying to drink the water too fast.

"Slow down sir," Viv said in a soothing and friendly way. "Take your time."

The man was too weak to hold the bottle himself, so Viv held it for him. It took a good couple of minutes for him to finish it.

"Could you get me another bottle Bill? He needs more," asked Viv.

After another bottle was brought to Viv, she opened that and started to slowly pour the water into the man's mouth, but this time he reached up to hold the bottle himself, and when the man's throat was partially hydrated, he began to speak.

"Thank you...thank you. My name is Darren," he whispered.

"How long have you been out here Darren?" Bill asked.

"I'm not sure, maybe a couple of days? I don't know. I was being chased by some people with guns. They were trying to kill me. I ran under this car to hide from them, and obviously, they never found me." Darren explained.

"Where do you live" asked Viv.

"Nowhere. I'm homeless. Been homeless for years. I've been living in a tent off the Highline Canal for the last year or so. I've just been looking for food or water somewhere, anywhere. I was going house to house when a man came running out of a house across the street from where I was, and then he took a shot at me."

He swallowed hard before continuing on.

"I started running down the street, then turned on University with five or six of them chasing me and taking shots at me. I had a pretty good head start on them. They almost hit me, hitting a tree instead right next to my head, then I came upon this parking lot and hid under this car, and I've been under here ever since." Darren replied between sips from the water bottle.

"You were in pretty bad shape a few minutes ago, but it looks like you're coming around now", said Bill.

"Where are you guys going?" Darren asked.

"No place you're going Pal" Bill barked.

"Please…take me with you" pled Darren.

Viv looked up at Bill with puppy dog eyes, as if to suggest he should join them.

Bill then reached for Viv's hand and picked her up from her knees and started walking back to the carts with Viv in hand.

"No Viv. Don't start collecting strays on me now. He doesn't belong with us and will only slow us down.

"He's dying Bill," she said.

"Not anymore he's not. We just saved his life to live another day. He's probably not going to be the last one we see today Viv. By the looks of the sun, it's probably close to nine already. We have to get moving. Don't debate this with me ok?" Bill asserted.

Viv knew not to push it too far with Bill. He was her husband, which meant he was in charge. That's the way she always wanted it to be, so she would have to respect his decision and forget about this man.

"C'mon gang…we've got territory to cover. Let's move" Bill ordered the crew as they rejoined them.

With Bill at the lead and more downtime than he had wanted to allow for, they continued up University Blvd., a caravan of seven brightly colored tarp-covered shopping carts, followed by a wheelchair with lots of miles on it.

With the delay, they still made good time and Bill hoped to make the I-25 overpass on Belleview Avenue by 1:00 that afternoon.

Jim Laudner had just set up camp. He, his wife, and his daughter had arrived at New Hope a few days prior, and he was damn glad to be as far away from the hunters terrifying his neighborhood as possible.

The people he was unexpectedly with were decent enough folk, though they were nervous about Jim at first. Most of them had gotten to what they now call New Hope first, with some families arriving afterward. Jim and his family were the newest additions.

What spooked the camp's inhabitants the most was the possibility that they could be eaters of human flesh and not normal people like the rest of them. It took watching Jim and his family eating normal food before they were fully accepted as one of them. After that, everything was fine. All the inhabitants had come from neighborhoods a good distance away, but not too far away. They had made the trip to the closest water source for their survival, with all of them on the same page on how to survive this 24/7 nightmare they were living in.

All of them shared a belief in God and prayed nightly before dinner, and they all ate together. They all found a way to contribute to the whole of the group, whether it be catching fish, hunting for stray elk that wandered near their campsite, or building things, things they would need to make their lives easier.

One project that had just begun was turning an old bicycle stationed by the water into a water pump, turning a paddle that pushed water up to a big basket covered with a huge trash bag, thereby filling it with water to wash clothes and dishes, then rinse them as well. It was an ingenious idea and worked out well.

Another project someone had just completed was building a brick oven to bake bread. The bricks were found in a utility shed by the old bathrooms no longer in use, along with a bunch of bags of cement. There were even mason's tools in there, making the project a whole lot easier than it might have been without them.

A giant hole was also dug, with a real honest-to-goodness outhouse constructed over it, complete with a half-moon carved into the door. The damn thing even had a toilet seat, though toilet paper was at a premium, at least until some of them made a trip to the local market to get more.

They still had many projects to complete before the winter snow would start to fly, but at the rate they were going, they hoped to finish by sometime in October.

There had to have been close to sixty people total living at New Hope, and everyone had a job to do, contributing to the health and wellbeing of this newly established community.

It was like a tent city with a communal fire pit dug in the center of the tents, a commune in the best sense of the word. They had gathered many of the picnic tables throughout the park and placed them next to each other so everyone could eat together as a family next to the giant BBQ pit and the new brick oven.

One of the ongoing things was the constant boiling of water in giant pots, water to be used for drinking, and making sun tea and Kool-Aid. On one picnic table alone, there had to be at least twenty to twenty five gallon jugs of drinks brewing, with more on the way.

The laundry station they had devised was not far from the dining area, so when they needed water for consumption, they just diverted the water meant for the laundry area to the pots for boiling, making it a lot easier to carry the pots to the fire pit instead of carting it up from the lake.

No one had yet figured out a good use for all the shopping carts people used to cart their stuff, other than to get things that were needed, so they all sat together at the edge of the encampment, looking lonely and bored.

It was 12:30 when they made it to the I-25 overpass, and God was listening.

They were half an hour ahead of schedule, and unlike Arapahoe Road, there were no cars underneath, just plenty of shade and cool cement to stretch out on. They had gone just over ten miles since about 4:30 that morning, and every single one of them, even Julie, could feel it in every bone in their bodies.

For the first time since that morning, when Bill laid in bed and questioned in his mind whether they could physically make this trip, he had a total turnaround in his thinking and was now pretty damn certain they were going to not only make it but make it in time to have enough light to set up tents.

They must have spent at least half an hour in the shade of the overpass, but eventually Bill got up and announced "We are so close now, and we have to move on. There's a supermarket up ahead that might have some stuff we could use, so we need to keep moving!"

Naturally, this was met with a host of moans and groans, but all knew that Bill was the master and commander of this caravan, and he had gotten them that far, so with a grunt and an ow sound, the group got up and continued, with Bill at the helm.

Before long, they arrived at the King Soopers shopping center, right where Bill said it would be.

They parked their carts outside and made a plan.

Viv, Julie, and Kate had to go to the bathroom in the worst way, as they had been holding it all day, to the point of stomach cramps. The women took the pistol with them to look for a bathroom, while Bill, Mark, and Rocky scoured the aisles as they looked for anything resembling food, water, and possibly toilet paper. Jack and Brian were left outside with the shotgun to watch over their possessions.

When the rest of them went into the market, they gagged from the abominable stench coming from the few leftover vegetables that had rotted, along with rotted meat left behind that had wafted across from the other side of the store, but they continued onward.

After grabbing a cart, Bill and Rocky took the food and water aisles, while Mark took the paper aisle.

Bill was able to find a few bags of noodles and a couple of jars of spaghetti sauce, while Rocky came back to the cart with a few half-gallon bottles of prune juice. Seems no one wanted prune juice, and why would they? The last thing they needed was to be regular. All other things resembling liquid were completely gone, except the prune juice, and there was as much of it as they wanted. Bill thought the prune juice Rocky had gotten would suffice. After all, they still had four cases of water left in the cart outside.

Mark was not able to find any toilet paper, but he was able to find a few rolls of paper towels, which would be like heaven after having to use half of his wardrobe to wipe with. He knew the women especially would appreciate it.

The men were out of the store first and waited on the women to finish their business inside.

Eventually, they strolled out of the store, looking much relieved and happy about their success at finding toilet paper still in the stalls of the bathroom.

After packing away the items they found in the store, they began their final three miles to their destination.

Going up the steep incline of Cherry Creek Dam Road almost killed them, but they made it up to the top and stopped, with all of them looking down over the vast expanse of the reservoir, over to the camping area, where they spotted numerous tents and tarp shelters scattered all around, but still close to one another.

"Looks like great minds think alike. There are people down there that had the same idea as us" said Bill as he grabbed the binoculars out of the cart to take a look.

After a minute, Mark asked, "Dad, what if they are hunters?"

"Well son, if those are cannibals down there, they're the weirdest cannibals I've ever seen. Take a look," said Bill as he handed Mark the binoculars. "See that table off to the side where those men are standing? They're cutting the heads off of fish and filleting them. I don't think cannibals eat fish." Bill added.

"You're right," said Mark.

Mark then handed the binoculars to Jack, then Jack to Rocky, and so on, and so on, until everyone had seen the campsite through them.

"Well, we only have a mile left to go and it's 2:30, so what do you say we go down there and see if they're friendly?" Bill said with a smile.

Jack then offered up a prayer that they would all be ok, saying they had much to be thankful for, and he praised the Lord for his help in getting them there.

They had been at it for ten hours and were ready to stop but going another mile would be cake for them.

Whiskers had moved over and sat in Julie's lap most of the trip, as he had enough of the vibrating and noisy cart. He was ready for this to be over as well, but he too had another mile in him.

⊰⌢⊱

It was a woman baking bread that spotted them first, and she called some of the men in earshot to come over and look.

As they looked to the top of the dam, they could see the orange and green tarps shining bright, along with the shopping carts glistening in the rays of the sun, coming down the dam road which led to where they were.

"Looks like they are heading our way. Sure, hope they like fish. If they don't, we might have a problem" said one of the men.

New Hope had no limit to the number of people they were accepting into their new little township. The more hands, the more help. The only requirement was that you didn't want to eat them upon your arrival.

EIGHTEEN

Welcome to New Hope

Coming off of Parker Road, they turned into Cherry Creek State Park, and the caravan was on its last legs. Two of the carts had wobbly wheels, with one wheel about ready to fall off on Kate's, making the cart much harder to push. Mark switched carts with her, much to Kate's appreciation.

After passing the little shack meant for checking in to the park, they made their turn toward the camping area and they could see a large group of men well up ahead, standing on the side of the road, waiting for the caravan to arrive.

As they got closer, they could see several of the men had rifles, and when it seemed they had gone as far as they could go, they stopped just before the group of men approached them.

Most of them stayed back a bit behind the man designated to greet them, although not exactly the warmest of greetings.

The man approached Bill, standing back about twenty yards.

"You can stop right there. State your business," he called out.

The man was now pointing his rifle at Bill, especially after seeing the shotgun laying on top of Bill's cart. The rest of the men, about eight or nine of them, stepped up about ten yards behind the leader.

The smell of freshly baked bread was filling the air, making the mouths of the weary travelers water.

"No business here," said Bill. "Looks like you guys beat us to it. We've walked a long way to get here. We've come here to camp, just like you."

"Where did you walk from?" said the man up front.

"Centennial. Arapahoe and University. We've been walking these carts since 4:30 this morning."

The man with the rifle pointing at Bill turned around to look at his posse, looking for a little direction.

"Hey Pal, do you mind pointing that rifle in another direction? This is my family, and we aren't here to cause any trouble." Bill was not having any of it.

The man looked Bill dead in his eyes for a moment, then let the muzzle of the rifle lower toward the ground.

"I'm sorry, but we are all kind of skittish. I'm sure you know what I mean. I got a question for you…do you eat people?" the man asked.

Bill chuckled a little, then answered him.

"Nope…we're not people eaters. Couldn't tell you what a human being tastes like. None of us can, and we're hoping you couldn't tell us either."

The man's whole demeanor seemed to change with Bill's answer. He lowered his guard both mentally and physically and walked over to Bill with his hand outstretched to shake Bill's hand.

"We've got fish fry tonight with fresh bread. Hope you're hungry. We'll know for sure when we see you eating the fish. Welcome to New Hope" said the man as he smiled. This signaled the other men behind him. They joined their leader shaking hands and smiling as well.

Viv started to cry. Bill wasn't sure if it was because she was tired, scared, or just overcome with emotion. It had been a long day for sure, quite possibly the longest day of any of their lives.

The caravan was encouraged to leave their carts where they sat and follow the men up toward the wonderful smell of the baked bread, coming from a plethora of loaves cooling on one of the picnic benches pushed together by the brick oven.

More people started circling them from throughout the camp, greeting them and introducing themselves, and it was a little overwhelming to be around this many people again, people that were welcoming and nice, even to Whiskers.

Julie was holding Whiskers tightly, which suited the cat just fine, as he was in unfamiliar territory. People were petting the cat, with some getting hissed at, as they were introducing themselves to Julie.

There were a few boys Brian and Rocky's age, and as boys do, they made fast friends, and after five minutes, it was like they had all known each other for a lifetime.

The man with the rifle then turned to Bill and said, "My name is Terry. Terry Pryor. Good to meet you. What's yours?"

"Likewise. Bill Jenkins," Bill returned.

"Man Boss, you've sure got a big family" stated Terry.

"We are two families, but I guess you can call us one big family now"

The people began lining up to a gigantic pile of fried fish and more bread than could have been eaten. They urged Bill and his crew to get in front of the line as hospitality was the rule of the day.

Bill then turned to his wife and began introducing people.

"This is Vivian, my wife. Behind her is our dear friend Julie Price, and behind her is her daughter Kate, right next to her is my son Mark, and behind him is Julie's son Jack, and bringing up the rear is my son Brian and his friend, and Julie's son, Rocky.

Whiskers could smell the fish and he became almost uncontrollable in Julie's arms, so he jumped away from her and headed straight for the large pile of fish. He stole a big fat fish and carried it over to a tree nearby and begin eating it.

No one remembered that poor Whiskers had not had anything to eat all day, except for the offering of part of a Clif Bar, which he had no interest in.

After grabbing plates and silverware from a huge pile on the table, the hungry travelers piled their plates high with different kinds of fish that had been caught in the reservoir, along with the baked bread. Some filled their glasses with Kool-Aid while others opted for sun tea, a treat they hadn't had in months, especially since they had been on a strict water diet. All of those in the caravan sat at one of the many picnic tables nearby.

Just as Bill was sitting down, Terry Pryor came over to where they were sitting.

"Bill, would you mind bringing your food over to this other table to sit with me and some of the other men? We'd like to talk to you for a bit."

"Sure" Bill replied and proceeded to join him at the other table, which started to fill up fast with other men in the group.

They were all well into their meals and introductions had been made, which would take a while for Bill to register, when Terry brought up the camp.

"Me, Joe Bird, Bob Hawkins, and our families were the first to arrive here a couple of months ago with the same idea the rest of us had, just like you, to set up camp near a fresh supply of water and someplace we could hunt for food. Over the last couple of months, we've been joined by the rest of these families, and so far, it's worked out pretty well. Without counting you folks, we have sixty three people here. Everybody pitches in according to what they are good at, and we make it work. Needless to say, we eat a lot of fish, and recently, a lot of bread too. Skip Holden recently built that brick oven over there and the women have been baking bread almost nonstop ever since.

Down by the lake, you'll see a bicycle set up to peddle water up here to wash dishes and do laundry, and whatever else we need water for. That was Billy Haggerty's invention."

Bill nodded his head in agreement while feasting on the most delicious meal he'd eaten for a while. It was nothing special for sure, but as much as he appreciated it, he knew his family was loving it even more, and he was glad his wife wouldn't have to cook that night.

Terry continued. "We call this place New Hope because that's what it is, a new hope, a new beginning. We've been listening to these dumbass emergency announcements on the NOAA channel and the things Biden has been saying. The bottom line is this…Nothing has changed at all since this whole thing started. We've never seen any military trucks with food or medicine like Biden said there would be, and the people eaters are still killing people and eating them. There's no law at all and we are basically left to fend for ourselves. We're lucky right now because the snow hasn't started to fly yet, but when that happens, it's going to be a whole new ballgame."

"I have to tell you when we were up on top of the Dam Road and looked down here and saw all of you, my heart skipped a beat, because we didn't know what kind of people you are. This was our last hurrah. There was no way we could have gone anywhere else. This was it, so I have to say that this is a Godsend for us." offered Bill.

"What did you do before the bright light?" asked one of the men.

"I work for the Department of Agriculture. It's a long story and kind of confusing, so I will save that for another time, but the plan is to get the country up and running within twelve to eighteen months, but from what I saw in D.C., that plan isn't going to happen in time for this country to get back on its feet. We were attacked and an EMP is what wiped us out. They say that ninety percent of the population will be dead within a year, but I don't think they ever considered people eating each other. It's been three months now and I think we are already close to that number," stated Bill with authority.

"I should tell you, we have brought something to the table that can ensure the longevity of some of us, depending on the malady. We have two backpacks filled with pharmaceuticals…antibiotics right out of a pharmacy still in their packaging, along with a Physician's Desk Reference, explaining the different drugs, doses, etc.

No one should be dying from an infection."

The men all looked at each other in amazement.

"We were just talking about this very thing last week. We were thinking of heading up the road to the nearest pharmacy to see what we could find, but I don't think any of us has a real knowledge of the difference between an antibiotic and a pain pill. With winter coming, we know people are going to get sick, and we are going to have to self-treat." said Terry.

"What about the hunters? Have you had any interactions with them since you've been here?" Bill queried.

"Knock on wood…no. We've been pretty lucky that way so far, but I don't know how long our luck will last. Eventually, they are going to run out of people to hunt and they will spread out way past their comfort zone. Could be this Winter or next Spring, but to think we won't see them is wishful thinking. They will come and we will have to deal with them, pure and simple, and hopefully, we'll be ready for them. Most of us are armed, locked, and loaded. We have plenty of weapons and a good deal of ammo, but we could always use more, and eventually, with hunting elk, we will run out. I believe a scouting expedition is in our future. What we are most concerned about now is preparing for Winter. We've been thinking about constructing a large shed or room with a fireplace in it, big enough for all of us to fit comfortably in it, but we'd have to do it before very long. As you can see, although it was pretty hot today, the nights are starting to cool down and it's sleeping bag weather. The problem we have is wood. There are a few sheets of plywood and some two-by-fours here and there, but not nearly enough for a project that big. Skip says there are enough bricks in the maintenance shed to build a pretty good size fireplace, though he's not sure there's enough cement, so there's that." said one of the men.

"Is there a Home Depot anywhere close to here?" Bill asked.

"There is, but I don't know if you could say it's close. It's one street over on Arapahoe Road by I-25, but that's a good seven-mile walk from here. We could put materials on those orange carts they use in the store, but it would take forever and a day to push everything over here. I'm pretty sure that's our only option though." answered Terry.

It was fast becoming twilight as the men were wrapping up their pow-wow with Bill. The women at the other tables were having a whale of a time, laughing and talking up a storm. It was good for Bill to see his girl so engaged, and comfortable. Even Julie was happier than she had been since this whole thing began.

Jack and Mark had already taken it upon themselves to start setting up the tents. They grabbed them out of the carts and walked them over to where all the other tents were set up, creating a little village, or fortress if you prefer.

Some of the women were boiling water to wash dishes, while others were collecting the plates off of the men's tables and emptying fish bones into the firepit, located just south of the tent village.

This was their gathering place at night. It had various camp chairs and homemade benches made by some of the men, all circling the pit, which was full of wood and ready to be lit.

Bill turned to Terry as they walked next to each other as they headed toward the lake.

"So, Terry...is there a leader of this group of people, or does everyone kind of do as they please? In other words, if something were to happen, like an argument between a couple here, or worse, say the hunters came into camp, who would be the one to intervene?

"We don't tell anybody what they can and can't do, that's for sure, and we haven't had anything like what you are talking about happen, but if the shit *did* hit the fan and somebody would make the first move to stop it, that would probably be Bob Hawkins. I guess he's the de-facto Sheriff of New Hope." Terry answered.

Bob Hawkins was one of the men holding a rifle directly behind Terry Pryor when the group of men first greeted the caravan, and Bob was also sitting at the end of the table while they ate.

Bob Hawkins looked like no one to mess with, kind of like Jim from Jim Croce's song *"You Don't Mess Around with Jim."*

He was in his early forties and built like a tank. He was every bit of six foot three inches tall and weighed probably close to 270 to 280 pounds, and not a bit of fat on him. Bob didn't say much at the table, but it was apparent he did his talking in other ways.

He had a big full beard, which wasn't saying a lot since all the other men had beards as well. Hell, even Bill's son Mark and Jack had beards. Bill was the only man in the camp to be anything close to clean-shaven, but soon Bill would catch up to the rest. He hadn't shaved since the morning he left Mt. Weather, which was two days prior, but it wouldn't take long for Bill to have a decent beard of his own. Viv would probably have something to say about it, but given the circumstances, it wouldn't be much.

Yes, Bill could see Bob Hawkins as the Leader of the Pack. As far as he could tell, not only was Bob a scary sight - if you had to go up against him, but he also seemed to have the temperament needed for the job.

The women had already discovered the outhouse and utilized it, much to their delight. Viv contributed the two rolls of paper towels they had absconded with earlier in the day.

The fire was roaring in the fire pit, with several of the New Hope residents gathered around it, but sleep was in the cards for the Jenkins/ Price group, so they would give their apologies and go to bed early. Bill thanked Terry for their hospitality and assured him they would discuss more in the morning; he then headed for the sleeping bag in his tent. Viv was already there, almost in the throes of dreamland, but managed to hug and kiss Bill goodnight, and Bill was not far behind her.

This had turned out to be one of the best things to happen to these weary travelers, Bill thought as he laid his head down. Not only did they arrive safely, but he could sleep extra soundly that night, knowing he was surrounded by good God-fearing folk that he could fight next to if need be, and not have to fight against.

NINETEEN

A New Day's Dawn

Viv found Bill standing outside of the tent, sipping a cup of coffee he had gotten over at the fire pit from a percolator sitting among a group of percolators on the flat rocks along the side.

For the first time in what seemed like forever, Viv had awoken in peace, and not in fear.

Many people were up and scurrying about, while others were late sleepers still in their tents.

There were already two boats out on the reservoir, fishing for the day's meals, and sitting next to the percolators of coffee, a big industrial-size pot full of freshly cooked oatmeal next to the fire to keep warm, with bowls, spoons, and sugar, all set up on the tables next to where they had received last night's dinner.

To Viv, it felt like another camping trip that she, Bill, and the boys had taken so many times before.

Off to the end of the settlement on the shore was a series of colorful tarps tied to tree branches that overhung the lake, serving as temporary walls that provided privacy for those wishing to bathe.

Wow, Bill thought to himself. These guys have almost thought of everything!

And then, just like a whirlwind of thought, images popped into his mind depicting a war between the other superpowers of the world, fighting over the spoils of what was once known as America. It was a horrible image to have that early before the morning had even begun, but the horror was the reality of it.

Bill knew damn well that life as they knew it was over and it would never come back, at least not in his lifetime. Replaying all the world events that had happened over the last few years, leading up to this, left him shaking his head in disbelief that not only could this have happened under America's nose, but how could this country have allowed life to go on as long as it did without preparing for a moment such as this?

So many trillions of dollars had been spent needlessly on things nobody could remember, except those on the receiving end, and not one single dollar was spent reinforcing the United States of America's electrical infrastructure, other than in parts of D.C. and a select few military bases across the country.

As a nation, America was a sitting duck.

Had they spent a fraction of what they had wasted American tax dollars on, this would have never happened, and his boys would have grown up in a world that still resembled the same world Bill had grown up in, less the simplicity of its time.

It was August 28 and winter would be here before they knew it; Bill also knew that for all of its ingenuity, the camp was not ready for it, and many would not survive. If they were to make progress in ensuring the survivability rate, they must act now in getting things prepared and ready for what could be the dying season if they did not act fast.

Eventually, other nations would fight for this land because of all its natural resources, and its beauty. America was once again the new world waiting to be rediscovered.

Would it be China?

Or would it be Russia?

Or maybe even England?

Would it be resettled, or just stripped of its resources?

What would become of the survivors, the last denizens of this defeated monolith?

These were all questions running through Bill's brain and had to be the same questions running through the minds of every surviving American.

What was next on the horizon for them and their children?

Bill's feeling was what they were seeing now around them, people living outside with none of the creature comforts everyone was accustomed to, was the best it would get, at least in the next ten years or more.

Being privy to the other side of this now rustic way of life, meaning what lies beneath the Earth's surface, with all of the underground military bases housing the elite and the important, leaving the common man to suffer the consequences of the decisions made by those that knew hardly of their existence. It struck Bill that this was the way things had always been, between the haves and the have-nots.

In the end, the haves always end up being the survivors, whereas the have-nots struggle for air and the ability to be free, only this time, it would be the have-nots having the freedom to start over again, no matter the cost or the struggle,

The haves would end up choking to death until they would be forced to come out from under the ground and then succumb to the new oppressive powers forced on them, as they would become the new slaves of Babylon.

Bill knew for a fact that help could have come in some form, somehow, but it was left by the government to be addressed and handled by the whimsical nature of our once close allies, and worse, our enemies.

So, this would be where life begins again, to be reborn under the love and protection of the Lord Jesus Christ…and Bill was going to be a part of it.

Beginning that day, Bill would become an integral part of the planning and implementation of New Hope. By helping to coordinate missions to retrieve supplies that were needed, by organizing the men of the community into specific tasks that would lead to the progress needed to be made.

The most important thing that needed to be done immediately was securing the lumber and hardware needed for the construction of the Great Building, needed to protect the community from the oncoming winter storms.

After consulting with the man most equipped with the knowledge to build this structure, they came up with a supply list to be filled by a series of men that would alternate making trips to the Home Depot. These would be groups of ten men, to be followed by ten more men, then followed again by the first ten men, and so on, and so on, etc.

Supplies would include plywood, two-by-fours, roofing shingles and felt for the roof, nails, screws, hammers, saws, pencils, tape measures, anything at all to complete the project promptly more cement for the fireplace, all in all, tons of materials that would have to be moved without any mechanical help, but instead the old fashioned way, by blood, sweat, tears, and brawn, and no man would get a pass when it came to the work.

Two days later, the lists were made, and the transportation began.

There would be many trips to the Home Depot in the following two weeks, and as arduous as they were, Bill managed to keep everyone inspired to do their part.

In a sense, he became the Mayor of New Hope with his relentless attention to detail, his fiery determination, and his willingness to endure anything he was asking of anyone else.

By the end of September, the building had been constructed right next to where the washing station was, and it was a beautiful sight to behold, and bigger than they had originally envisioned.

Built with a lean-to style roof, the building was functional, with clean lines and even surfaces, and even had a wood floor, which was more than they had planned for before Bill's arrival. The roof was watertight, and the fireplace was gigantic and enough to keep the whole building warm in the coldest of winters and perfect for cooking.

When it was completed, all of them, including Bill, were astonished and amazed at what they could do if they set their minds to it.

Surpassing any and all improvements they had made in the past, this new structure was by far the greatest thing they had been a part of since the beginning of New Hope. They were all proud, deservedly so, because every single one of them had a hand in its erection.

The best part was that they had finished it before the first frost, giving them plenty of time to arrange its contents and move on to the next project, constructing a shower house that would separate the men from the women.

In some ways, this would be even more ambitious than the Great Building.

They would need to come up with a system that would push the heated water from the fire to the pipe over the shower head and be able to temper the hot water with cold water, so no one would get burned while cleaning themselves.

This would take some inventing, but there were men in camp more than capable of pulling this off, so the construction began.

It was also critical not to pull all the men to work on this, as it was for the Great Building. Lots of firewood would have to be chopped to get through the winter, and this would require a lot of hands. Even the women would chop wood when they were not cleaning dishes or washing clothes.

It was in October when the first snowstorm hit New Hope, and they hadn't completed the shower house a moment too soon. Though the building was constructed and was sound, the water distribution system had not yet been perfected, but it still enabled everyone to sponge bathe in privacy after hauling in the hot water from the newly dug fire pit outside the door of the shower house.

Although it wasn't what they had hoped for, it was worlds better than the alternative, which was what they had been doing before… standing in the lake bathing, hidden behind the tarps.

The house enabled them to take off all their clothes and not freeze to death, instead of bathing in the freezing water and air.

The Great Building proved crucial to their survival during that first snowstorm. The temperature had dipped down to the teens, and most were not prepared for cold weather sleeping, as they did not have zero or below sleeping bags, nor did they have the proper sleeping attire. Many of them would have froze throughout the night and were grateful to be inside of a warm, dry place to sleep, albeit cramped with no privacy.

Bill and Viv had done a lot of cold weather camping throughout their marriage, and they knew how to survive a snowstorm, whereas Julie, not so much, but they made sure she was warm, dry, and comfortable.

The days throughout the winter were much the same, hunting for elk that strayed into the camp and beyond, baking bread, pumping water up from the reservoir, the constant boiling of water for bathing and cooking, and most importantly, chopping wood.

Christmas was a special time in the camp. With the sanctity of life ever-present, as they were all aware of the alternative had they ended up on the plates of the hunters. Dealing with the hardships of winter, in a way none of them had ever had to before, you would think their spirits would dampen, but just the opposite happened. Everyone was extremely glad to be alive when so many they knew had passed on, some in ways no man would want to die.

Christmas carols could be heard throughout the camp on Christmas Eve, lulling to sleep those who chose to go to bed early and sleep their way through to Christmas morning.

Jack had steadily grown in his faith and was hosting Bible study every Wednesday night in the Great Building. Those who wanted to highlight a certain scripture could do so, then open it up for discussion. At first, it started off slow with little attendance but gradually gained steam, becoming a focal point of the week for the majority of New Hope residents. Many brought their own Bibles into the study, and by the light of the propane lanterns, they read and prayed out loud, giving thanks to the Lord for their many blessings.

Jack had also become the camp pseudo/quasi doctor/pharmacist, mostly distributing ibuprofen to bring down fevers and reduce pain, but also gave out antibiotics to two of the residents, one for a suspected bladder infection, and the other for an infected hangnail. After consulting the PDR, he came up with the correct antibiotic and dosage, with spectacular results in both cases. Doing this particular task made Jack feel important and needed while making him feel close to his late father.

New Hope had benefitted from the arrival of the Jenkins/Price families and was thankful for their presence in camp. The gratitude was shared because Bill Jenkins firmly believed that the camp and its citizens had saved the lives of their families.

The winter would have been especially rough for any of the families had they had to go it alone. Becoming a community of like-minded individuals willing to work together for the common good made it possible for them to prepare for the worst and brave the storm.

Two thousand twenty three had come and gone without so much

as a whoop and a holler, but they did tie one on as they brought in the New Year.

Celebration was not something they thought about as they drank the liquor they snagged from the liquor store on their last supply run, because the New Year felt eerily similar to the Old Year.

It wasn't as much about bringing in the new but trying to drown out and bury the old, putting the final nail in its coffin. Though they weren't cognizant of it, their drinking together signified the lack of fear they had felt not too long ago. The hunters were not thought about as much as they used to be, because in their little community they felt shielded, in a sense, from the outside world. Letting their guard down for one evening felt safe and needed no one's permission. They felt no one knew of their existence because they were so far off the beaten path, and they all felt safe in the company of each other.

At times throughout that night, it became solemn, and that's when the damage to their psyche, caused by the events of the year was most apparent. As optimistic as they all tried to be, they all deep down felt the pain of losing what was once theirs that would never return to them, and this was their way of saying goodbye.

New Year's Eve was also a night of communion.

Mark and Kate had become increasingly close with each passing day, their love grew to an intensity that it might not have otherwise.

They managed to avoid their feelings ever since Bill had come back and led them on the trek to New Hope. Life became arduous, keeping them both busy contributing to the camp, but they never missed an opportunity to wave at each other from afar or touch one another in passing.

This night was the perfect opportunity for them to share a first kiss and profess their love for one another, while the adults became inebriated and preoccupied with adult conversation and laughter.

They walked out together past the perimeter of the camp, holding hands and realizing the bond they had created.

Kate had always liked Mark growing up across the street from him, but because Mark was a couple of years older and a couple of grades higher, she could never get his attention, especially in a romantic way. She knew she was in love with him then, but it wasn't until the bright light hit that he began to notice her, mostly because their lives had intertwined as the result of living under the same roof.

He immediately began to see her in a completely different light than at any time in the past. He noticed that she was not a little girl anymore, but instead becoming a woman, a very appealing woman. He even had dreams about her, and it wasn't long before he had developed a full-blown crush on her. But because of the situation they were in, he decided it would be best if he kept his feelings about her stuffed in the closet. Besides, who was to say that she felt the same way about him? Had he let his feelings be known and she didn't feel the same way, it could have been a source of great embarrassment for him with no escape because they shared the same roof, but as fate would have it, he discovered otherwise.

One day he was digging a new hole for the latrine in the backyard, and she sat on the back porch staring at him as if he were a steak and she was a hungry lioness.

He caught a glimpse of her adoration, and it was then he knew how she felt about him. He didn't react at that moment, but it locked into his brain that the feelings he had for her were mutual. Knowing this created some confusion for Mark, and he had no idea how to proceed with her, or if he should at all.

Over the final weeks, before his father came home, he was walking out of his bedroom and she walked out of hers, both at the same time, practically crashing into each other, and it was then that they shared the moment...*that* moment...staring into each other's eyes and not saying a word, because their eyes said everything that needed to be said.

It was the unmistakable look of love. The kind of love sung about in love songs, love letters, and marriage vows.

Mark unzipped the tent, allowing Kate to go in first, the same tent Mark shared with Jack, then he carefully and quietly went in behind her, zipping the tent back up. It was in that tent on that New Year's Eve, that they consummated their love for each other with great abandon, and there would be no turning back.

They stayed locked in each other's arms, not knowing how to act or behave, but knew that whatever life had in store for them, it would be for both of them together, and no matter what appeared on the road before them, they would face it together because their love would conquer anything that got in their way.

It was destiny. It was meant to be. And it was in the eyes of Christ, our Lord.

TWENTY

Old Chevy's Never Die

The groundhog must not have seen his shadow, because Springtime rolled into Cherry Creek State Park the same way Winter came; strong-willed, unannounced, and determined.

The cherry blossoms were already in bloom and the birds were singing in a way they only sang in the Springtime.

A lot had transpired over the Winter; Mark and Kate had announced to the parents their love for each other and their desire to be married, sooner rather than later, so the decision had to be made if their marriage would even be possible.

Who would marry them? Would it be legal?

In the absence of any legal authority, it only mattered if it was legal in the eyes of God.

Jack was asked if he would lead their ceremony, and he gladly accepted.

He had no idea how to proceed but would spend countless hours trying to figure it out. He would ask questions of anyone that could help him craft a wedding ceremony for his sister and best friend, talk to those that could remember their wedding vows, scour the Bible for any help, and pray to Jesus to give him the words to pull it off.

Kate had been late, then missed another period, so in early March, after consulting with her mother Julie and Viv, she was relatively sure she was pregnant with Mark's child.

This was the catalyst of their early marriage, as both Kate and Mark, especially Mark, did not want their child to be born a bastard in the eyes of God; hence the wedding was on.

Two weeks later they would be wed on March 15th, under the bright Colorado sun in the last week of winter, and the weather could not have been more cooperative.

It was more springlike than winter; another early sign that spring was on the way.

Kate was barely beginning to show, so getting a dress for her would not be an issue in fitting as much as it would be getting her a dress in general. The women took Kate's measurements the best they could and wrote them down on a piece of paper, and gave them to Mark, Jack, Terry, and Bill. The four men would then make the five-mile walk to a bridal shop in Aurora to pick out a dress for Kate, according to the measurements given to them.

When they got to the bridal shop, it was locked, so they found a nearby shopping cart and threw it through the plate glass window for entry.

Inside, they were like cowboys on an ice-skating rink and felt as out of place as anyone could, yet they used each other's eyeballs to make the best-uneducated guess they could make, and selected a beautiful dress being displayed on a mannequin that looked to be close enough to Kate's size. Throwing it in a bag, they got out of there and back to camp in record time.

The dress turned out to be almost perfect and needed little alteration, and at the sight of the dress, Julie broke out in tears, knowing that she was losing her little girl faster than she had ever imagined she would.

It was a beautiful ceremony and Kate was stunning in her brand-new white wedding dress, standing next to Mark in the best clothes he could find. They never thought to get Mark a suit or anything dressy, probably because they never thought they would find anything for Kate.

Nevertheless, Jack's ceremony was excellently written, and he delivered.

Kate Price was now Kate Jenkins, and Bill and Viv were bursting with pride.

Afterward, there was drinking and singing, and instead of cutting the cake, they cut some homemade cranberry bread baked by the women using canned cranberries.

Jack and his mother Julie were now living solo, as Mark and Kate had gotten their own tent to bed down in, living as man and wife, with child.

Other things had happened during the winter as well, but nothing as exciting as a wedding.

New Hope had decided they should start operating like a township, with a loosely run government run by elected officials, so they adopted a town council with a very short list of rules to live by. They would hold weekly meetings in the Great Building attended by the residents of New Hope, and they would even take minutes.

Bob Hawkins was appointed the Constable, in charge of law and order. Though he had no jail and no plans of ever putting someone in it even if he had, he still was recognized as the rule of law.

Terry Pryor was appointed Mayor of New Hope since he was the original resident and founder, which only made sense.

Bill Jenkins was appointed Town Planner, in charge of all projects projected for New Hope, since he had done such a bang-up job making sure the Great Building and shower house were completed before winter had set in. Jack Price was officially named Pastor and Pharmacist, two positions, both of which would have made his father proud.

Mark had also used his Eagle Scout skills by contributing to the camp, devising a shower, which he created by using a construction grade, heavy-duty trash bag to be filled with hot and cold water mixed, with water then slowly let out of the bag, which created more of a rinse than an actual shower, but it was a step in the right direction and was most effective for rinsing the shampoo out of your hair, which the women appreciated the most.

The American dream was alive and well in the little tight-knit community and patterned after the true spirit of the American West.

There was talk of finding and corralling horses somewhere if they could find some, and possibly start a cattle ranch where they could raise beef.

A garden was already in the works with seeds ready to be planted, and it would be enough to feed the entire community of New Hope.

It had been the first week of February, when they heard their last transmission over the NOAA Emergency weather channel, talking about how it would still take time, possibly now two to five years before they could notice a significant source of help coming their way, which might as well have been a lifetime to them.

Bill knew this was bullshit.

America as he knew it was over, and it would be anyone's guess before other countries would start to explore the possibilities of this new and vast available land to the world.

Bill had imagined that Canada and Mexico were already staking their claims, and it would only be a matter of time before choppers, airplanes, and drones would begin to appear in the skies above them scouting out the territory.

Had Bill and his family gone back to Mt. Weather, he wondered where they would be.

He imagined the resources there had long since been used up and all people there must have had to exit the facility, and possibly left to fend for themselves. It had been months since Biden had made any kind of speech or announcement, and for all anyone knew, he could be dead and the country already in the hands of a foreign entity.

There was no way to know for certain what the truth was and what was happening, but they all knew what was happening in New Hope. Life was beginning again.

Mark was throwing the football to his dad, Brian, and Rocky on this sunny and gorgeous first day of spring. The newlyweds had only been married a week, and love was in the air.

Kate was helping her mother cut up elk steaks from a kill the day before, while the rest of the women were in various stages of butchering the rest of the elk and salting it for its preservation.

This particular bull elk had been brought down by none other than Bill himself.

Bill had just moseyed out of his tent early in the morning, and there it was, only thirty feet away, drinking Kool-Aid out of a cup left out on one of the picnic tables, with another smaller elk close by. Bill's bow and quiver of arrows were right there in arm's reach, and before the elk could finish his drink, Bill put an arrow through its neck, right under its jaw, and out of the elk's mouth. He ran a few feet, but then dropped to the ground and died.

Before the butchering began, the men had skinned the elk and draped the hide over one of the picnic tables they never used, leaving it to dry out to cure.

Viv was relaxing with a book in a lawn chair not far from the women, and Jack was reading Psalms in his dad's Bible.

A couple of nights prior when the moon was almost full, Terry Prior and one of the other men were talking about the new garden about to be planted and how it would be irrigated, when they would plant the seeds, and when they could expect their first harvest.

Upon looking over the Dam Road, he thought he had spotted two figures up on the road, but after squinting and rubbing his eyes, then looking again, whatever he thought he had seen was no longer there, so he didn't give it a second thought and never mentioned it to anyone, not even Bob Hawkins.

Now Terry was sewing up a rip in his jeans on the grass by the road leading to the campground, and he was the first one to hear it.

"You hear that?" he shouted to Bill.

"Hear what? I don't hear anything" Bill answered him.

Everyone got quiet, and sure enough, it was the sound of a car, but quite a way off in the distance.

Most of them had not heard that sound for almost a year, whereas Bill had heard it as recently as last August, riding in the MRAP.

A few minutes went by and the sound drifted off into the quiet of the day.

About half an hour later, they all heard the engine this time without any prompting from Terry. The sound was much closer now, and they all looked at each other in silent bewilderment.

Bill wondered if it could be one of those military vehicles that were supposed to be coming to their rescue months ago, but he couldn't be sure.

Now the sound was unmistakable. It sounded like more than one vehicle, possibly two, coming from around the corner, they then both appeared and stopped a good 100 yards away, to the horror of everyone in the camp.

Kate had run to Mark's side, with baby just beginning to show.

Bill and Viv were holding hands next to Julie, who was sitting at a picnic table with Whiskers in her lap.

Bob Hawkins was acutely alert to the presence of the two vehicles, just sitting there idling, not moving at all.

Terry was still sitting in the same place he was before and was much closer to both vehicles than anyone else. He could see that the vehicle in front was a police cruiser and the one behind was an old Chevy.

The one in front was a late model Arapahoe County Sheriff's Department Cruiser, and if his eyes weren't playing tricks on him, the car behind was an old 1950 Chevy Styleline Sedan. It had been tricked out, painted pearl white. Its top had been chopped and lowered, its springs shortened to make it ride lower to the ground, and its windows were tinted solid jet black so you could not see in, but those inside could see out.

The cars then began to move slowly toward the campground.

Behind the wheel of the Sheriff's cruiser was an exceptionally large man, accompanied by a younger man that could easily have been his son. Both were looking at the residents of New Hope like they were hamburgers and hot dogs, the same way the cartoon cat looks at the cartoon mouse.

In the car behind, no one could be seen because the windows were blacked out.

When they approached the campground, they stopped again and idled for what seemed like forever.

Everyone outside of their tents saw the vehicles. Everyone took a collective hard swallow of what little saliva was left in their throat.

Mouths became dry like the desert and sweat began to leak from their pores.

"I'm going to get my rifle" Bob said softly, but Bill stopped him before he could move an inch.

"NO Bob…DON'T," Bill whispered. "Don't let them know we are armed or that we suspect them of anything. Don't let them know we are scared. Just stay calm."

The cars then suddenly began to move again, slowly up the road, then turning around and coming back the way they came. As they passed a second time, everyone looked on in horror as they could see the trunk of the second car covered in blood, which stood out because of the pearl white paint job, and then they drove away.

Viv thought she recognized the cruiser as the car used by Deputy's Tipton and Engleart.

She immediately got weak in the knees and slid down to the ground while she held Bill's hand. She knew perfectly well who was in those cars and what they were there for.

And so did everyone else.

The women began to panic, as did some of the men.

The guys in the cars were hunters and the community's cover was blown.

Whiskers had hissed at the cars because even he knew.

Because they all had been at New Hope for so long, they lulled themselves to sleep, believing that the hunters had died out by running out of food sources, giving them all a false sense of security.

They came to believe they were shielded by the trees around the camp, combined with being so far away from the main roads, but they had always been visible from the Cherry Creek Dam Road, which is the route most of them probably arrived in the beginning, and most certainly the point of discovery two nights before when Terry Pryor thought he saw something up there in the moonlight.

Everything had suddenly changed, and their Shangri-La was now in danger of being attacked, and its residents barbequed on the very fire pits they had cooked their meals these last seven or eight months.

So many nightmares were had by so many people, nightmares that had finally vanished but would now come with a vengeance.

The evil that walks in the dark, just as it walks in the light, does push-ups while the innocents sleep, gaining strength for their attacks on their prey.

Satan has dominion over the Earth and eventually takes what he believes is rightfully his.

Now the residents of New Hope must change gear in mid-stream and plan for the worst, while praying to the Lord for protection. They are dug in with nowhere left to go, so they must stand and fight to the death if they must. Their fight is a fight not only for their survival, but a fight for the legacy of mankind.

As Bill Sigler and his son drove away from the campground, they were already making plans for how they would extend this food supply as long as they could.

They were most concerned with the man riding in the car behind them because he scared them both to death.

For days they had traveled in all directions, many miles from their home, looking for new food supplies, and they had not eaten for days. Thanks to this discovery accidentally made two nights prior, they would be able to hold the man riding in the car behind them at bay for a while, keeping him from eating *them*…until it was time for him to feed again.

Printed in the United States
by Baker & Taylor Publisher Services